SURPRISE ATTACK!

In an earsplitting crash, the rear door of the house splintered inward, and One Eye stood there filling the open doorway, his warriors behind him.

In just seconds all five Apaches had burst into the room, eyes blazing, pistols at the ready.

"What the hell?" Parrish said loudly. He thought they were white men at first, and then saw their faces.

Dan'l was under no such illusion. "Get down! Find cover!" he yelled. He tipped the table over for Molly to hide behind. Then he turned and ran for the back wall of the kitchen for the Kentucky Rifle he took with him on all of his ventures into the wilderness.

By then, though, the Apaches had begun shooting.

The room was suddenly filled with deafening gunfire that shook the glass in the window. Dan'l was hit in the back by One Eye's first shot, and then in the side, as he fell, by Lone Wolf's hot lead. He never got to his rifle. He smacked the wall hard beside the fireplace, and slid to the floor.

One Eye walked over to Dan'l and looked down on him. Dan'l lay on his back, motionless, looking very dead. One Eye grinned an ugly grin.

"It was too easy, Sheltowee. Where is your reputation now? Where is your great medicine?"

THE LOST WILDERNESS TALES

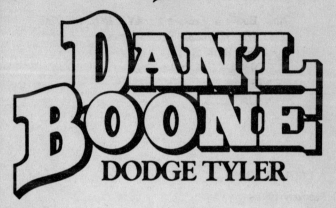

DAN'L BOONE

DODGE TYLER

APACHE REVENGE

LEISURE BOOKS   NEW YORK CITY

A LEISURE BOOK®

February 1997

Published by

Dorchester Publishing Co., Inc.
276 Fifth Avenue
New York, NY 10001

Printed in the United States of America.

APACHE
REVENGE

Prologue

The bearded, aging frontiersman sat on the narrow stoop before his cabin and carefully cleaned the Kentucky rifle that lay across his knees. As he worked, he watched the approaching rider. Gradually the horseman loomed larger, coming through the corn, rocking in his saddle. Finally the rider stopped just a few yards away. He wore a bowler hat and wire spectacles; he gave the impression of being a preacher.

"They told me in town where to find you. Are you really the great Indian fighter and explorer Dan'l Boone?"

The old man set the rifle aside and squinted up at the mounted stranger through clear, penetrating eyes. Boone was bareheaded; his hair was thinning and almost white. He had a tooth missing at the corner of his mouth.

"What if I was?" he asked suspiciously.

The rider dismounted, retrieved a large notebook from a saddlebag, and came up onto the porch, where the old fellow sat on a willow chair. The musket leaned against the log wall of the cabin beside the frontiersman, but Boone saw no need for it.

"I'm Adam Hollis. I've come all the way from Boston to find you, Dan'l. I'm pleased and mighty proud to finally meet up with you."

"I don't talk to newspaper people." When Hollis smiled, Dan'l liked the eyes behind the glasses.

"I'm just a library clerk. Mind if I shake the riding cramps out on your porch?" Hollis asked.

When Dan'l motioned grudgingly to a second chair not far away, Hollis slumped onto it and stretched his legs. The aroma of cooking food came to him from inside. He looked out past the cornfield to the woods and admired the view.

"Thanks," he said wearily. "People have been coming to me for years, selling me bits and pieces of your life story because of my special interest."

Dan'l grunted. "Most of them is selling swamp fog."

Hollis grinned. "I figured as much. But all those stories got my curiosity up, sir, and I came to realize your own story could be one of the great untold legends of the frontier. So I spent my life savings to get out here, hoping you might talk to me some about yourself."

The old hunter regarded Hollis sidewise. "You want to write down all that stuff? Hell, ain't nobody'll want to read about them times. We're in a whole different century, by Jesus. Nobody gives a tinker's damn about that early stuff no more."

Hollis shook his head. "You'd be surprised, Dan'l. You're already something of a legend—even in Europe, I hear. But I think that's just the beginning. If you let me document your life while it's all still in your head, generations to come will know what wild adventures you had."

The great hunter rose from his chair. He no longer enjoyed the renowned robustness or grace of his youth, but he still looked as hard as sacked salt. Dan'l went to the far end of the porch and stared out into the green forest beyond the fields, the kind of country that had been his home for all of his life. He finally turned back to Hollis.

"What would you do with these stories once you got it all writ down on paper?"

Hollis shrugged. "Publish them, but only if you wanted me to. At least we'd have them all down. For safekeeping, you might say."

Dan'l shook his head. "I can't say I'd want them in no book. Not in my lifetime. Not the real stuff. Most of them are too damned private. There's too many people out there who might not want them told. Or they might be moved to correct them, so to speak. Come out with their own versions so they would look better."

A resolve settled over Hollis. "All right. It can all be hidden away till long after you're gone if that's what you'd like. Then if the stories don't get lost somewhere down the line, maybe they will all come out later, at a better time, and be given over to some book people. That's what I would hope for."

Dan'l thought for a long moment. "You'd promise that in writing?"

Hollis nodded. "I will."

A laugh rattled out of the old man's throat. "I guess you'd want even the bear mauling and the wolf eating and the nasty ways some redskins liked to treat a white man when they caught him?"

"Yes, everything," Hollis said.

"There's treks into the West, the far side of the Mississippi, that hardly a man alive now knows about," Dan'l said, reflecting. "And these eyes have seen things that nobody's going to believe."

Hollis was becoming excited. "I'd want it all."

Dan'l took a deep breath in and called, "Rebecca! You better put a big pot of coffee on! Looks like we got company for a spell!"

As Hollis relaxed and smiled, Dan'l heaved himself back onto the primitive chair and closed his eyes for a moment. Finally, he said, "I reckon we might as well get going on it then."

Hollis was caught off guard. He fumbled in a pocket for a quill pen and a small ink pot, then opened up the thick but empty notebook. Hollis dipped his pen into the ink and waited.

"Most of it happened in about thirty years," Dan'l said quietly. "The important stuff. The stuff most folks don't know nothing about. That's when I got this raw hunger for the wild places, the far-off country where no settlers had been.

"I was just a stripling when I first started hearing about the land west of the Alleghenies," Dan'l said, his gaze wandering off toward the woods.

Hollis did not hesitate or interrupt with any questions. As the old man talked, he just began writing steadily in the thick book with an urgency he had never before experienced. He had to get every sentence down exactly as Dan'l said it. He could not miss a single word.

Chapter One

They did not look like Apache warriors, sitting silently on their mustang ponies there in the Missouri sun.

There was not much about them to reveal that they were five horse soldiers from the most feared tribe of the West, savage killers who had sliced scalps off screaming enemies with cruel pleasure, and flayed men alive to walk in their oiled skins. Wearing the eastern clothing that was stolen from now-dead victims—dark shirts and trousers, and hats that hid their long black hair—there was little to identify them with their blood-soaked past, or with their vengeful, murderous intentions.

They had even mounted stolen saddles on their horses to help disguise their real identity.

They had ridden all the way from south of Soccoro into unknown Missouri territory, with but one deadly purpose.

They had come to kill Dan'l Boone.

The small knot of them now stared expectantly down a gentle slope toward the Boone farmhouse below as they sweated slightly in the unfamiliar clothing. One Eye, their leader, turned to a broad-coupled, bronze warrior who had just ridden up from the house and was still short of breath.

"Are you sure he is there?"

The one to whom he spoke was Little Crow. He had been ostracized from his own clan when he killed a fellow Apache, severed the man's head and stuck it atop a pole, because the fellow had stolen from him. He had fought against Dan'l Boone three years previously, when Dan'l had helped lead a successful campaign against the warlike Apache chief called Yellow Horse, and he knew Dan'l by sight, which was important.

"I saw him clearly. Through the window. There are two other men, and a young woman."

Sitting beside One Eye on another mustang pony was his brother, Lone Wolf. In contrast to his sibling, Lone Wolf was handsome, with an aquiline face and an athlete's body. He was a steadying influence on his brother, even though he was younger. They were nephews of the great Yellow Horse, whom Dan'l had killed by his own hand, and they were considered by other Apaches to have royal blood.

"The girl would be his daughter," Lone Wolf said quietly.

A fourth Apache sat hunched forward on his mount behind One Eye. He was Gray Hawk, a recent recruit to One Eye's camp. He grinned tightly, staring down the slope. "The girl could make it interesting." He was very muscular, with cold, black eyes and a hawk nose. He had always liked white women, and had taken part with One Eye in the rapes of a couple of Spanish Mexican women.

The fifth rider, named Crooked Leg because of a birth defect, frowned at Gray Hawk. "Apache women do not suit your taste now, my brother warrior?"

But One Eye quickly intervened. "Enough of women. Keep your minds fixed on our purpose for being here." He was a rather ugly young man. His eye had been gouged out in adolescence, and he wore a thin but livid scar on his right cheek. The lid of his missing eye was shriveled and drawn over the hole in his face. "We are here to destroy the murderer of Yellow Horse and our cousin Running Dog. He is a defiler of sacred places and the scourge of the Apache."

Crooked Leg muttered his sober concurrence.

One Eye looked again toward the farmhouse. He had been talking wildly of Apache vengeance on the notorious fierce fighter called

Sheltowee ever since Dan'l had left the Apache hunting grounds. But because other Apaches exhibited no interest in revenge, One Eye had finally begun receiving taunts from other warriors about his boasts of going after Dan'l. Now he had formed his own small band of followers, violent men who were amenable to his plans of revenge and glory. One Eye figured that when he had killed Dan'l, his name would live forever in Apache annals, and he would become a great chieftain.

"We will not forget, One Eye," Crooked Leg assured him.

"They had no idea I was looking in on them," Little Crow added. "We should surprise them totally."

One Eye nodded. "Then the time has come," he said with a tense finality. "Make your weapons ready."

Each man had a Charleville rifled musket holstered in a saddle scabbard, all part of contraband taken from Mexican soldiers in skirmishes. But for this special assault they had even better hardware. They were all armed with Mortimer repeating pistols, also stolen, that fired eight shots without reloading. The weapons would be perfect for the in-close fighting they were sure was about to occur.

They all drew the pistols and quickly primed and cocked them. One Eye took a deep breath.

"Now we become Apache legend," he said in a half-whisper.

He dug his moccasined heels into his horse's flanks and led the others down the slope toward the farmhouse.

Inside the house, the four of them sat around a kitchen table, joking and laughing softly. Dan'l Boone was relaxed and happy, enjoying the company of relatives and friends. The girl sitting across the table was not his daughter, as Lone Wolf had guessed, but Molly Morgan. Molly was a second cousin to Dan'l, the daughter of a cousin, Ethan, whom Dan'l had had to kill by his own hand to keep him from being tortured by Shawnee.

All of that, though, was in the distant past now. Molly had traveled from Carolina to Missouri to marry Jock Parrish, who had preceded her there by six months and owned a small farm near the Boone place. Molly had arrived less than a week before, and the Boones—Dan'l, wife Rebecca, and their grown daughter, Jemima—were reacquainting themselves with the ebullient Molly and enjoying her verve and her infectious buoyancy.

The other men at the table were Parrish, who was to wed Molly in another week, and Uriah Gabriel, a suitor of Jemima. At that moment, Jemima and Rebecca were off at a nearby village to buy Molly and Parrish a modest wedding present.

Because of the sounds of conversation among them, Dan'l had not heard Little Crow outside the house moments before, and had no thought of danger as Molly described an incident on her trip west.

"I was sitting on the back of the wagon, right on the edge, mind you, and we hit this enormous bump. Well, I flew right off my perch like a bird, and landed on the ground on—well, on a soft part of me!"

Dan'l and Gabriel laughed loudly, but Parrish only smiled and blushed slightly, because his bride-to-be was referring indirectly to her backside.

Dan'l shook his head, grinning through a full graying beard. "You remind me so damn much of Ethan," he said softly to her.

Her pretty face slowly became serious. She knew how Ethan had died, and what Dan'l had had to do to save him from a horrible death. "Thanks, Dan'l." She was in her late twenties, with long, auburn hair and deep green eyes. In a tight-fitting gingham dress, she looked very womanly sitting there among the three men. She and Dan'l's Jemima had become childhood friends back in Carolina, and both had grown into rather willful, spunky young women. Parrish liked that in Molly.

"I wish I'd known your father," Parrish said to her. He was tall and thin, and Dan'l had met him just a few weeks ago but liked his quiet assurance. "He was in the Frenchie war, wasn't he?"

Molly was caught off guard. She looked down at the table.

"Just the beginning of it," Dan'l said for her. The great Indian fighter and explorer ran a hand through wild, graying hair. He was much older than the other two men at the table, but had a brawny, hard look about him, a primitive look that made some men cross the street to avoid him when he went store-shopping in St. Louis, just an hour's ride away.

Uriah Gabriel felt the mood shift in the room, and changed the subject. "I told Jemima you ought to get married in St. Louis, Molly. In a real church. That's what I'd want to do. If the time come, of course."

Dan'l smiled at him. They all knew that Gabriel was enamored of Jemima, but so far she had not returned the interest. A rather short man with thinning hair despite his youth, Gabriel could not in any way be considered handsome. But he was a very pleasant fellow, and Dan'l thought he would make some woman a good husband, whether or not that woman was Jemima.

"Oh, I'm sure the time will come, lad," Dan'l offered. "One way or the other."

Gabriel noted that Dan'l had made no reference to Jemima. He was being careful.

"I'm hoping that, Dan'l," Gabriel said quietly.

"Wouldn't it have been nice to have a double wedding?" Molly blurted out brightly.

All the men were slightly embarrassed. Gabriel shot a quick look at Dan'l, who smiled to himself. "Well, I reckon the timing waren't just right on that," he managed.

Molly had a dreamy look on her lovely face. "I can't wait, Dan'l!" She reached over and took hold of Parrish's bony hand. Parrish grinned sheepishly, and she sighed. "I wish it was happening tomorrow! I don't need a big church affair in town. I just want it done. Why, I—"

Dan'l held up his thick hand for silence, and Molly regarded him curiously.

"What is it, Dan'l?" Gabriel said.

Dan'l was listening carefully, head cocked slightly. "I thought I heard something," he said. He looked toward a window, where dull sunlight streaked inward.

"Maybe it's the women, back from the village," Parrish suggested. A neighbor friend of Dan'l, Sam Cahill, had driven them to the store in the farm buggy.

"No, it's too soon," Dan'l said, a frown creasing his brow. He rose slowly from his chair.

In that moment, there was another sound outside, which seemed to be right near the back door, not far from where they all sat. Dan'l saw a shadow cross the window, and then the sun went under and cast a sudden gloom over the room.

"What's the matter?" Molly asked innocently.

"Is either of you armed?" Dan'l said, his whole demeanor changed.

"Why, no," Gabriel said. Parrish shook his head and also rose.

"Maybe I'll just—" Dan'l started to say.

But then, in an earsplitting crash, the rear door of the house splintered inward, flying wide open, and One Eye stood there filling the opening.

"Jesus!" Gabriel hissed.

In just seconds all five warriors had burst into the room, eyes blazing, pistols at the ready.

"What the hell?" Parrish said loudly. He thought they were white men at first. Then he saw their faces.

Dan'l was under no such illusion. *"Get down! Find cover!"* he yelled. He tipped the table over for Molly to hide behind. Then he turned and ran to the back wall of the kitchen to get the Kentucky rifle he took with him on all of his ventures into the wilderness.

By then, though, the Apaches had begun shooting.

The room was suddenly filled with deafening gunfire that shook the glass in the window. Dan'l was hit in the back by One Eye's first shot, and then in the side, as he fell, by Lone Wolf's hot lead. He never got to his rifle. He smacked the wall hard beside the big fireplace and slid to the floor.

In the meantime, the other Apaches had fired off their Mortimers, too. Little Crow's shot hit Parrish over the heart, exploded it, and shattered a posterior rib on exiting. Parrish went flying over the upended table and hit the floor. Molly began screaming uncontrollably.

Gray Hawk hit Gabriel in the stomach and made his eyes widen in shock, then Crooked Leg's shot struck Gabriel in the side of his face and blew gray matter all over a side wall.

When Gabriel hit the floor dead, Lone Wolf moved over to Molly and backhanded her across her cheek, almost knocking her unconscious. She fell against the wall, then slid to the floor and sat there dazed.

One Eye and Gray Hawk had reprimed quickly, and now Gray Hawk came and stood over Parrish and fired again, tearing up the dead man's face. One Eye walked over to Dan'l and looked down on him. Dan'l lay on his back, motionless, looking very dead. One Eye grinned an ugly grin.

"It was too easy, Sheltowee. Where is your great reputation now? Where is your great medicine?"

Crooked Leg had reprimed too. He stood beside One Eye and aimed his pistol at Dan'l's face. "I will make sure of him."

One Eye put his hand over the muzzle of the gun. "He is dead, can you not see?" He bent down and pulled Dan'l's eyelid open, exhibiting a blank stare. "To continue to assault him now demeans the ease with which we defeated him. Use your head, my cousin."

Little Crow was kneeling over Jock Parrish, whose face was a bloody mess, and was cutting the scalp off his head. Molly regained her senses in the middle of that and began screaming again. One Eye's brother, Lone Wolf, went over to her, pulled her to her feet, and punched her in the face. She went out cold and hit the floor again. Lone Wolf stood beside Crooked Leg, who was bending over Dan'l.

"If anybody takes the scalp of Sheltowee, it should be my brother," Lone Wolf said.

One Eye had been distracted momentarily, looking about at the carnage. Now he turned back to Crooked Leg.

"We do not want his scalp. There are those in our nation who would believe it to be bad medicine. Let him lie."

Crooked Leg reluctantly backed off, and One Eye took one last look at Dan'l, then raised his arms high into the air and began issuing a series of triumphant war-whoops, which were echoed by the other Apaches. The house rang with their shouting.

Then One Eye walked over to Molly's unconscious form. He looked her over, pulled her skirts up, and grunted. "This will be our trophy," he said after a moment. "Sheltowee's offspring. We will take her with us."

Crooked Leg protested. "We do not need any extra baggage, One Eye. We must travel fast to rid ourselves of this territory. She will be a burden."

But One Eye's appetite had been whetted by his look at the pretty white woman. He turned to Crooked Leg and slapped him hard across his weathered face.

"It is I who will decide what is a burden and what is not!" One Eye said fiercely.

Crooked Leg was shocked, but made no further protest. It was apparent that the killer of Sheltowee was already feeling the importance of his new status.

"Very well," Crooked Leg muttered.

"Carry the girl out to my horse," One Eye commanded them. "She will ride with me."

"Let us remove ourselves from this place," Lone Wolf said, looking about at the three bloody figures on the floor. "As quickly as possible."

"Our vengeance is complete!" One Eye announced to the room. "Let us return to our homeland in triumph!"

Little Crow held up the blood-soaked scalp of Jock Parrish, the fiancé of Molly Morgan who had not lived to make her his bride. He let out another bloodcurdling cry, and then the five of them hurried from the house and mounted up outside. Molly was propped up on One Eye's mount, and he held her upright as they galloped off into the lowering sun.

In the slaughterhouse that had been the Boone kitchen, three bloody figures lay inert on the floor. Flies had already begun buzzing dully around them.

* * *

Almost an hour later, Sam Cahill drove Rebecca and Jemima up to the yard of the farmhouse and reined in. Rebecca and Jemima were still talking excitedly about the bed clothing they had purchased for the prospective bride and groom, and Cahill was smiling at their happiness. Cahill went back a long way with the family. Back in Carolina, when he and Dan'l were mere striplings, he had driven a supply wagon alongside Dan'l on the first Fort Duquesne expedition, and then helped Dan'l find and kill the villainous Henri Duvall after his military defeat in the second campaign. Dan'l had saved Cahill from drowning on a river trip to Fort Cumberland. A couple of years before, Cahill had followed Dan'l to Missouri from Kentucky, at Dan'l's suggestion, and now owned a farm a few miles from Dan'l's. He was a widower, but had his son and daughter-in-law with him.

Now, sitting there on the buckboard and listening to the women's soft laughter, Cahill squinted his eyes down on the yard and house, and his lined face lost its smile. Behind him, Rebecca noticed the change in his demeanor.

"What is it, Sam?"

He hesitated a long moment. "There's tracks of horses out here, and it looks like they go to the back of the house. Maybe a half-dozen riders. And the horses are unshod."

Rebecca and Jemima exchanged a look. "Indians?" Jemima said lightly. "They're all friendly around here. They probably came to talk Father out of some flour or dried beans."

"I don't like it," Cahill said quietly. "It's awful still here. I better check it out."

"You just drive us around to the back first," Rebecca told him firmly. "That's where the tracks lead."

Cahill sighed. "Well. All right."

He drove them around to the rear entrance, where the ground had been scuffed up by horses. Cahill saw the wide-open door, and tensed up inside.

Rebecca looked toward it curiously. "Dan'l don't leave the door open ordinarily. *Dan'l!*" she called out.

Cahill had noted now that tracks led away from the house. Whoever had been here was gone. Also, there was still no sound from inside.

"You two stay right here a minute," he said to the women. "I'll take a look inside."

"Oh, Sam. You're scaring us," Rebecca scolded him. "We'll go in with—"

"Stay here!" Cahill said loudly.

Rebecca jumped slightly, and she and Jemima turned and stared at each other. In all the years they had known Cahill, he had never spoken to either of them like that.

Cahill regained some control. "Please," he said urgently. Then he jumped down from the buggy and walked over to the open doorway.

He stepped inside.

He caught his breath. The flies buzzed loudly

25

around the horrible scene. Jock Parrish lay there, his face destroyed and his scalp gone. There were a lot of flies on his head. Uriah Gabriel lay in an awkward position only corpses could attain, his brains all over the nearby wall. And then there was Cahill's old friend Dan'l, over by the cold fireplace, lying in a pool of blood, looking as dead as cordwood.

"Oh, my God!" Cahill gasped. *"Oh, my God!"*

He moved quickly to Dan'l's side and knelt over him and felt for a pulse, but could not find one. *"Son of a bitch!"* he said angrily, tears welling in his eyes.

Then he heard the scream from behind him at the doorway. He turned in a daze and saw Rebecca there, her face contorted with sudden shock and pain.

Jemima's face appeared beside her mother's, and her eyes widened in terror. "Jesus and Mary!"

Rebecca walked through the room like a sleepwalker and stood over Dan'l's still, bloody form. "Is he . . ."

Cahill paused, then nodded. "Yes. They're all dead."

Rebecca leaned against the fireplace stones, felt a great dizziness come over her, and almost fell to the floor. She had been dreading a day like this for thirty years, since she and Dan'l were both in their teens and he had gone off to the war with the French. But she had known she would never be prepared for it.

26

Jemima was leaning against the doorjamb and sobbing. She had seen what they did to Uriah Gabriel, and even though she had rejected him as a suitor, he had been a good friend to her. She could not look at Molly's Jock Parrish, and whenever she let her gaze fall on the inert form of her father, she began sobbing all over again.

Rebecca opened her eyes suddenly and looked around the bloody room. "Where's Molly?"

Cahill shrugged. "They must've took her. One set of hoofprints was extra deep out there. She was on one of them horses."

"Oh, my heaven!" Rebecca exclaimed weakly.

Jemima, a rather pretty dark-haired girl who looked a lot like her mother, shook her head slowly. "It would have been better if they had killed her here."

Rebecca turned toward her distraught daughter and started to object, but then realized she might be right. "I don't . . . understand. The Sioux hereabouts are friendly. They trade with us."

"This waren't Sioux, ma'am," Cahill said heavily. He was a slim, well-built older man, with thinning hair and small brown eyes, which were now watery and dull. "This was Apaches."

Rebecca stared hard at him, and he saw the doubt in her face. It was hundreds of miles to Apache territory, and Indians almost never ventured very far outside their own hunting grounds.

But Cahill repeated solemnly, "It was Apaches, Rebecca. Nothing else makes sense."

"Oh, God, Dan'l," Rebecca muttered, tearing up.

At the door, Jemima began sobbing all over again. She had not approached her father's still figure on the floor. She could not bear to see it close up.

"Well," Cahill said, as if he would never speak again. "I got a job to do that I never thought I'd have. I'll carry these three outside and go get a shovel. If you got the strength, Rebecca, you might like to go get the parson."

Rebecca nodded. "I'll have to find him, Sam. I want some words spoke over them."

Cahill bent over the mutilated corpse of Jock Parrish, but he suddenly stopped when Rebecca issued a small gasp. He looked up at her.

"His hand moved!" Rebecca said tremulously.

Both Cahill and Jemima came dubiously over to Dan'l's prone figure. Jemima held her breath tightly. Cahill bent over his old friend a second time and pried an eyelid up. "I don't know, Rebecca. These things happen after—"

Then came a low groan from the depths of Dan'l Boone's chest.

Cahill jumped backward as if a snake had struck at him. The groan had been almost inaudible, and it had sounded as if it came from the far end of a long tunnel. But it had been very real.

"*Jesus!*" Cahill exclaimed. He bent closely over Dan'l and put his ear to Dan'l's face. Then he tried again for a pulse, in Dan'l's throat.

"By God! There *is* a pulse!" he said excitedly. "It's just barely there!"

Rebecca's hand went to her mouth, and hope irradiated her pretty face. "Are . . . you sure, Sam?"

Cahill nodded with a tight grin, and Jemima let out a little cry of ragged relief.

Cahill stood quickly. "He was hit in the back and side. Pack them wounds up tight so he won't lose any more blood! I'm riding for Doc Purvis! I'll be back within the hour!"

Both women were bending over Dan'l now. Rebecca looked up at Cahill tearfully. "Ride hard, Sam. We'll take care of him till you get back."

Then Cahill disappeared out the doorway.

There was a full moon that evening.

The Apaches had been riding hard to get out of Missouri territory and away from Sioux villages. They had taken turns carrying Molly to make better time, and Crooked Leg deeply resented the inconvenience. He had never been attractive to women, not even those of his own village, and impatiently tolerated One Eye's interest in these whiteface females.

Because of the full moon, One Eye kept

them riding until almost midnight to get them into safer territory. Finally, they encamped on the bank of a small stream in a stand of poplars.

Molly had come around in early evening, while riding with Lone Wolf on his mount, immediately remembered the slaughter at the Boone cabin and the killing of Jock Parrish, and began screaming hysterically again. Lone Wolf struck her to keep her quiet, and she rode the rest of the evening in a dazed silence, realizing slowly what had happened at the farm and what was happening to her now.

It was a terrible thought.

When they made their camp, Molly was taken off Crooked Leg's horse by One Eye himself, and he looked her over more carefully. He liked what he saw. This one was even more attractive than the Spanish women he had raped and killed in raids on small settlements in New Mexico.

One Eye trussed Molly up, hand and foot, and leaned her against a small tree near the low fire they had built. Nobody paid much attention to her for a while. The Indians took food from their gear and ate quietly at the fire. They were very tired, but exhilarated with the flush of triumph over their hated enemy. They would go back home as heroes, and Apaches from far around would ask to join their small clan to serve under One Eye.

Molly watched them eat from a short distance. She had heard stories back in Carolina about white women taken by Shawnees being raped and tortured. A fear crept into her chest slowly and shoved out her grief for Parrish and her cousin Dan'l. She began trembling gently inside, sitting there and wondering what would happen next.

One Eye finished eating first. He got up from a log bench and took a chunk of dried buffalo meat over to her at the tree while the others watched.

"Here. You eat," One Eye told her.

She looked up at him with fear and hatred, and saw his ugly, scarred face. He had removed the hat from his head, and his long black hair flowed over his shoulders.

As scared as she was, Molly glared fiercely at him, then spat at his feet. "Keep your damn meat, you murderer!" she said angrily.

One Eye knew only very primitive English, and the others at the fire knew none. But they all understood. Little Crow and Gray Hawk laughed boisterously.

One Eye smiled and nodded. He was beginning to like this white woman. He squatted down beside Molly.

"You do not speak Athabaskan?"

Molly glared at him and tried to ignore the lurching inside her stomach. "Leave me alone or kill me!" she said breathlessly.

"She does not seem very friendly," Lone Wolf said with a grin.

31

One Eye ignored him. He reached out and touched Molly's hair, and she flinched away from him. "You are very beautiful. Like the golden eagle. Do you understand?"

Molly closed her eyes to be rid of his image.

One Eye turned to the others. "She is quite beautiful. I did not notice at the house."

"She is a white woman," Crooked Leg said sourly.

"Undress her," Gray Hawk said casually. He ripped his dark shirt open at the buttons, because he hated white men's clothing. Another day of riding and he would shed them entirely. His hard muscles rippled in the soft light from the fire. He looked toward One Eye. "We will take turns on her. She will entertain us for days on the long ride back."

Little Crow stood up, looking brawny and hard. "Yes, untie her, One Eye. I will undress her myself. She is not Apache, but she excites my interest."

One Eye's brother, Lone Wolf, turned to see One Eye's reaction. He was more cautious with One Eye than the others, because he knew him better.

"I say have your pleasure with her, and then kill her tonight," Crooked Leg said.

When One Eye turned toward the fire, Lone Wolf saw the somberness in his scarred face.

"You think I stole Sheltowee's daughter to give you weasels pleasure?"

Nobody answered him. Lone Wolf smiled slightly.

One Eye turned back to Molly. "You," he said in English. "My squaw."

Crooked Leg made a grunting sound in his throat and spat into the fire. Little Crow and Gray Hawk exchanged a dark look.

Molly could not believe her ears. "Your woman! Are you mad? Give me a gun and I'll shoot myself in the head, you damn redskin monster!"

One Eye did not understand the insult, but knew she was rejecting the idea. He slapped her hard across the face. She felt the pain rocket through her, and suddenly she was breathing hard. At the fire, Little Crow laughed loudly.

"My squaw," One Eye said in her face.

He untied a rawhide cord at her wrists, then placed the meat in her hand. "Eat."

Molly saw the handle of a war knife at his waist, very close to her. In a quick movement that surprised him, she grabbed the knife and drew it from its sheath. Then she started to stab herself in the chest.

One Eye lashed out and caught her hand just before the dagger plunged into her flesh, between her breasts. She struggled weakly for a moment, but he held her hand away easily. Then he twisted the knife from her grasp.

He stood up and stepped away from her, thrusting the knife back into its sheath.

"Did you see that?" he said to the others.

"She *must* have Sheltowee's blood in her," Little Crow exclaimed.

"She shows her utter hatred for you. And us," Crooked Leg offered.

But Lone Wolf was impressed too. "She has fire," he said.

One Eye turned to his brother. "Exactly."

"Aiwee!" Gray Hawk hissed quietly, realizing there would be no molestation of the white woman.

One Eye was staring at Molly with even greater interest, and he spoke to his comrades while his eyes were still on her. "She will be my woman. When we return to our village, I will make it official."

"Well," Little Crow said with a sigh. "It is your right, Cousin."

"By the ancient spirits!" Crooked Leg grunted.

Lone Wolf, who also had a taste for white women, nodded. "A good choice, my brother."

"No one will touch her but me," One Eye said, turning to them. "Is it understood?"

They nodded and mumbled their replies.

One Eye knelt again before Molly, who was still dazed from the blow on the face, grabbed her by her chin, and looked deep into her green eyes.

"You. My woman."

Molly did not reply this time. She just sat there wishing that somehow a miracle would happen and it would all be over.

Wishing she were dead.

Chapter Two

The area doctor had arrived at the Boone farm in just over an hour to tend Dan'l on that bloody afternoon. The women had already stopped Dan'l's bleeding temporarily, so the doctor put him on the kitchen table and cut the bullet out of his back. The second bullet had passed through his side. Dan'l was unconscious through the entire procedure, and through that whole evening and night. But in early morning he began mumbling incoherently, and not long after dawn on that following day, his eyelids fluttered open while Rebecca and Sam Cahill were sitting with him in the bedroom.

Rebecca had prayed all through the night that her husband would survive. Doc Purvis had left in mid-evening, telling the family that Dan'l's chances were maybe fifty-fifty. But Purvis did not know his patient. He had no idea what a fighter Dan'l Boone was.

When Dan'l finally opened his eyes on a sunny Missouri morning and looked around trying to figure out where he was, Rebecca broke down and sobbed again.

"I'll be damned!" Cahill said in wonder. He had almost lost hope.

"Jemima!" Rebecca called to the kitchen. *"He's awake! He's going to live!"*

Jemima came running into the room, eyes wide. Her dark hair hung down onto her shoulders, and her pretty face looked suddenly radiant. "Oh, God! Oh, God!"

Dan'l was coming back from some dark place where he did not want to be. He focused on Rebecca, then on Cahill.

"What the hell," he said thickly.

Rebecca took his meaty hand. "Thank God you're back!"

Dan'l looked at Jemima, who was kneeling beside the bed. "Where am I? What happened?"

Cahill cleared his throat and ran a hand through his thinning hair. "It was Indians, Dan'l. You was in the kitchen with Molly and the men."

It came flooding back into Dan'l's head, the door busting open, him running for the rifle.

"You was shot twice," Cahill went on. "Busted up inside. Doc says the lead nicked your left lung, and it's got to heal. You lost a lot of blood."

Dan'l stared at him. "Indians?"

"Doc says most men would be dead," Cahill added.

"The others," Dan'l said, not wanting to hear the answer. "What happened to the others?"

Cahill turned away. Rebecca sighed heavily. "Jock and Uriah are dead, Dan'l," she said.

Dan'l closed his eyes against the harsh reality of her words. "And Molly?" he croaked. "What about Molly?"

"She's . . . gone."

Dan'l looked into his wife's tired-looking face. "They took her?"

Jemima nodded. "They took her, Father," she said tearfully. Dan'l's boys had always called him Paw, as he had his own father. But Jemima had begun using the more educated-sounding word when she had reached puberty, and Dan'l rather liked it.

Dan'l turned away, staring grimly out through a window on the near wall, where the sunlight filtered in brightly past muslin curtains. "Good Jesus."

"Doc Purvis reported this to the authorities in St. Louis," Rebecca said. "They'll be sending somebody out."

Dan'l turned and looked sternly at Cahill. "What kind of Indians?" he said. But he figured he knew the answer. There had been a rumor that a few Apaches were talking about revenge against him after his defeat of Yellow Horse. And the quick look he had gotten of the men before they shot him had reminded him of the look of Yellow Horse and Running Dog.

"They was Apaches, Dan'l," Cahill said heavily. "The horses was unshod, and they scrawled a mark in the dirt outside before they rode off. It was a bear claw, the sign of Yellow Horse."

Dan'l nodded. "There's some nephew, they say. Called One Eye. He's the one. He's the son of a bitch took Molly."

The women averted their eyes at the obscenity. But suddenly Dan'l pushed himself up off the bed, a new fire in his eyes.

"I got to get out of here! I got to go after—"

He grimaced in raw pain and collapsed heavily onto the bed, perspiration popping out on his upper lip. He was breathing shallowly.

"You ain't going nowhere," Cahill told him, "till you get healed up."

"Oh, Christ!" Dan'l muttered.

Rebecca put a hand on his hot forehead. "Please rest, dear Dan'l. Others will take care of this. It can't be you every time. The law will catch them and bring Molly back to us."

Dan'l looked at her. "They're out of Missouri by now. Making their way through Kiowa territory. I have to—"

He tried again to raise himself, and passed out.

Rebecca smoothed his wild-looking hair on the pillow. "Rest well, dear husband. Rest and heal."

"Amen," Cahill said.

*   *   *

Several days passed. Then one morning Dan'l got out of bed and hobbled across the room while the women were at the other end of the house.

His chest still hurt when he moved. But the lung had healed, and he could breathe easily again. Doc Purvis had been there the previous afternoon and said Dan'l was making a miraculous recovery. But the only miracle Dan'l was interested in was getting Molly back from the Apaches.

He was not kidding himself. He guessed she had been sexually assaulted by now, maybe by all of them. He just hoped she was not dead. But that was a good possibility, too. And the longer he waited, the more ugly things could happen to her.

Without Rebecca's knowledge, he stayed on his feet that morning, pacing up and down the room, getting his strength back. His breath came shallow, he sweated a lot, and pain wracked his torso, but he knew he had to go through all of that to get well.

About midmorning Rebecca came in with some broth, and he was up again, walking back and forth, holding his chest.

"Dan'l!" Rebecca cried out when she saw him. "What are you doing?"

He leaned on a bedpost. "Getting well," he said.

"You get back into bed!" she admonished

him. "The doc says you shouldn't be up for another week!"

"Purvis don't know what's going on inside me," Dan'l said irritably. "I'm getting well. I'm building my strength back up. I'm going to need it."

Rebecca was very tense. She went and closed the door so Jemima, in the kitchen, could not hear them.

"Damn it, husband! We've been through this! You're thinking of Molly again. But you ain't fit! There ain't nothing you can do!"

Dan'l scowled at her. Standing there in flannel pajama bottoms and nothing else, with his thick hair and beard and hairy chest, he looked more animal than man. "If I'd been paying attention, Becky, she'd still be here. She was under my roof, giving herself over to my protection. She was getting married, with a great future in front of her. Now Jock is six feet under. And Molly—"

"We all feel terrible about Molly," Rebecca said. "Just like you. But it wasn't your fault that happened. Them heathens have tricky ways, we know that from Kentucky. Remember when the Shawnee took little Jemima, and you had to go get her back? You couldn't have stopped that."

"That's right," he said. "But I did go after her."

"By God, you'll kill yourself if you hurry this!" Rebecca declared. "You shouldn't got yourself involved in that Yellow Horse war at all, and we wouldn't had this trouble!"

Dan'l looked at her but said nothing.

She hesitated, then went to him and hugged him. "Oh, God, I'm sorry! I didn't mean that."

He touched her face with a thick hand. "I know." He took her with him to the bed, and they sat down on its edge. "But it did all start with me. It's my fight, not Molly's. She has the right to hope I'm going to do something about this. And I am."

Rebecca knew she could not dissuade him. She nodded. "I figured you was. Just don't go till you're able, Dan'l. If not for me, or Jemima, or yourself, then for Molly. You'll need to be strong to help her. If she ain't beyond help."

Dan'l met her gaze. "I know that."

The next afternoon, Sam Cahill stopped by to see how Dan'l was doing. The women had taken the buggy to see Doc Purvis for more medicine for Dan'l's wounds, so Dan'l was there alone. Cahill was surprised to find him in the kitchen, warming some stew over a woodstove.

"What the hell!" Cahill said when he walked into the kitchen.

Dan'l turned to him and grinned. He was clothed in his usual buckskins, but was in his stocking feet and had his left arm in a sling. "Well, look who's here. Good to see you, Sam."

"Are you supposed to be up and around?"

"I'm feeling a lot better. I been a lot worse off than this with a head cold."

Cahill grinned.

"I'm surprised One Eye thought he had me

killed with just two bullets. He ought to know you ain't got a bear killed—"

"I know," Cahill said. "Till you got him skinned."

They both laughed softly.

"Can I give you some stew? It's some of Rebecca's best."

Cahill shook his head. "I just et, Dan'l."

Dan'l served himself some of the stew on a tin plate, then sat down and began eating it with a thick chunk of dark bread.

Cahill shook his head slowly, watching him. "If you don't beat all. Most fellows would be eating soup through a strainer about now. If they survived at all."

"Well, you and me is from Carolina, Sam. We run Frenchie out of Fort Duquesne. We ain't like most folks."

Cahill smiled. "We got that old Henri Duvall, didn't we, partner? We got him good."

Dan'l grinned through his chewing.

"By God, you do look pretty good."

"I'm doing better every day." Dan'l looked up at his old friend. "I'll be leaving in a few more days, Sam. Whether Rebecca wants me to or not."

"Leaving?"

Dan'l grunted. "Don't act dumb, Sam. You know where I'm going."

"After One Eye?"

Dan'l nodded.

"Dan'l. If you waited a few *months* you

wouldn't be what you was before the shooting. You ain't in no condition for hard riding."

"I got myself another Appaloosa. Bought him in St. Louis just before all this happened. Never rode a smoother animal. He just flows over the ground, Sam. He'll carry me out there without no trouble."

"You're riding out of here by yourself?"

Dan'l held his look. "If I have to."

Cahill sighed heavily. "Hell. If you didn't pull me out of that river on the way to Cumberland, I wouldn't be here talking about this. If you're going, I'm going."

Dan'l frowned at him. "Are you sure?"

Cahill shrugged. "If you fall off your goddamn saddle, I can put you back on."

Dan'l was grinning now. "You know I appreciate that, Sam. I wouldn't want no better partner out there."

"Hell," Cahill said, looking away.

"I guess you know it could get dangerous," Dan'l reminded him.

Cahill regarded him solemnly. "I guess *you* know she could be dead, with the buzzards picking her bones," he said quietly. It was a harsh reminder, but one he felt ought to be voiced.

"I ain't forgetting that," Dan'l told him. "But I got a feeling about this. I think maybe One Eye will think of her like some kind of trophy that he'll want to show off. He'll figure she's related somehow, and that will make it better for him."

43

"I hope it works out that way," Cahill said. He pondered for a long moment. "We can't go against the Apache with just you and me, Dan'l."

Dan'l nodded, wiping a sleeve across his mouth. "I know that. I'm hoping to find somebody when we get out there. Maybe in Santa Fe."

"It would be good if we could pick up one or two good old boys right around here."

"You're right. But there ain't none of these farmers would want to go off on a chase like this. Rebecca even thinks I'm a damn fool to go." He smiled through the beard.

"I'll keep my ears open," Cahill told him.

"I reckon I'll be ready within the week," Dan'l said. "I'm going then, no matter what."

"Rebecca will be glad to hear that," Cahill said sarcastically.

"I can't help it, Sam. Time is a-wasting."

Dan'l rode into a tiny cantina in a crossroads village between the farm and St. Louis four nights later. Cahill met him there, and they had a few drinks together. Rebecca was getting tense about Dan'l's leaving so soon with his chest still hurting, and he just wanted to get out of the house for a few hours.

The cantina was run by a Spaniard named Gomez, but most of its patrons were emigrants from the East, come to make their fortunes in the new territories across the Mississippi. On that evening there were only three other customers present, with the slick-haired Gomez behind a long counter. Two of the other customers were obviously drifters from more civilized parts, wearing narrow-brim hats and fancy vests and carrying pistols openly in their belts. They were drinking at the counter-bar and kept throwing glances at the fifth customer, who sat at a table not far from the one Dan'l and Cahill occupied. He was a mountain man wearing rawhide clothing, like Dan'l.

"Maybe you know him," Cahill suggested. "He looks like a trapper."

Dan'l shook his head. "No, he must be new to these parts. They come in from the West every now and then to get a good bath and trade their pelts."

One of the drifters at the bar turned and stared openly at the mountain man, grinning slightly. The drifter was rather tall like the mountain man, but did not have the hard, wiry look of the trapper. His companion, a shorter man with a potbelly, also turned.

"Do you smell something in here?" the tall one said rather loudly. "I just got a whiff of buffalo shit."

The mountain man looked up at them but said nothing. Dan'l liked the looks of him. He had a long, bony face and a brown handlebar mustache, and his hair flowed over his shoulders. He looked as if he were put together with iron cables.

"That's what it smells like to me," Potbelly agreed. "Or maybe somebody dragged a dead skunk in here. It's kind of putrid."

They both laughed loudly, the liquor in them showing itself. The tall one swigged another drink. "I think it's coming off of that hunter sitting over there. Could that be?"

"By God, I think you're right," his comrade said.

They had another big laugh. The trapper just sat there, making no comment. Cahill looked at Dan'l and shook his head. "Couple of greenhorns. Probably selling shoes in Philadelphia last week."

"Their mothers should've taught them some manners," Dan'l said. He rubbed at the left side of his chest and made a face.

"Say, bartender," the tall drifter went on. "You expect civilized folks to have to drink in the same room with that smell?"

Gomez came from down the counter and gave the twosome a stern look. "I don't want any trouble in here tonight, gentlemen."

The tall man suddenly pulled a pearl-handled pistol from his waistband and let it hang loosely in his hand. "Why don't you ask that piece of buffalo shit to move his smelly ass out of here?"

The two were not laughing anymore, and a quick tension had mounted in the room. The owner looked grave. "I can't do that, boys," he said in accented English. "I have to serve everybody, you see."

The tall drifter turned to his partner. "Did you hear that? A goddamn *frijole*-eater tells me he can't fumigate his own cantina. Damn, what a world they got out here!"

Now Potbelly pulled his gun too. Both guns were loaded and primed, and the drifters cocked them in unison. "Hell. Maybe we'll have to do the job ourselfs."

The mountain man did not even look at them. He just swigged a whiskey and stared at his glass. Dan'l noticed for the first time that the trapper had a long rifle propped against the table beside him. But it did not look loaded or primed.

"I think maybe the hunter's got hisself some trouble," Cahill said quietly to Dan'l. Cahill was wearing a rifled cavalry pistol in a handmade rawhide holster, but Dan'l was unarmed.

Dan'l nodded. "It kind of looks that way."

The tall drifter walked over to the mountain man's table, Potbelly following close behind. Potbelly glanced toward Dan'l's table on the way.

"Hell, we got two of them in here. Looky over there." He gestured toward Dan'l.

The tall one nodded. "Yeah, but it's this one stinks the most. Maybe you better just drink the rest of that bottle outside, mister, so we can all breathe easier."

The trapper looked up at him with hard, cold eyes. "You orter put them peashooters away afore you shoot yourselfs in some tender place."

The tall man's face turned red slowly. "What did you say, hunter?"

"Maybe we ought to try to stop this," Cahill half-whispered to Dan'l.

Dan'l saw the trapper rise from his chair and take the rifle with him. "Just a minute. Maybe he's going."

The trapper moved around the table, closer to his two tormentors. They both had the pistols aimed at his chest. "Maybe you're right," he said.

The tall man relaxed some. "Well. That's better."

But the trapper went on. "Maybe this little place is too small for all of us."

As the tall man's face changed, the trapper kicked hard at Potbelly's shin, and the sound of cracked bone was heard distinctly in the room. Potbelly screamed in pain and bent double, and his gun fired loudly into the floor at the trapper's feet, chipping wood. While the tall one was reacting to that, the trapper swung the butt of the rifle into the tall fellow's jaw, and there was further cracking of bone. The tall drifter hit the floor on his back, throwing his pistol across the room, where it clattered against a wall.

"Damn!" Cahill said softly with a smile.

"*Madre de Dios!*" Gomez said, crossing himself.

Both drifters were on the floor now, but Potbelly was reloading and priming as the trapper turned his back on him to take his seat at the

table again as if nothing had happened. Dan'l
smiled at his nonchalance. Then he saw Potbelly finish priming, cock the pistol again, and
aim it at the mountain man's back. Dan'l rose
from his chair like a grizzly bear, unarmed but
wild-looking.

"You do that and I'll kill you," he growled at
the man on the floor.

The trapper turned, saw the gun aimed at
him, and shook his head slowly. Cahill glanced
tensely up at Dan'l.

"Kill me?" Potbelly said. "You ain't even
armed."

"He don't have to be," Cahill said with some
satisfaction. "This here is Dan'l Boone."

Potbelly's face changed. Dan'l moved away
from the table, and Potbelly turned the gun on
him.

"Go ahead," Cahill said, still seated. "Bullets
bounce off'n Dan'l like hail on a tin roof. When
you get through shooting, he'll come over there
and skin you like a goddamn rabbit."

Behind the counter, Gomez smiled. He knew
Dan'l's reputation.

Potbelly slowly lowered the muzzle of the
gun. "He's *the* Dan'l Boone?"

"In the flesh," Cahill said. "Now, why don't
you drag your partner out of here before Dan'l
gets in a *real* nasty mood?"

Potbelly did not utter another word. He
hauled the tall drifter to his feet and they stumbled out of the place together. Dan'l sat back

down and grimaced with pain. It had all been a bluff. He was not fit for fighting yet. But he had not wanted to see that little coward put a hole in the mountain man.

When Dan'l looked up, the trapper was standing beside their table. "I want to thank you for that."

Dan'l nodded. "That little weasel."

"So you're Boone, heh?" the trapper said.

"That's me. This here is Sam Cahill. It's his big mouth that saved you from a hole in your back."

Dan'l and Cahill grinned, but not the trapper.

"Well. Anyway, I'm much obliged. The name is Luther McGill. I been in the Rockies hunting beaver. I reckon I do smell."

Dan'l looked into his eyes. They were the hardest, coldest eyes he had seen in a long while. They looked a lot like the eyes of some Apaches Dan'l had come face-to-face with. There was no friendliness in his face, either, even though he had come over to express appreciation for Dan'l's action.

But Dan'l recognized a strength in the man's face that he liked. He pointed to a chair. "Let us buy you a drink, McGill."

McGill hesitated, then sat down. He looked over at Dan'l. "I been hearing about you since I sucked. They say you cleaned the Frenchies out of Fort Duquesne almost single-handed."

Dan'l ordered whiskeys, then said, "No, Cahill here give me a little help."

Dan'l grinned at that, and so did Cahill. Mc-Gill watched the exchange straight-faced. Cahill concluded that the man must never smile. Maybe he did not know how.

They all swigged another round of whiskey without talking. Then Dan'l looked over at Mc-Gill. "You handled yourself real well with them emigrants."

McGill shrugged. "If they was Kiowa, I'd be dead."

Dan'l nodded understanding. "You got plans to head back west real soon?"

McGill sighed and pulled at his long mustache. "Didn't get much for the hides this time. Might have to get a job for a spell. Just to get back out there."

"The beaver was running thin this year," Cahill offered.

"Thin as rainwater on a groundsheet," McGill said.

"How would you like a job that would take you back out there?" Dan'l said slowly, watching McGill's bony face.

McGill met his gaze. "What kind of job?"

Dan'l told him briefly what had happened, and McGill listened with interest. He was younger than Dan'l and Cahill, in his thirties, but he looked older.

"We're going after her," Dan'l concluded. "Sam here and me. We was hoping to get a couple others to ride with us."

McGill nodded and stared past them for a

long moment. "I hate Apaches," he finally said.

Cahill grunted. "Is that a yes?"

McGill looked at him, then at Dan'l.

"When do we leave?" he said.

A couple of days later, Dan'l was ready to go. The chest pain was getting better every day, and he was not going to wait any longer. He would be riding long hours, but he figured he would continue to heal.

Rebecca was very upset with all of this, but she knew that she could not get in the way of her husband when his mind was set on something. She had tried many times before.

On the day before they were to leave, Cahill came to Dan'l in the early morning with a suggestion for a fourth man to ride out with them.

He called Dan'l out into the yard so Rebecca would not hear their conversation. Just the talk of the proposed trek made her jumpy.

"I just remembered this neighbor of mine, Dan'l," Cahill began, standing in a warm breeze with Dan'l. "Name of Finney. He used to be a gunsmith, and they say he's real good with all kinds of weapons."

"Cyrus Finney?" Dan'l said.

"That's the man."

"I heard he was in prison."

"He was," Cahill admitted. "He caught his wife with another man. Shot the poor bastard through the head. He was paroled out a year ago. His wife left him while he was inside. Run off to New Orleans with a drummer."

Dan'l nodded. "I guess he had cause. But he's still a killer, Sam."

Cahill took a deep breath. "I've talked to him a couple times, Dan'l. He 'pears like a pretty regular fellow. And he'd be ripe for something like this. He ain't scratching much of a living out of that little farm of his. Why don't you go talk with him?"

"Well," Dan'l said.

"Maybe McGill would like to go over there with us."

Dan'l shook his head and glanced toward the small barn where McGill had been sleeping. "McGill rode into St. Louis to get some supplies for us. Come on, we'll go now."

It was a half-hour ride to the small Finney farm. Dan'l was surprised by the makeshift look of the cabin when they arrived. The door had leather hinges, and there was no glass in the windows. A chestnut gelding was hitched to a post outside.

They had just dismounted when the door flew open. There stood a broad-set, fierce-looking man with reddish hair and squinted eyes. He was holding a Mortimer pistol in his right hand, ready to fire.

"Hold it right there!" he commanded.

Dan'l looked into the muzzle of the gun. Finney looked from him to Cahill, then squinted even harder.

"Cahill?" he asked gruffly.

"It's me, Finney. Put the goddamn gun down!"

"Oh," Finney said. He lowered the gun and came on out into the yard. He had a pinched-together, sour-looking face, and a way of holding his mouth so it looked as if he were sucking on a peach pit. "Didn't recognize you. A couple of drifters rode past last week, gave me some trouble."

"I think we met them at the cantina," Cahill said with a grin.

Finney squinted at Dan'l again. "Well. Come on in."

Dan'l gave Cahill a look as they followed Finney into the cabin. Finney looked kind of funny from behind, because he was so bowlegged. But there was nothing humorous about his manner.

Inside, the place was a mess. There was a bunk on one wall, a table littered with dirty tin dishes, a couple of straight chairs, and a dry sink on another wall. The place smelled slightly of sweat and urine.

"Nice place," Dan'l said.

"It ain't much, but I own it," Finney commented. He put the gun in his belt and waved at the chairs. "Have a seat."

Dan'l and Cahill seated themselves, and Finney leaned against the double bunk not far away.

"What can I do for you, Sam?" he finally said.

Once again the Apache story was told, this

time by Cahill. When it was finished, Finney said, "So?"

Dan'l furrowed his brow slightly at the lack of empathy. He wondered if the trip had been worth the effort.

"Look, Finney," he said. "My cousin Molly is in big trouble. I got to get her out of it. We'd like to have another man that can use a gun. Sam here says you fill that bill."

Finney frowned. "Ride clear out to Mexico land to try to find a kid that's probably already been had by half the tribe? That don't seem real smart, Boone."

Finney had not heard of Dan'l Boone, and was not impressed by him. But when he saw the anger rise into Dan'l's square face something in him made him soften his attitude quickly.

"Hey. I'm sorry if I talked out of turn."

Dan'l rose from the chair. "I think we made a mistake, Sam. Let's ride on back."

Finney came off the bunk, looking apologetic. "What would the pay be?"

Dan'l regarded him balefully. "More than you'd make here on this rock pile you call a farm," he said evenly.

Finney smiled for the first time. But it was a sour, cynical smile. "If you'll still take me, I'd be interested," he said. "I can kill Apaches. Better than most, I'd guess."

"Nobody said anything about killing," Dan'l reminded him.

"Oh. Sure. You know what I mean. My gun

will be your gun. That's all I meant."

Dan'l looked down at the table. "How long was you in that stinkhole of a prison, Finney?"

Finney cast a glance toward Cahill. "Seven years."

"I reckon it tends to make a man hard inside," Dan'l said.

"That's right."

"You come across some pretty tough men inside, and you pride yourself on being one of the toughest. After all, you survived."

Finney shrugged eloquently and put on an arrogant grin. "You got it about right, Boone."

Dan'l walked over to Finney and threw a cast-iron fist into his face.

There was a loud smacking sound, and Finney flew back hard against the bunk, hitting it solidly and cracking a board there. He slid to the floor, dazed.

"What the . . . hell!" he mumbled thickly. Blood ran down his chin.

"That's for the remark about Molly," Dan'l growled at him.

Cahill suppressed a grin.

"You ain't seen tough till you seen an Apache," Dan'l said to Finney. "Am I getting through to you, boy?"

Finney spat a tooth out onto the floor. "You son of a bitch!" But he made no move toward Dan'l. He just slowly raised himself to his feet, watching Dan'l carefully. "You damn near busted my jaw!"

"If I'd wanted it busted," Dan'l said, "it'd be hanging loose." He paused. "And I ain't even got my strength back yet from two bullets in me."

Finney leaned against the bunk again and wiped at his bloody chin. "You go the distance to make a point, damn you!" Finney said, scowling at Dan'l. "I could shoot you full of holes, you know."

Cahill laughed softly. "You're lucky you didn't try that, Finney," he offered.

Finney narrowed his dark eyes on Dan'l again, and suddenly understood Cahill's meaning.

"If you go out where we're headed," Dan'l said, "you got to have a lot of humility. If you think you can find some, you're hired. But you have to be ready to go tomorrow before first light."

Finney looked from Dan'l to Cahill and wondered what kind of man Cahill had brought into his cabin. He looked away for a moment, then back at Dan'l.

"All right, you made your point. I guess it's still the prison working inside me. Hell, I'll go."

Dan'l nodded. "Be at my place at five. And make sure you got a mount that can keep up with us."

Finney spit some blood onto the floor. "I'll be there."

Chapter Three

It had been well over a week since the attack on the Boone farm, and One Eye's party was far into Kiowa territory, heading swiftly for their home ground.

The night before, Molly had been raped by One Eye.

She had bitten and scratched him, and screamed into the night until he hit her hard across her pretty face. Then she had lain there and numbly succumbed to the assault.

Two of the other four men had watched.

It was the most humiliating and traumatic thing that had ever happened to her, and she was a different person the next morning. There were no more defiant outbursts. She had become silent, and let something hard settle deep inside her. The world was not a pretty place, after all. It was full of ugliness and death and terror.

At least for her.

The only small consolation was that One Eye considered her his woman. If he had not, they all would have violated her. And perhaps worse.

But now, at this brief rest stop on this warm, early-summer morning, Molly felt a depression well up forcefully within her until it threatened to engulf her entirely and destroy her sanity.

As for One Eye, he was very angry. He had expected some consideration from Molly, since he had, after all, made himself her protector. Even after he had consummated the marriage act with her and made her his, he was greatly disappointed that he had gotten nothing back from her at all. He expected her to forget her past and accept the fact that she was now an Apache squaw, and he did not understand her lack of acquiescence.

He had spoken to her just once that morning, and when he learned that she would not respond, he had not tried again.

The men now squatted in a tight circle, chewing on dried buffalo meat, talking quietly among themselves. Molly was propped against a nearby boulder, staring blankly off into the distance. Her auburn hair was wild-looking, and a smudge of dirt marred her right cheek. Her gingham dress was torn at the bodice. She was not tied, because One Eye knew she could not escape them.

"The woman still looks at you with hatred," Little Crow said to One Eye, smiling as he chewed on his meat.

One Eye glanced toward her. "She is an Apache now. She will learn our ways. She will sit beside me in the Great Lodge, and will have the respect of the entire tribe."

Little Crow and Gray Hawk exchanged dubious looks. Crooked Leg shook his head slowly. Lone Wolf just took in a deep breath and let it out audibly.

"Do not expect too much, my brother. She does not have our blood. The ways of the white woman are mysterious."

"It has always been so," Little Crow agreed.

Gray Hawk drank some water from a buffalo udder pouch, then rose to his feet. They had removed the dark, eastern-style clothing now, and all wore rawhide trousers, knee-high moccasins, and beaded cloth shirts. Gray Hawk rubbed a hand across his shirt and walked over to Molly. His hair hung long and black onto his shoulders, held by a headband with one eagle feather stuck into it. The others wore nothing on their heads.

"You. Drink!" Gray Hawk said to Molly, offering the flask.

Molly glanced upward and said nothing. She stared back down at the ground.

Gray Hawk narrowed his cold, dark eyes on

her. He grabbed her right arm and pulled her violently to her feet, and she felt the strength of his athletic frame.

"Drink!" he commanded in Athabaskan.

Molly got the idea but still did not respond. Gray Hawk poured water from the flask over her head, laughing.

Crooked Leg laughed too. But the others knew it was not a laughing matter. One Eye rose swiftly and walked over to Gray Hawk. He grabbed him from behind, taking Gray Hawk by complete surprise, and hurled him to the ground.

Gray Hawk hit hard, a look of shock on his face. Molly had flinched away from the sudden violence, and now huddled against the boulder.

At the circle of men, Lone Wolf rose too, in case he had to defend his older brother.

Gray Hawk stared up at One Eye with a deep frown. "What are you doing?"

"Have you lost your hearing?" One Eye yelled down at him. *"I told you to leave the woman alone!"*

Gray Hawk scrambled to his feet, very angry. "I wanted to give her water! She acts crazy! Is this my fault?"

"You are not to touch the woman!" One Eye repeated, the scar on his cheek livid in the sunlight.

"You defend a whiteface woman against your own warrior?" Gray Hawk said hotly. "Are you Apache or paleface?"

One Eye pulled his long war knife from a sheath and held it out in front of him grimly. "Maybe I must remind you what I am," he said through his teeth. "Royal blood runs through my veins, and my brother's. You are nothing."

Gray Hawk squared off with him but did not draw his own knife, or the gun that was stuck into his waistband.

Lone Wolf stepped up beside them. "You were wrong, Gray Hawk. The white woman is my brother's property. To pour water on her is to do the same to him."

Gray Hawk eyed Lone Wolf sideways, and his look softened.

"My brother will not have to demonstrate for you what it means to violate the property of a royal. Because I know you will realize the folly of your actions and ask my brother's forgiveness."

Gray Hawk took a long look at him, then at One Eye, then at One Eye's knife. Even with his skill with all kinds of weapons, he knew he was no match for the very fierce One Eye, who had proved his physical superiority over and over again.

He finally averted his eyes. "You are right, Lone Wolf. I meant no disrespect, but I should not have disciplined the woman. My heart is heavy for your embarrassment, One Eye, and I request you overlook my failing."

"Aiwaa!" Crooked Leg said to himself.

One Eye nodded and replaced the knife in its

sheath. "The matter is forgotten," he said.

Gray Hawk turned and walked back to the others, and the brothers exchanged a small smile. Then One Eye turned to Molly, who had sat back down on the ground.

"Do you see the trouble you cause, woman?" Without warning, he kicked her hard in her left thigh.

Molly cried out in pain and hid her head in her hands, afraid. But then her old self came alive in her, and she looked up at him with fire in her green eyes.

"Damn you!" she yelled. *"Damn all of you!"*

One Eye's face brightened, and a smile broke across it. He turned to the others. "There, you see! Is she not worth the effort?"

By the time they rode out, with Molly riding behind One Eye again on his spotted mustang, the incident was forgotten.

One Eye found that he liked having Molly ride with him on his mount, and from that point onward, he did not let her ride with anybody else. When she was on his horse, she had to hold on to him, if loosely, for balance. That gave him the feeling that she was his, and that she needed him for protection. It also developed a physical intimacy that could not easily be attained in any other way.

One Eye was certain that by the time they arrived back at his small village, she would be his, body and soul.

Late that afternoon, One Eye's party finally ran into other Indians.

They were still not out of Kiowa territory, and it was a small party of Kiowa that spotted them. The Kiowa were out hunting, and thought as they approached that they were coming upon other Kiowa. There were six of them, and when they stopped thirty yards away, their faces became very grim.

One Eye did the smart thing, though, and held his hand up as a gesture of peace. The Kiowa, who had rifles but not side arms, reluctantly gave the sign back. Then they came in closer. Two of them spoke Athabaskan.

"You are Apache," the heavy one in front said harshly, as if he were calling them criminals.

"Yes," One Eye admitted.

"You have violated Kiowa territory. That is the death penalty for Apache."

One Eye nodded, and rested his hand on his Mortimer pistol. "Do you wish to enforce the punishment?"

The Kiowa hesitated. He had them outnumbered six to five, but The Apaches had the short shooting sticks that fired quickly. He looked past One Eye to the others, saw Molly, and strained to get a better look at her. He also saw an antelope that Little Crow had killed earlier in the afternoon, hanging over the rump of his mustang.

"Perhaps a deal can be made," the Kiowa said.

One Eye nodded. "Perhaps." He knew that if they killed these men, there might be other Kiowa coming after them tomorrow.

"You have a white woman," the Kiowa said.

"Yes."

"Is she healthy?"

One Eye sighed heavily. Maybe there would be a fight, after all. He did not respond.

"Let's kill them," Gray Hawk said. "They are Kiowa."

"We will take the woman," the lead Kiowa said. "And the antelope. Then you may pass on without trouble. I will guarantee it."

"Give her to them," Crooked Leg said under his breath.

Molly had seen the Kiowa point at her, and she was suddenly even more scared than she had been earlier.

"What's he saying?" she said from behind One Eye.

One Eye ignored her. "The woman is my squaw," he said to the Kiowa. "She is not for trading. You can have the antelope."

"The antelope is not sufficient!" the Kiowa said loudly. He turned to the others and explained the rejection of his offer.

"The clothing," Lone Wolf said to his brother.

One Eye had kept the dark clothing they all had worn at the Boone cabin in his saddlebags. He dismounted, leaving Molly on the horse alone, and unpacked the bags, then walked up boldly to the Kiowa. They watched him warily.

"I give you all of this. The clothes of the whiteface. Good material. Warm cloth. All of it is yours. And the antelope."

The Kiowa reached down, took a shirt and examined it closely, then passed it back to the others. One Eye offered him the rest, and he hesitated, then took it.

"All right. The deal is made," the heavy Kiowa told him. "But be out of this area before the sun sets twice. Or you will not leave at all."

One Eye did not take offense at the threat. He knew it was all part of bargaining.

"We will be gone by this time tomorrow," he replied.

Gray Hawk took the antelope and threw it over the rump of a Kiowa's mount, and a few moments later One Eye's party rode on, unmolested by their traditional enemies.

By sunset that evening, they were at the far edge of Kiowa territory.

The next morning, in the darkness of a cool predawn, Dan'l set out after One Eye. Finney arrived at the farm promptly at five, as Dan'l had requested. The three other men were already saddling up, stuffing saddlebags with light provisions, checking guns and ammunition. Cahill had wanted Dan'l to take a packhorse, but Dan'l had explained to him that no packhorse would be able to keep up with them.

"Are you sure?" Cahill now asked him again.

"I don't think I made myself clear, Sam,"

Dan'l told him, cinching up the saddle on his sleek, gray-spotted Appaloosa. "We're going to be riding hard. I mean hard. Maybe twelve hours or more a day."

"Even then it could take a couple weeks," Cahill said.

Dan'l looked at him. The four men were all standing beside their mounts, making things ready. Jemima stood off at a small distance, teary-eyed, and Rebecca was over at the front door of the house, looking desolate.

"It ain't going to take no couple weeks," Dan'l said firmly. "Molly needs us. Now. I want to be in Santa Fe in eight or nine days. I'll ride all night if I have to."

Cahill nodded. "I understand, Dan'l."

"If we get there in a week or a little more, they'll have to bury us on arrival," Finney joked. Then he looked over at Dan'l and lost his smile quickly.

"We can do it," McGill said. He and Dan'l were the two roughest-looking of the group. McGill was wearing an old coonskin cap, with the tail hanging down over his long hair. Dan'l still wore a dark, wide-brim Quaker hat, which had become his trademark. They both wore rawhides with fringe on the tunic sleeves and bottom, and Dan'l had the small figure of a bear sewn onto his, over his heart, put there by Rebecca. It was a protection totem given to him by the Taos Indians who had fought with him against Yellow Horse.

Dan'l would not have worn that shirt but for Rebecca. He did not like the implication that the symbol identified him as an ancient Apache god, which he had always vigorously denied. But Rebecca would not remove it before he left, because she felt it would be bad luck.

"I figure we can cover most of a hundred miles in a day," Dan'l said. "If we make sure the horses get plenty of rest and water. But that's riding hard and long."

"We'll keep up, Dan'l," Cahill said. "I just hope you're able."

"I'm feeling good," Dan'l lied. He still had a lot of pain inside him, and he knew that what lay ahead would be grueling. But it had to be done.

The three others had their saddlebags full and everything in place. One by one they mounted up. Dan'l went over to his daughter.

"Please take care of yourself, Father," she told him, her blue eyes moist.

Dan'l grinned widely for her. "I always do, don't I?"

She smiled in return. "Yes. You always do."

Dan'l looked past her to Rebecca, twenty yards away. "Is your mother going to be all right?"

"I'll take care of her. You better go say good-bye again. She needs it."

Dan'l nodded and walked over to the house while Jemima said goodbye to Cahill.

Rebecca stood there with the dim light of the

house behind her. She looked older to Dan'l this morning, with wisps of gray hair straggling down beside her face, and dark spots under her eyes from worrying and crying.

"I'm sorry, Becky. I'm right sorry things got to be this way. But you know I'm doing what's right. We can't abandon that girl out there."

"I know," Rebecca said to him. She looked away.

He came closer. "Everything's going to be just fine, woman. I'll get some help from Alvarado, and we'll go get Molly back in a hurry. Trust me on that."

"In your condition, you might not even get to Santa Fe," Rebecca said, her voice unsteady.

He took her chin in his hand. "You know better than that. I'm tough as an old weathered board. Look at me."

She met his gaze.

"I'm coming back. With Molly."

She suddenly threw herself onto him, hugging him with silent desperation. "All right, Dan'l. I believe you."

"I'll see you before you know it," he said.

She nodded. Then he pulled away from her and returned to his mount. A few minutes later, they rode off into the darkness.

They rode very hard that first day, through the woodlands of Missouri, and then on to open grasslands. Hour after hour they rode at a half-gallop, so they would not wear the horses out.

The rest stops were few and brief. Anytime they crossed a stream, they let the horses drink. In midafternoon it became clear that Finney's mount was not up to the rigor of it, so when they came to a lonely ranch out in the middle of nowhere, they traded the animal for a fleeter one that Dan'l picked out himself.

They kept going after dark, and Dan'l would not let them stop to sleep until almost midnight.

They were worn out.

The horses' flanks were sweaty and required currying. Finney looked as if he might fall off his horse before he dismounted. He was thinking seriously of turning back when he collapsed on a bedroll without eating.

Dan'l was wracked with chest pain, but did not mention it to anybody. The bullet hole in his back started draining again through a light bandage. He had needed a couple more weeks of rest, but he could not afford it. Every day would count in recovering Molly.

They built a low fire as soon as they encamped, and all four of them put their bedrolls down near it. Cahill was bone-weary, but resolved he would not make anything of it to Dan'l. The mountain man, Luther McGill, was old-leather tough like Dan'l, and was not intimidated by the long ride. He was accustomed to privation and hardship.

All except Finney sat on their bedrolls and ate a light meal of dried meat and hardtack. Finney was already snoring by the time the coffee was boiling in a small pot that Cahill carried on a thong beside a saddlebag. He also carried four tin cups that fit inside the pot for traveling.

The three of them sat there in a dull moonlight and chewed their hardship-camp food and swigged the hot coffee. They did not speak at all for a long while. Finally Cahill threw some coffee dregs onto the fire, making it sizzle briefly, and broke the silence.

"I better take a look at that bandage, Dan'l," he said. He rose, walked over to Dan'l, and pulled up the back of his rawhide shirt.

"Damn," he muttered. "It's weeping again."

"Leave it be," Dan'l told him. "I'm all right."

"We can't leave that bandage on there," Cahill argued. "The wound can reinfect."

"Goddamn it, Sam," Dan'l said crossly. "I didn't bring you along for no nursemaid. I feel right good."

Cahill was too old a friend to take offense. He came around and looked Dan'l in the eye. "Listen to me, by God! If you want to make it to Santa Fe and have any chance of getting Molly back, you got to take care of yourself. Now, by Jesus, I'm going to change that bandage!"

Dan'l saw the resolve in Cahill's square, lined face with the rather small, intent eyes and the busted nose. A slow grin tugged the corners of Dan'l's mouth.

"I reckon you are."

Cahill got some gauze out of a saddlebag over near where the horses were tethered, and Dan'l pulled his shirt off. McGill was still chewing on a tough hunk of dried antelope meat that was brought from Dan'l's farm, and watched the bandage changing while he ate.

"I knowed a trapper once that got this arrow in his side fighting off a couple of renegade Sioux. He got the arrow out clean and packed the hole all up with a poultice. Then went on about his business, hunting and trapping beaver. The wound seemed like it was healing, but it never did. It went on for months like that, with yellow stuff coming out of it off and on, and the place getting kind of a reddish-blue color. He didn't pay it any mind, but he begun losing his appetite. Damn if he didn't wither right up finally. Weighed maybe a hundred pounds. I'd started hunting with him then, and one morning he just didn't wake up. I pulled his shirt up and took a look at the wound, and there was a place around it swolled up big as a grapefruit and all purple. Never seen nothing like it in my life." He swigged some coffee. "That boy never thought nothing of that hole in him, right up to the day he died."

Dan'l gave him a sour look. "Much obliged for the comforting words."

McGill shrugged. "That's just the way it was. Me, I always tend the smallest scratch out here in the big country. You never know what little bugs is a-picking away at you."

Cahill was finished, and Dan'l pulled his shirt

back down. "I'll keep that in mind, McGill," he said.

Dan'l had had doubts about both of the men he had hired ever since he met them. He figured he would never be able to get really close to McGill—close enough to make any assessment of McGill's loyalty or trustworthiness. McGill was too closemouthed, too secretive about his feelings. As for Finney, Dan'l thought he may have made a mistake in taking him on. Finney gave the impression that he had been a pretty cold character long before the incident that sent him off to prison, and also maybe that he had learned some things there that did not make him a better man. Dan'l hoped Finney had learned a little humility back there at his cabin, but he was sure that the ex-gunsmith still had the potential to be trouble.

There were two other things Dan'l was certain of, as well. One was that both men were good with guns, and the other was that neither of them would shy away from a fight. And both of those things were very important to Dan'l.

"That campsite we found this afternoon," McGill said to Dan'l as Cahill returned the gauze to his saddlebag. "That was old One Eye, wasn't it?"

Right after a midday break, they had ridden through the first campsite of One Eye and his men. Dan'l and Cahill had stopped and examined it closely, but Dan'l had not wanted to talk about it at the time.

Dan'l looked over at the hunter. "Yes. It was."

"Looks like we'll gain some time on him as we go."

"That's what I'm hoping," Dan'l said.

"Did you see all them scuff marks on the ground by that tree?" McGill asked.

Cahill was back at the fire. "Why don't you let it go, McGill?"

McGill looked up at him in mild surprise.

"It's all right, Sam," Dan'l said quietly. He met McGill's look. "Yes, I seen the marks. There was a scuffle there. It might've involved Molly."

"There ain't no way of knowing," Cahill said quickly.

Dan'l sighed. "I know how it looks," he said. "They're already causing her pain. Maybe raping her."

"At least there ain't no evidence they killed her," McGill offered.

Dan'l looked over at him. "If I thought she was dead, I wouldn't be out here."

Cahill sat down on his bedroll. "She ain't dead," he said with slow assurance. "I feel it right in here." He tapped on his chest.

Dan'l smiled. Cahill was always trying to take care of him. He would never forget that Dan'l had saved his life on that river a thousand years ago. He had resettled in Missouri just because Dan'l was there.

"Me too," Dan'l said. He looked into the flickering fire. "Reminds me of the time the Shawnee took Jemima."

Cahill nodded. He had still been in Carolina at that time, while Dan'l was in Boonesborough in Kentucky, but he knew the story well.

"Her and a friend was playing down by the river, outside the fort," Dan'l went on, as if talking to himself. "They was just kids, but beginning to look like women. The Shawnee snuck up on them and grabbed them afore they knowed what was happening. They just carried them away on foot."

Cahill shook his head.

"We heard the yelling," Dan'l went on, "and I knowed right away what happened. There wasn't nobody around that could help right then, so I went after them."

"Alone?" McGill wondered.

Dan'l nodded. "When it's your kin, you don't think twice. I run after them Shawnee for five hours. They didn't know I was onto them. They finally camped in the deep woods, the five of them, and they staked the girls out on the ground and was going to take their turns on them. I got there just when that was about to begin."

He stared into the fire, remembering.

"Jemima seen me right off but didn't make a peep. That girl was smarter than her paw even then. I stuck a knife in the back of the nearest Indian, then pulled it out and thrown it at a second one. They was both down afore the others knowed I was there. I blowed most of another one's head off with my Kentucky rifle, then smashed the fourth one's face in with the butt. The last one run off so fast, I let him go."

Cahill and McGill exchanged a look, and Cahill saw new respect in McGill's face.

"When Chief Blackfish heard about it, he found that fifth Shawnee and had him skinned alive," Dan'l concluded. "The chief and me always did get along."

McGill grinned and shook his head. "I'm beginning to be glad I won't be one of them Apaches when you catch up to them," he said easily.

Dan'l grunted. "When we catch them Apaches, it won't be a few men caught by surprise in the woods, McGill. It might make that other time seem like a Sunday picnic at the Boston Commons."

McGill regarded Dan'l soberly. "I'll be ready for it, if that's your point," he said.

"I'm glad to hear that," Dan'l said. "Now, let's try to get a few hours' sleep."

"That suits me right down to the ground," Cahill concurred.

Chapter Four

The following morning, One Eye and his straggling warriors arrived back at their home village.

A sentry spotted them at a distance, and when they rode into the small enclosure of tipis and lodges, the entire village came to welcome them back. Women and children yelled and screamed, and young warriors strode alongside their mounts, looking Molly over openly.

Molly still rode behind One Eye, and she watched the procession with wonder and fear. She had never been west of St. Louis, had never seen any Apaches except for the men who had brought her here. She listened to the foreign, odd-sounding language, and peered fascinated at the cloth-and-buckskin garb, much of it bead-worked, and tried to understand what kind of world she had been brought to.

Through the last couple of days she had been in the hot, dry country south of Santa Fe, and that, too, was all new to her. She had never seen a butte, or a dry riverbed, or a rocky canyon. Under other circumstances, it could have been a wonderful experience. As it was, she just sat on One Eye's horse rather numb through it all.

As the small party arrived in the center of the village, they reined in and One Eye held his hand up to catch the attention of the assemblage.

The chattering and yelling settled down.

"The murderer of Yellow Horse is dead!" he announced.

The yelling broke out again with renewed intensity.

"May the gods reward One Eye!"

"One Eye is the greatest Apache!"

"His story will be told forever!"

Lone Wolf turned to his older brother and smiled. The others just looked weary.

One Eye raised his hand again. "This woman is the offspring of Sheltowee, and she is the trophy of our victorious journey!"

A hush fell over the Indians as they stared soberly at Molly. A young woman, called Nalin, stood nearby and let a scowl mar her pretty features. She had been a kind of mistress of One Eye before his departure, and he had not even caught her eye yet.

"Give her over to us women!" Nalin called to One Eye. "We will know what to do with her!"

Several other women joined in and supported Nalin's proposal. One Eye, though, looked down at Nalin seriously.

"She will not be harmed. As a trophy of war, she will be my woman."

Nalin's face revealed quick shock and anger. Many of the women also showed disapproval. The men did not care. Many of them cheered One Eye again.

"She will become an Apache!" One Eye said loudly. "And I want her treated like an Apache!"

Again, the mixed reaction. Nalin spat onto the ground and walked away toward a tipi. One Eye ignored her.

"Now let us celebrate our great victory!" he concluded. "There will be a feast!"

There was more yelling as One Eye and his four warriors dismounted and their horses were led away by others. Molly was placed in a lodge made of branches and skins, with a young warrior on guard at the doorway. One Eye and his men went to a nearby stream to be bathed by some of the young women.

Later that day, in early afternoon, the village shaman, an older man named Eagle Spirit, got the men of the village together and voted to name One Eye its official chief. When they made the announcement One Eye was very pleased, but he had fully expected the honor. Now he had status, and so did the village.

Young men would flock to him, and the village would grow in size and importance, all because he was the Apache who had killed the great Sheltowee, the much-feared warrior whom some Apaches still credited with spiritual powers because he resembled their image of an ancestral god called Ancient Bear.

While the feast was being prepared out on the compound, the young woman called Nalin went to One Eye's lodge with a friend, carrying a gourd bowl of porridge with her.

"What do you want?" the guard asked her.

"One Eye asked us to bring the white woman food," Nalin lied. Actually, One Eye had not even spoken to Nalin privately since his arrival. He did not want to make excuses for taking Molly as his woman. Not to Nalin. Not to anyone.

"All right," the guard said. "Keep watch over her until I return. I must speak with One Eye."

"We will watch her well," Nalin told him.

She and her small, thin friend entered the lodge and found Molly sitting on a stool at the far wall, looking very forlorn. When she saw the women with the bowl, Molly thought she might at last find some kindness in this wilderness they had brought her to.

But she saw by Nalin's sober face that her first impression had been wrong. Nalin came and put the bowl at Molly's feet in an offhand way.

"What is your name?" Nalin asked.

Molly regarded her quizzically. "What?"

"Do you speak our language?"

"I don't understand," Molly said with a shrug.

Nalin slapped her hard across the face.

Molly was stunned. She rose with her cheek burning and fire in her green eyes. "Damn you!"

Nalin, a smug smile on her brown face, turned to her companion and nodded. The other woman came forward a step. *"Habla español?"*

Molly turned to her, still angry. Her mother had sent her to Charleston for a while after Molly's father's death, to stay with an aunt there and learn to be a lady. Molly had befriended a Spanish-speaking servant, and had absorbed some of her language before returning to the Yadkin Valley in Carolina.

"Un poquito, sí," Molly said glumly.

"She says yes," the smaller woman said in Athabaskan.

Nalin nodded. "What do you think you are about?" she said icily to Molly. "Did you flaunt your white skin before my man?"

The other woman, called Three Tongues, translated. It was too complex for Molly, but she got the sense of it.

"Do you think I want to take your place with that murderer?" Molly said in English, a look of incredulity on her face. "I'd rather be dead and buried with pennies on my eyes!"

Nalin frowned and looked at the one called Three Tongues, then Molly remembered and translated it into rough Spanish.

"She says she would rather be dead than One Eye's woman."

Nalin was angry now. "You add insult to deception and treachery, you white whore!"

Three Tongues did not translate.

"You look like a sick she-buffalo," Nalin said loudly. "How can he stand to lie with you?"

Three Tongues hesitated, then translated roughly. Molly's face clouded over. Then she mustered her rudimentary Spanish.

"One Eye is murderer. You are all murderers. I wish to be be free of you, that is all."

As translation followed, Nalin's eyes narrowed quickly, and she slapped Molly again with more force.

Molly staggered backward but did not fall. She acted out of pure instinct. She swung hard at Nalin, and her closed fist connected with Nalin's cheek with a loud smack.

Nalin fell back, then just stood there, looking stunned. When she touched her mouth there was a small smear of blood on her hand.

"By the holy spirits!" she hissed. "You must be insane as well as stupid." She hurled herself at Molly.

They went down in a heap on the rugs that covered the floor, with Nalin beating Molly with her fists and tearing at her auburn hair. Molly was too surprised by the ferocity of the attack to fight back. Three Tongues reluctantly joined in, grabbing Molly's arms so she could not properly defend herself. Then Nalin reached for a small, thin knife at her belt and held it up to Molly's face.

"We will see how One Eye likes you after I have scarred your pallid face!" she said in a grating voice. Molly saw the razor-sharp blade come down to her cheek and let out a muffled yell.

"Nalin!" Three Tongues protested. "She is One Eye's woman! There will be consequences!"

"I don't care," Nalin said huskily. "I don't care what he does to me!"

But at that very moment, the guard appeared in the doorway of the lodge and took in the scene at a glance. Three Tongues released her hold on Molly and moved away.

"What are you doing there?" the warrior said sharply.

Nalin glanced over her shoulder, then turned back to Molly. She lowered the knife to Molly's flesh.

Rough hands grabbed her and yanked her back.

"You fool!" the guard said. Nalin struggled in his grasp for a moment, then relaxed. He took the knife from her.

"What were you thinking?" he admonished her. "Have you hurt her?" He looked down and saw the bruises beginning on Molly's face.

Nalin took a deep breath. "She insulted our people. I was teaching her to be an Apache."

"With this?" the guard said. "Please leave, both of you. Now."

Nalin and Three Tongues moved to the entrance, where Nalin turned to him. "She is trouble," she said in a cold voice.

He nodded. "Many of us feel the same way. But the brothers like their white women, and they rule the clan. It is just a physical thing, and will not last. As for this thing, I will have to report it, of course."

"Of course," Nalin said darkly. "You and the brothers are all fellow warriors, and I am a mere woman. I expected nothing more from you."

The guard watched them leave, shaking his head. Molly had risen to the stool again, her hand up to a bruise on her face. *"Gracias,"* she said heavily to him, hoping he would understand.

He nodded with an acid look. *"De nada,"* he replied.

After several days had passed, Dan'l's riders were well over halfway to Santa Fe. Dan'l had kept them on their horses twelve hours a day and more, and they were all worn out, as were the horses. One day, Cahill finally insisted that they stop at dark to give them all a needed rest. Dan'l agreed, but just before the sun went down, they met a lone Ute Indian on the trail.

The Ute's people had settled their differences with the Mexicans and white settlers long ago, but he still approached Dan'l's riders warily. Individual murders were still committed on both sides, and you never knew whom you would meet out on the trail.

It was McGill who recognized the Ute first, because he had trapped all through that area. So all of them kept their guns out of sight as they approached the Indian. The Ute raised his hand in the traditional peace sign, and Dan'l responded.

"I was right. He's a Ute," McGill said. "He's all right."

"You talk it some, don't you?" Dan'l asked.

McGill nodded. "Enough to get by."

"Ask him about One Eye," Cahill said.

"Hell, let's just get on with finding a place to sleep tonight," the ragged-looking Finney suggested.

Dan'l gave him a look. "Go ahead, McGill. Be friendly."

The tall, rugged McGill nodded. "May peace rule in your tribe," he began.

The Ute was expressionless. "You have whiskey?"

McGill turned to Dan'l. "He wants liquor," he said.

"Tell him to go to hell," Finney said in a fit of temper.

Cahill glared at him. "You keep to hell out of it!"

All their tempers were short.

"Ain't you got some rotgut in your bags?" Dan'l said to McGill.

"I got part of a bottle left."

"Give it to him," Dan'l said.

McGill eyed him narrowly.

"I said give it to him," Dan'l repeated.

McGill hesitated, then fished in a saddlebag and came up with the bottle. He spurred his mount forward and handed the whiskey to the Ute. The Indian, a heavyset, middle-aged fellow, opened the bottle and swigged half of the liquid in one gulp. Then he belched loudly and grinned.

"Good whiskey."

Dan'l came up closer to McGill. "Tell him we're looking for some Apaches," he said.

McGill watched his whiskey disappear into a saddle pouch on the Indian's pony. "How long do you ride this trail?"

The Ute regarded him straight-faced. "It makes many days I come here from the south."

"You have possibly met with Apaches?"

"Yes. I felt surprise at the sight, because they were in Comanche territory. They were going to Apache land."

"How many were there?" McGill asked.

"Five. They had a white woman. I recognized one of them. The Apaches call him One Eye."

McGill again translated for Dan'l, and Dan'l nodded. It was the first confirmation they had had that One Eye was the killer at Dan'l's house, and the abductor of Molly Morgan.

"It's them, all right, a few days ahead of us. One Eye's kept the girl alive," McGill said to the others.

"Thank God," Dan'l muttered.

"That probably means you're right, Dan'l. She'll be kept for a while, at least. As a trophy."

Dan'l met McGill's gaze. "The question is, how long?" he said quietly. "All right, boys. Let's find us a spot to camp. Tell the Ute we're through with him."

"Do you have tobacco?" the Ute asked McGill.

McGill grunted. "Now he wants tobacco."

Dan'l moved his Appaloosa up close to the Indian. "Get on your way, damn it!" he said with a jerk of his thumb over his shoulder.

The Ute looked into Dan'l's face and was suddenly very frightened. He nodded and moved off, looking twice behind him as he disappeared over a rise of ground.

They found a comfortable campsite against a low cliff wall that night, and all had a good rest despite taking turns standing sentry duty. The next day, Dan'l was up in the dark, more eager than ever to get moving now that he knew Molly was still alive.

They rode without incident through Comanche territory all that day. They were in the dry country now, with dust under their horses' hooves and high buttes all around them. Desert country lay just ahead, and they were already running into prickly pear and yucca, and getting glimpses of coyotes. In midafternoon, when Dan'l figured they were pretty well past any Comanche threat, things changed for them in a hurry.

Dan'l saw them first, just specks on the horizon. There were six of them, a Comanche war party itching for a fight with a whiteface because a clan member had been murdered out on the trail by a Mexican.

"We got us company," Dan'l said when he saw them riding hard toward his group.

Finney could not even see them for a couple of minutes. McGill saw them as soon as Dan'l pointed them out.

"Comanch!" he announced rather loudly.

"Oh, hell," Cahill said with fatigue in his voice. That was exactly what they did not need, a shoot-out with hostiles.

Dan'l was looking around quickly. "That ravine over there to our left," he said. "It's shallow, just a small, dry riverbed. But it'll do. Let's get over there."

In just moments, the four of them had dismounted in the shallow, head-high depression in the ground, pulled their horses off their feet so they would present smaller targets, and drawn their rifles for defense. Now the Comanches were just two hundred yards away and galloping hard, dust kicking up behind them.

"Pick off as many as you can before they get here!" Dan'l called to the others as he primed his famous Kentucky rifle, which other men had called Ticklicker because of its extreme accuracy. "That might kill their enthusiasm some!"

The Comanches were only a hundred yards off now and had begun yelling raucously. They all wore full eagle feather headdresses and were dressed in beaded rawhide pants, but they were naked above the waist, with bright colors painted on their chests and faces. They all carried brightly decorated lances, and their leader held above his head a long pole with feathers attached from top to bottom. Only two of the Comanches wielded rifles, while all wore short bows and quivers of arrows on their backs.

These were the deadly enemy of One Eye and his Apaches, and One Eye had been very lucky to pass through without a bloody battle.

"Now!" Dan'l yelled. *"Fire now!"*

All four rifles exploded loudly, and three of the attackers were thrown wildly off their charging mounts. Cahill had missed with his first shot.

The Indians stopped momentarily and looked at their fallen comrades, then with some more loud yelling came on again, fifty yards away.

Dan'l and McGill were reloaded and ready for the charge, but Cahill and Finney were still operating their ramrods when the Comanches arrived. Lances came flying into the riverbed. One grazed Cahill's right arm and thudded into the ground across the small ravine. Another one missed Dan'l's head by inches. Then the Indians were riding up and down the bank of the ravine, firing arrows into the depression.

Chaos ensued. Dan'l knocked a fourth Comanche off his mount and he came plunging into the ravine, falling dead at Finney's feet.

Suddenly the mounted Comanches realized that there were just two of them left, and both wheeled their mounts and rode off the way they had come. McGill aimed his rifle at their retreating backs, but Dan'l put a hand on the gun's muzzle and pushed it down. McGill eyed him curiously.

Behind Dan'l's back, Finney walked over to the dying Comanche in the gulley, aimed his gun at the Indian's head, and fired. The fellow jumped spasmodically and died.

Dan'l saw what had happened and sighed audibly. "There wasn't no need for that, neither," he said to Finney.

"Did you want me to let him throw a knife into your back?" Finney said defensively. "He was alive and kicking."

"Hell, forget it," Dan'l said. He watched as the two uninjured Comanches picked up a comrade who was still alive out there and carried him away.

"They'll be back for the dead ones later," he added.

McGill looked into Dan'l's square, bearded face and dropped his rifle to his side. "I hope you ain't fixing to be that nice to One Eye."

Dan'l grunted softly. "When we catch One Eye, it'll be him or me," he said. "I thought you knowed that."

A few minutes later they were saddled up again and riding hard to get out of Comanche territory.

Cahill's wound was just a scratch, so he did not even bandage it before they rode out.

They had been lucky this time.

Tomorrow, they would be in the country of the Apache.

Chapter Five

Molly did not know when One Eye was told it was Nalin who had beaten and almost killed her. But the following morning Molly caught a glimpse of Nalin with a blackened left eye and looking very morose. One Eye had administered a mild punishment, just enough to remind Nalin that he was the chief of their clan and would not tolerate rebellion against his wishes in any form.

Molly was formally married to One Eye that afternoon. Four women came to One Eye's lodge, stripped her clothing off her despite her physical protests, and put on her a deerskin dress decorated with fancy beading and feathers. They also made her wear leggings, an ermine cape, and a headband with one golden eagle feather affixed. When they were done with her, she looked like an Indian princess, which she would soon become, in a modest way.

Everybody attended the outdoor ceremony, where Eagle Spirit chanted and danced and laid a garland of desert blossoms around Molly's neck. One Eye looked very regal, with a feather headdress, a large ermine cape, and a gold breastplate hanging on a rawhide cord worked with beads. Lone Wolf, proud and handsome, stood beside him through the ceremony. Molly got another glimpse of Nalin in the assembled crowd, looking very glum and hostile.

When it was over, Molly was made to sit with One Eye near a council fire, eat antelope meat and cassava, and drink something that tasted alcoholic, which the Mexicans called *pombe*. Surprisingly, though, after that she was escorted back to her lodge, with One Eye paying almost no attention to her. The celebration went on into the evening, well past dark, with drums, chanting, and dances. She heard all of that from the lodge, and waited tensely for One Eye to appear.

When he did, he was inebriated and entirely impatient with any coyness or resistance on her part. When she tried to pull away from him he slapped her hard across the face, bringing tears to her eyes. Then he forced her just as he had done on the trail, while she closed her eyes tightly and waited until it was over. One Eye then talked to her in a slurred voice for a few minutes, but she understood nothing of it. Finally, he fell into a heavy sleep beside her, both of them nude.

Molly lay there and wondered if this would ever end. Her only hope was for Dan'l to somehow still be alive, because she knew her cousin would come after her if he could. But she could not just wait and hope. She looked over at her new "husband," and thoughts of murdering him ran through her head. She could wait for an hour until he was fast asleep, then get his war knife and stab him in the heart with it. A man could not defend himself when he was asleep, no matter how strong he was.

She lay there feeling violated and dirty. She had saved herself for Jock Parrish, had anticipated their marriage with great pleasure. Now Jock was dead at the hands of the savage brute who was taking Jock's place with her. It was too much to bear, to think of this going on night after night, month after month. Until he tired of her, and then what? He might just give her to someone else, or even kill her. There was no way for her to know, and that was perhaps the worst part.

Even if she killed One Eye, though, her situation would not be improved. In fact, they might kill her immediately if she harmed him in any way. Some of the women, she knew now, were already hostile toward her. Even though some of the men seemed to like the idea of taking a white woman as a mate, most of the women probably resented it greatly.

But there was an alternative to killing One Eye. Not suicide; she had gotten past that. Suicide meant the end of all hope. Maybe Dan'l would come eventually. Maybe she could escape.

Molly lay there and let the last idea sink in for a while. There was no guard outside their lodge now. They felt One Eye could handle her, it seemed. The rest of the village would be sleeping, too, with maybe only a sentry or two out there. The idea of escape filled her chest with renewed hope. She waited for another half hour, until One Eye was snoring softly beside her. Then she edged away from him and pulled on her Apache clothing. They had burned her other things. She looked down at the Apache chief who had just taken her by force and would continue doing so for as long as he pleased.

Yes, there was no time like the present. If she waited very long, she would become more accustomed to it, perhaps numb to it. Her spirit would be crushed, and she would not be able to fight back. If that happened, she might as well be dead.

She went to One Eye's things, found his knife, and stuck it in her beaded belt. She was ready. She looked back at him. Maybe she would never see his ugly face again.

She turned, pulled a skin aside, and left the lodge.

Outside there was a bright moon. The village

tipis and lodges crouched in silhouette in the darkness. The council fire had almost guttered out, but bright coals still remained.

There was no one in sight. Over to her right was a small corral where the horses were kept, but she knew she could not possibly cut a horse out of the bunch without attracting attention. So she started out of the village on foot, in a half-crouch.

She moved quietly to the perimeter of the village. She looked for sentries but could see none. She knew they had complete confidence in their ability to find her and bring her back if she got away. And they were probably right. But there was an outside chance that she could avoid them for a while, hide away from them, and then find help from some traveler or wagon train on its way to Santa Fe.

She was fifty yards outside the village now. It sat at the mouth of a gorge, with high cliffs on either side and a few straggly cottonwoods beyond the entrance. Molly tried to keep in the shadows of the few trees, but she was in the open a lot in the first fifty yards.

She did not hear him come. She had just reached the apparent cover of a small tree when she finally heard the scrape of gravel underfoot behind her, and a strong arm wrapped itself around her throat.

She managed a small yell, and her heart leapt into her upper chest and threatened to explode. She grabbed the arm and tried to struggle, but she was overpowered by its strength.

When the Apache turned her to him, she recognized Gray Hawk, who had happened to be on sentry duty that bright night.

"You fool!" he said into her face.

Molly was terrified. She struggled against him, and he suddenly enjoyed feeling her in his hands. "You stupid whiteface! I should take you too. Right here."

Molly quit struggling. She knew what he had said, even though she could not understand the words. She could see it in his dark eyes.

"Go ahead," she said breathlessly. "I'm sure One Eye will be pleased to know what happened!"

Gray Hawk recognized Molly's pronunciation of One Eye's Athabaskan name, and it stopped him. He gave her a hard look, then slapped her viciously. If he had not been holding her, she would have hit the ground.

"We will see what your husband thinks of you now," he declared. Then he began dragging her back to One Eye's lodge.

When they got there, Gray Hawk threw Molly into the lodge. She fell to the ground not far from the sleeping One Eye. Gray Hawk came in behind Molly as One Eye came awake.

"What? What is it?" One Eye said sleepily.

"Your woman!" Gray Hawk said harshly. "Maybe you had better tie her to a stake. I caught her trying to leave the village."

One Eye was still naked. He sat up and looked

over at Molly, who was propped on her elbow, looking disheveled and desperate, her long hair wild.

"You tried to escape?" One Eye said to her.

Molly hung her head, wanting it all to go away. Maybe, she thought, she should have cut her own throat when she had the chance. Gray Hawk had taken the knife from her belt, and now hurled it into the ground beside One Eye.

"There must be punishment!" Gray Hawk said to him.

One Eye rose and pulled on a pair of rawhide trousers. Then he walked over to Molly and kicked her in the side of the head with his bare foot.

Molly cried out in pain, fell onto her back, and began sobbing uncontrollably.

One Eye moved over to Gray Hawk. He grabbed the muscular, hawk-nosed warrior by the throat with one powerful hand and slowly forced him to his knees. Gray Hawk was gasping for breath when One Eye released him.

"You are one of my favorite warriors, and you will belong to our newly formed *akacita* society as one of its leaders. But do not ever tell me when or how I must punish one of my people!"

Gray Hawk stayed on his knees, seeing the fury in One Eye's good eye. "But she is a—"

"*She is my woman!*" One Eye shouted at him. "She is an Apache now! Make a place for that in your heart, Cousin, or I will disown you!"

Gray Hawk knew One Eye was sober now,

and that he meant every word he said. "All right. Chief One Eye."

One Eye nodded his approval of Gray Hawk's use of his new title. "You may go. Your finding of my woman will be rewarded."

A moment later, One Eye and Molly were alone in the lodge. One Eye went over and sat down beside her, touched the side of her face gently, and looked at it.

"You will be all right."

She pulled away from him. The sobbing had stopped, but her eyes were teary.

"You must not try to leave us. You are Apache now. You will learn to like it here among us." He turned away. "*Aiwaa!* I wish you could speak."

"Do not strike me," she suddenly said in Spanish.

One Eye turned back to her. He knew some Spanish, and understood. His bronze face brightened, and his good eye revealed pleasure. "They told me about Spanish. I forgot. You can speak."

"Do not strike me again," Molly said quietly. *"No me dar golpes nuevamente."*

One Eye nodded soberly. *"Comprendo.* We will attempt to share my lodge in peace." The last was said in his own language, but Molly got the gist of it.

"But I am chief," One Eye added. *"Jefe. No se olvide."* Don't forget, he warned her.

"I don't think that's possible," Molly mumbled in English.

As she lay beside him the rest of that night and listened to his deep breathing, she said over and over in her mind, "Be alive, Dan'l. Come after me."

The next day, as a continuation of the celebration of One Eye's appointment as chief of the village, and also his marriage to Molly Morgan, One Eye led his warriors against a newly formed Spanish settlement half a day's ride to the north, toward Santa Fe.

One Eye had grand plans. He had vowed to carry on the war against the whites that Yellow Horse had started, and rid the area of all pale-faces. Maybe even attack Santa Fe again, as Yellow Horse had done years ago.

Most Apaches in the area wanted no more of war, and One Eye regarded them as cowards. But he was certain that, once he had had some victories from his forays into the white man's world, warriors from other tribes would flock to him in great numbers, and the Apache would rule the south country once again.

It took most of the morning to reach the small settlement of thirty or so Mexicans. One Eye's war party of two dozen warriors, including Lone Wolf and the others he had had with him in Missouri, all had rifles and muskets stolen from the Mexican army and other sources, and were ready for a big fight.

One Eye sat his mount quietly out in front of the settlement. It was just a collection of huts and shanties, surrounded by a partially constructed adobe wall that did not even have a gate yet. One Eye would have no trouble getting in.

His warriors were all gathered around him. He raised a war lance high above his head to get their attention. He wore a full headdress of an Apache chief, but was naked to the waist for hard fighting. In his other hand he carried a Charleville rifle.

"Now we will carry on with the great fight begun by the heroic and immortal Yellow Horse!" he said loudly into a slight, warm breeze.

There were some shouts of excitement.

"Now we go in!" One Eye yelled. "Death to the whiteface!"

There was a roar of wild whooping as they charged at the Mexican village.

As they rode in, they saw Mexican men in the streets, running in all directions, going for weapons. Women carried children to safety behind closed doors, and cowards slunk off into dark corners to wait out the chaos.

The Apaches shot anyone they found out in the open. One Eye immediately killed a young fellow running for his house, blowing the fellow's face away and spraying blood and matter onto the ground. Women went down, too, with holes in their backs and chests. Two children were caught in the open, and one ended up on the end of Crooked Leg's war lance.

Apaches felt no guilt in killing women and children. The whites were all infidel intruders into sacred Apache land, and to spare children would only be to cause themselves further trouble in a few more years, they reasoned. So any whiteface—Spaniard, *mestizo*, or Anglo—was fair game.

For the settlers, the attack was horrific. It was all hot gunfire, wild yelling, and blood. In minutes the central plaza was littered with bodies and drenched with crimson. Soon Apaches were breaking into the small houses, riding their mounts in, and killing anyone inside. Skulls were split wide open with tomahawks, and women were run through with bloody lances. Most men could not get to their guns, and had to fight off the Indians with their bare hands. Within fifteen minutes, all the men and boys were dead, well-hidden, or had run off. There were three Apaches down, bleeding onto the dirt of the compound, all dead.

Near the end of the uneven fight, Lone Wolf rode his pony right into a large hut and found a young woman there alone. Her name was Isabel Navarro, a widow who had come there with a relative who was now dead on the plaza. She was a dark-haired beauty, wearing a silk dress bought in Mexico City, and she looked resigned to her fate when Lone Wolf pointed his crimson-tipped lance at her.

When he saw her close her eyes against the

deadly thrust to accept death bravely, he hesitated and looked her over more carefully. He dismounted and walked over to her, and her eyes opened. They were dark and big, and he liked the beauty in her chiseled face.

"You will live, white woman," he said harshly to her.

She did not understand. He grabbed her at the waist, walked over to his mottled mustang, and lifted Isabel aboard. Then he mounted and walked the horse back out through the low doorway, with both of them leaning down to get through it.

Outside, the fighting was over. One Eye saw his brother with his captive, and rode over to him.

"What is this? Why is she still alive?"

Lone Wolf's handsome face was defiant and fierce with the war paint. "My renowned brother has taken a white woman to his lodge. Why may not I?"

"Por favor," Isabel sobbed. "Let me go!"

One Eye looked her over and saw why Lone Wolf wanted her. She was very attractive. Like One Eye himself, and a few other warriors close to him, Lone Wolf had always liked white women.

"Oh, very well. You may have her. Let us ride out!"

The looting was finished, too, and now they all rode back out of the settlement, whooping and yelling. In moments, they were gone.

On the dirt of the compound and in the huts, the dead and dying bore mute testimony to the brutal savagery of One Eye's raid.

The Apaches arrived back in their village, set between the high cliffs, in late afternoon.

All of the village—older men, young boys, and women—came to greet the victorious heroes, and there was much singing and noise. Molly was being watched by two older men, but she was allowed to come outside and watch the arrival. One Eye rode right past her and grinned down at her. She did not return his friendliness. Then she spotted Lone Wolf, with Isabel on the rump of his horse.

"Oh, my God!" she whispered.

Isabel, dirt-smeared and frightened, looked right at Molly, and her face changed. She had not expected to see a white woman there.

The horses were corralled, and loot was distributed among the residents of the village. Food, flour, liquor, clothing, bolts of cloth. There was a carnival spirit in the air. No thought was given to the dead white men and women at the settlement. This was war, and in a war your enemy died. If you were lucky. Otherwise, it was you. After all, three Apache corpses had been brought back too. Their mates were not celebrating.

Isabel Navarro was established in Lone Wolf's smaller lodge, and a guard was set to watch her. The Apache dead were taken away and another celebration was begun.

One Eye was beginning to look like a great chief.

He came to his lodge and found Molly outside. Three Tongues was teaching Molly some Athabaskan while they kneaded cassava root in large gourd bowls. One Eye spoke to his woman, and Molly looked up at him soberly.

"I learn your tongue," she said in clear Athabaskan.

One Eye grinned widely. "You speak! The ancient gods smile on you!"

Then, in Spanish, she said, "You killed Mexicans today?"

One Eye smiled. "Many."

Molly hung her head gravely.

"In time, you will celebrate with us after these great victories. You will think like an Apache."

This was all said in his language, and she did not understand much of it. "It is bad," she said. "*Muy malo.*"

One Eye's face darkened.

"She said the killing is bad," Three Tongues told him.

"I know what she said!" One Eye said loudly. He kicked Three Tongues in the side, and she fell over with a small yelp. "Get out of here!"

The woman skittered away from him, then rose quickly to her feet and departed, holding her side. Molly rose and confronted him angrily. "Damn you, you brute! You'll always be a vicious savage! You're not fit to lead these people!"

One Eye frowned and grabbed her by her long hair. "You white women have too long a tongue! Be careful I do not cut it out!"

They were exchanging emotions, not understandable words. But that was enough at that moment. Molly walked away from him, toward the center of the compound, and he did not try to stop her.

Molly found Lone Wolf out there, swigging the Mexican liquor, a tequila. She confronted him. "The woman. She is Spanish?" she asked in Spanish.

He understood her. *"Sí, español. Mas linda que usted, sí?"* Prettier than you.

"May I talk with her?" Molly asked, ignoring the gibe.

Lone Wolf hesitated. Then he nodded and swigged the liquor again, turning away from her.

Molly turned and walked to his lodge. On the way there she saw Little Crow and Crooked Leg talking together. Little Crow saw her and gave her a grin. She merely looked away.

At the lodge, a rather elderly Apache sat cross-legged beside the entrance, guarding the new captive. He frowned at Molly when she approached him.

"I have permission," she said in Spanish. "From Lone Wolf." She pointed. When she went on into the lodge, the guard did not try to stop her.

Isabel sat on a long bench at the back, crying softly. Molly figured she must look a lot like

Molly had on her arrival. Isabel looked up at her, and curiosity crept into her face.

"Are you Spanish?"

"American."

"Ah." She switched languages. "I speak English."

"Oh, thank God!" Molly sighed.

"You are a captive too?"

"Yes. I've been here just a week. I was brought all the way from Missouri." She sat down beside Isabel.

The dark-haired girl frowned slightly. "Missouri?"

"It is . . . a part of Louisiana. A civilized place."

Isabel averted her eyes. "I am from Mexico. Mérida. My husband died on the trip north. So I came to the frontier anyway. It was a terrible mistake."

"They attacked your village?"

Isabel nodded. "They killed . . . everyone. I was told the Apaches had been subdued. Now one of them has taken me as his woman."

Molly nodded. "The man who claims you is called Lone Wolf. His bother, the chief, called One Eye, has wedded me to him in a formal ceremony. You may have the same."

"I could kill myself!" Isabel said bitterly.

"I tried that. But now I'm glad I didn't. At least we're alive."

"What good is it?" Isabel wondered. "Tonight he will take me to his bed!"

"I know." Molly touched her arm. "Listen to me. Close your eyes and think of other things. Don't fight it. Don't think about it afterwards. He won't kill you if he likes you. Do you understand?"

Isabel met Molly's gaze. "Yes."

"I have hope that my people will come after me. If that happens, you will be freed too."

Isabel tried to smile, but it did not work. "At least I have you."

"Yes," Molly assured her. "We have each other. And our resolve must be strong. We must want to survive."

Isabel managed a better smile. "We will help each other," she said. She grasped Molly's hand and held it tightly.

"Yes, we will," Molly said, returning the smile. She felt a momentary guilt because Isabel's presence there had brightened her day. "I'm Molly, incidentally."

"And I am Isabel. We will—"

Suddenly a figure appeared in the lodge entrance, and Molly looked up. It was Nalin.

"What are you doing in here, whiteface!" she said loudly to Molly.

"*Dios mío!*" Isabel whispered, cowering.

Molly stood up and met Nalin eye to eye. Though she couldn't understand Nalin's words, her meaning was clear. "Lone Wolf gave me his permission," she said in Spanish. "I am the woman of One Eye. You do not say where I may go."

Isabel was shocked by Molly's response, and Nalin glared wide-eyed at her. Then her dark eyes narrowed to slits. "You are a dead woman! I myself will cut off your head and place it atop a medicine pole!" Then, in Spanish, she said "You. Dead. Understand?"

Molly stuck out her chin. "One Eye. Kill you. *You* understand?"

Nalin said nothing more. She made an angry gesture at Molly and stormed back out of the lodge.

"Jesus y Maria!" Isabel gasped.

Molly turned to her. "The women will hate us. You can't blame them. But watch out for Nalin. She attacked me with a knife."

Isabel swallowed hard. "You are very brave, Molly. I am pleased that you are here with me."

Molly tried a smile. "The same with me," she said.

In Santa Fe that same afternoon, Governor Luis Alvarado was meeting with an old friend to discuss the recent attacks by One Eye on Spanish settlements and ranches down south in the hot country. Alvarado sat behind a long French desk that had been imported from Europe and stared past his companion to a portrait on the wall, a picture of Alvarado's ancestor, who had been a lieutenant of the great Cortés.

"Who would have thought that almost three centuries after my illustrious predecessor had vanquished the Aztecs in Tenochtitlán, we would still be fighting their cousins here in Santa Fe?" he said heavily.

Pedro Rivera smiled at the governor. A swarthy, blocky fellow with a square face and graying hair, he was attired in the costume of a Spanish *vaquero*, with silver buttons on his tunic and down the trouser legs. He had recently retired from Alvarado's Santa Fe garrison with the rank of full colonel, and had fought with Dan'l Boone against Yellow Horse several years before.

"There is a parallel history between the Aztecs and the Apaches, Governor. The Aztecs migrated to the Valley of Mexico not long before the arrival of the *conquistadores*, but were at their military height. Also, the Apaches have been here for only a century or so, having also migrated from the north, and they, too, have been the scourge of other tribes in the area. They have not built great cities as the Aztecs did, but they are a proud and resourceful people, with considerable military skills."

Alvarado nodded. "I thought they were pacified until the rise of One Eye. Now the whole thing may start over again, unless something is done. Unfortunately, Mexico City has seen fit to reduce our garrison here to a skeleton force, because they think the trouble is past."

"Have you written to the viceroy, Mr. Governor?" Rivera asked.

Alvarado made a sound in his throat. He was a tall, elegant man with an aquiline face and silver hair, and his mere physical presence drew respect from others. He had been educated in Madrid and Paris. "I have sent two urgent messages directly to the Palacio Nacional. But I have received no response."

"I want you to know that if you need my service, Governor, I'll gladly put myself at your disposal. My ranch can run itself for a while."

Alvarado shook his silver head. "No, of course not, old friend. You would have no troops to lead. No, we must content ourselves with only the defense of Santa Fe at this time, and I doubt we could do even that successfully if a real war was mounted against us. Until we receive replacement troops from Mexico, One Eye will have a free hand to do pretty much as he wishes, I'm afraid. And all we can do is sit here and watch, and hope it does not get too bad."

A knock came at the dark-wood door behind Rivera, and Alvarado called for whoever it was to enter. A thin, young aide opened the door and stuck his head in.

"An Enrico Fuentes is here, Governor. For Colonel Rivera."

"Ah," Rivera said. "I asked him to come for me."

"Didn't he serve with you?" Alvarado asked.

"Yes, but he was discharged when our force was reduced. He works for me now, out on my ranch."

"Oh, good." Alvarado looked at the aide. "Send Fuentes in, please."

A moment later Fuentes came in, holding a hat shyly in both hands. He was a slim but well-muscled *mestizo* with rather dark skin. He had killed many Apaches and Comanches in his career with the garrison, and was an excellent shot.

"Mr. Governor," he said humbly. "Colonel."

Alvarado did not rise, but merely smiled at Fuentes. "Come on in, Fuentes. We were just discussing the Apache One Eye."

"Ah," Fuentes said. "That one."

"He is one bad fellow, heh, Fuentes?" Alvarado said.

"He is a dirty *cobarde!*" Fuentes offered. A distant relative of his had been killed the year before by One Eye's people, down southwest of Santa Fe.

Rivera asked, "Have you heard anything about him recently, Enrico?"

The *caballero* nodded. "Just now in the cantina. I was going to tell you on our way back. There was a fellow there who had just come up from the south."

"Yes?" Alvarado urged him.

"The new settlement of Santa Rosa has been attacked by One Eye's warriors," Fuentes said quietly. "The report is that all were killed except for a woman named Navarro, who was taken captive."

"Good God!" Alvarado muttered.

Rivera swore under his breath. He had been going to suggest to a cousin in Mexico City that he should buy ranchland at Santa Rosa. "That damned fiend!" he growled.

"There is something else, too," Fuentes told them.

They both turned to him.

"There is a rumor that he has a second white woman at the village where he hides out. It is said she is from the East, and is a relative of Dan'l Boone."

Alvarado's jaw dropped slightly. "What?"

"This is all rumor, Governor. The word is that One Eye rode all the way to Missouri to kill Boone, and abducted one of his children. She is said to be a grown daughter."

This came as news to both Alvarado and Rivera. A message was sent by wagon train to Alvarado from the authorities in St. Louis, but had never arrived.

"*Espiritu santo!*" Rivera said under his breath. Dan'l Boone had become one of Rivera's best friends when they fought together against One Eye's uncle, old Yellow Horse. "Dan'l Boone dead! I cannot believe it!"

"It is not confirmed," Fuentes reminded him.

"That is correct, Colonel," Alvarado said dully. "We cannot jump to conclusions until we have the facts. I can send a letter east. Maybe that will produce a reply."

"My God," Rivera said slowly, shaking his head. "Is there no end to this madness?"

"The Apaches are a vengeful people," Fuentes said. "The story has a ring of truth."

Rivera rose from his chair, grave-faced, and Alvarado stood too. "I will be going, Governor. If you hear anything about this, I would appreciate your advising me."

"It will be my duty," Alvarado said.

Then Rivera left the room with Fuentes.

He did not speak all the way to the buggy waiting outside the building.

Chapter Six

It was only a few hours later, after dark, that Dan'l arrived in Santa Fe.

There was a cantina only a couple blocks from the Governor's House that rented beds by the night. Dan'l took his people there and got them settled in. The place reeked of alcohol downstairs, where the drinking took place, and of sweat and other foul smells upstairs, where the foursome were to share a dormitory-style room with several drunks and drifters. It was called the Oso Blanco, the White Bear. A greasy-looking *mestizo* took Dan'l's money and advised them to dampen their bedcover with camphor, which he would sell to them at a very cheap price, to ward off the fleas. Dan'l declined.

They were bone-weary, but Finney and Mc-

Gill both wanted to go downstairs for a couple of drinks before turning in. When it was clear they were determined, Dan'l decided to join them to keep them out of trouble. Cahill made his excuses, saying he could not keep his eyes open.

Down in the saloon, the three of them found a table near the bar and ordered mescal, and the greasy bartender brought them a bottle and set it on the table. Finney swigged down two small glasses of it before Dan'l and McGill had even poured themselves a drink.

There were several other customers in the place, two at the long bar and one at a nearby table. The one at the table was a local named Miguel Zarate, called by some "El Loco" because of his sometimes strange behavior. He had strolled through the central plaza once in a state of inebriation with no clothing at all except his boots. In a small settlement north of Santa Fe, he had challenged its mayor to a duel with pistols because the fellow had insulted a prostitute. The mayor had fled. Zarate hated Apaches, had killed more of them than most soldiers, and had burned one at the stake once, because the redskin had scalped a friend and cut his belly open while the victim screamed in shock.

Zarate stared at the newcomers, particularly at Dan'l, as they had their drinks. Dan'l's curiosity was aroused, because Zarate seemed familiar to him. When the bartender came back to their table to see if more liquor was needed, Dan'l asked who the man at the next table was.

"Oh, that is Zarate, *señor*. Pay him no attention. He is, you know, crazy in the head. He causes much trouble in here."

Dan'l nodded. "I remember now. Years ago, he called me a name in this same cantina. I ignored him and he left. A right strange fellow."

"Sounds like some trappers I knowd," McGill said, casting a dour look toward Zarate and the big pistol on the Mexican's belt.

"He's a-staring at you, Boone," Finney said. "Maybe you'd like for me to give him a goddamn pistol-whipping."

Dan'l gave him a brittle glance. "Just mind your own p's and q's, Finney. We don't need no trouble here our first night in town."

"I don't tolerate no disrespect from nobody," Finney said, out of sorts because of the long ride.

McGill looked at Finney and chuckled. Finney's face colored briefly. "What's so damned funny, mountain man?"

"Just you, my boy," McGill said, looking into his glass.

Finney was angry. "Are you trying to hooraw me, hunter?"

But Dan'l interceded. "Come on, boys. We're out here to fight Apaches, not each other."

"The boy is funny," McGill insisted.

Finney would have responded again, but Zarate's voice interrupted from the next table.

"Hey, greenhorn! You are the Boone fellow, *sí*?"

Dan'l looked over at him. "And you're Zarate."

Zarate frowned. "Yes. Zarate." He wore a black mustache, a wide-brimmed black hat with silver decorations on the band, and a bandolier across his chest.

The bartender came, set a glass of tequila on Zarate's table, and left, looking apprehensive.

"You remember me from before, yes?" Zarate said to Dan'l.

Dan'l nodded. "Ain't you moved from that table for three years?"

He had meant it as a joke, but Zarate's face went straight. "You think I am *un borrachin*, yes?"

Dan'l did not respond.

"You come back to Santa Fe to boast of killing Yellow Horse, that weak old man?"

McGill turned an icy look on Zarate, and Finney, too now directed his anger at the Mexican, away from McGill. "Why don't you shut up and drink your cheap booze?" he said loudly to Zarate.

Anger flashed hot in the Mexican's face, and the two *peónes* at the bar turned to watch the exchange with new interest.

"Who is this, Boone?" Zarate asked. "Some milkweed clerk from Missouri who cannot even ride a horse?"

Dan'l thought it was rather humorous, but Finney did not. He rose in a flash and drew the

Mortimer pistol from his belt. He kept it primed at all times, so all he had to do was cock the hammer. He did so now, and all in the room heard it.

"I think I'll just blow your liver out through your back," he threatened.

Zarate rose, too, his hand poised over his own pistol, an old one-shot model. "*Excelente*. Then I will put one between your coward's eyes!" Zarate hissed.

"Finney!" Dan'l barked at him. "Put that damn gun away!"

Finney cast a quick look at him. "Keep out of this, Boone!"

"Damn it, Finney!" Dan'l roared.

"Hell, let him do it," McGill said casually.

"Did you hear what he called me?" Finney said hotly to Dan'l.

"It was you that drawed down," Dan'l said. "Now, put that gun away, or you're fired!"

"Don't bother to try to save his miserable life," Zarate said to Dan'l.

"God*damn!* Did you hear that?" Finney asked.

"I'm telling you, Finney," Dan'l said ominously, "you got a choice, and you got to make it now."

Finney hesitated, then shoved the gun back into his belt.

"I'm heading upstairs. You two can stay and get insulted if you want." Then he stormed past

Zarate, giving him a blistering look, and headed up the back stairs.

Zarate sat back down. "A crazy fellow, your friend. I hope your other one is smarter. I would not like to make a mess on the floor here."

McGill eyed him silently. "You got a big mouth, Mexican," he finally said. "How'd you ever live so long?"

Zarate grinned, and showed a missing tooth in the front of his mouth. "Just lucky, I guess."

That broke the tension, and Dan'l took a last drink of the mescal. "I think I'll go get some sleep too. I'm going to try to see the governor tomorrow."

Zarate was still eavesdropping. "Ah, the governor! Maybe you hope for a medal, heh? For killing an old man!"

Dan'l sighed, and McGill turned a diamond-hard look on the Mexican. "You just keep at it, don't you?" he said quietly.

Dan'l rose from his chair. "Zarate don't know no better, McGill," he said easily to his hireling. He knew that Zarate represented a certain portion of Santa Fe that resented Dan'l's receiving all the attention for the Yellow Horse victory, when they felt all the honor should be theirs. He stopped at Zarate's table a moment, while McGill got up too.

"I'm here to kill an Apache, *hombre*," Dan'l said to the Mexican. "If that's any of your business."

"Ah, I see. You wish to kill one Apache. Why

don't you go after One Eye, *amigo?* He would get you a big medal for your chest."

"He *is* going for One Eye," McGill said, now standing beside Dan'l at Zarate's table.

The Mexican's face changed. *"Caramba,"* he muttered softly. Zarate was a trader who led wagon trains through hostile territory regularly, but he had begun making wide detours around the area when One Eye was causing trouble.

Dan'l grinned slightly. "Don't drink too much of that bad tequila, *amigo.* It might burn the skin off'n your lips." Then he went back to the stairs, with McGill following.

Dan'l slept heavily that night. Despite the hard riding, his chest had healed on the way there, and he had almost no pain in it now. One Eye had made a mistake at Dan'l's cabin by not putting one more bullet into Dan'l's head. The Apache's arrogance had created a deadly enemy.

Dan'l slept past dawn for the first time since leaving Missouri, and was disgusted with himself for doing so. But he had badly needed the rest. Before he even had coffee downstairs, though, he sent a cantina employee over to the Governor's Palace to try to get Dan'l an appointment to see Alvarado later that day. While Dan'l was having a light breakfast with his three men, the messenger returned and reported that Alvarado would see Dan'l as soon as he could get there. Alvarado had been shocked to learn that

Dan'l was still alive, and suddenly here in Santa Fe.

Dan'l sent McGill and Finney out to buy some provisions, while he took Sam Cahill with him to see the governor. Cahill was surprised by the look of Santa Fe, with its brown adobe buildings and houses, and especially by the look of the government house, which was just a two-story affair built at one end of the grand plaza, looking very ordinary to a fellow who had seen the grandeur of Charleston and Richmond.

Inside, though, the place was extravagant, with high, vaulted ceilings, murals on the walls, and potted plants in the corridors. Dan'l and Cahill were met in a reception area by an officer of the almost-defunct garrison, who treated Dan'l like a visiting dignitary; then they were taken upstairs to Alvarado's private offices.

When an aide showed the two into Alvarado's office, Dan'l was surprised to see Pedro Rivera there too. He had been hastily informed of Dan'l's arrival, and had been invited by Alvarado to help welcome Dan'l back to their city.

"Captain Boone!" Rivera said warmly, standing before Alvarado's desk. The governor sat behind the desk, looking like a French general in the blue military uniform he wore on special occasions as titular head of the Santa Fe garrison.

Rivera came and embraced Dan'l, much to Dan'l's embarrassment. "Welcome back to Santa Fe!"

"Colonel," Dan'l said with a grin. He looked Rivera over. Rivera was wearing a dark maroon suit with heavy silver decorations. "You're looking great. I reckon retirement agrees with you."

The governor shook Dan'l's hand vigorously, his lean face beaming. He and Rivera both had affection for Dan'l, and great respect. "Mr. Boone, what a great pleasure!"

"Would everybody just call me Dan'l?" the Kentuckian asked with a grin. "I ain't no officer in your garrison anymore."

"We heard you were dead, my friend," Rivera said.

Dan'l shook his shaggy head. Standing there in his rawhides and full beard, he looked out of place in the room. "The rumors about me dying was what Bostonians would call *pre*mature."

"You can't know how pleased that makes us here in Santa Fe," Alvarado said.

Dan'l gestured toward Cahill. "This here is my friend Sam. It was him that helped save me after One Eye put a couple chunks of lead into my thick hide."

"One Eye went all the way to Missouri for revenge because of Yellow Horse?" Rivera said.

Dan'l grunted. "I doubt it had much to do with old Yellow Horse. I think One Eye went to Missouri for glory."

"We are told that he took your daughter," Alvarado said.

"No. A second cousin, a dead cousin's daughter. But he probably thinks Molly's my daughter. I've got to get her back, Governor."

Alvarado's face turned somber. "Please. Both of you, sit down."

They seated themselves in front of the large desk, while Alvarado walked back to his high-backed, overstuffed chair.

"You are going after One Eye?" Alvarado asked Dan'l.

"I have to," Dan'l said.

"We rode twelve hours a day just to get here," Cahill put in. "Dan'l's still hurting inside him."

Dan'l turned to him. "Sam."

But Cahill ignored him. "Dan'l figures time is agin' us, and I got to agree."

Alvarado nodded. "I understand."

"What I was hoping, Governor, is that you could lend us a few men. For a sneak attack on One Eye. We couldn't beat him in open battle, maybe, but I got some other plans."

Rivera looked down, embarrassed for the reply he knew the governor was about to give Dan'l.

Alvarado sighed. "I was afraid you would ask, *amigo*. Unfortunately, things are different here in Santa Fe from when you were here before. We have no garrison here, not a real one. They are trying to save money in Mexico City. They say the Apaches are subdued. I have just a few men now, not even enough to defend the city. I don't see how I could release any of them for such a venture."

Dan'l took a deep breath. "I see."

"The governor is right, Dan'l. He would be taking a big risk, sending his few men south with you. The city would be left defenseless."

"Damn!" Cahill said under his breath.

"I understand," Dan'l said, slowly crimping the edge of his hat brim as he considered the new situation. He had depended heavily on Alvarado's support.

"It tears at me inside to tell you this," Alvarado added.

Dan'l tried a smile. "It's all right, Governor. We'll work something out. I've got three men now, including Sam here. Maybe we can find a couple more in Santa Fe."

"It could be difficult," Alvarado said. "Everybody is tired of fighting Indians. We can't even find civilians to help with odd jobs at the garrison."

Rivera had been sitting there studying the floor. Now he looked over at Dan'l.

"If you'll have me, Dan'l, I would like to go with you."

Everybody else in the room registered surprise, including the governor. Dan'l stared into Rivera's square, swarthy face. "You don't have to do that, Colonel. You've got your ranch, and a new life. This will be risky business, and you don't need it."

Rivera had been a widower when Dan'l was there before, but he had married a young woman since then, and she was pregnant with their child. It would be a firstborn for both of them.

Rivera smiled. "Frankly, Dan'l, I am bored. All I have to do is tend my horses and watch my wife's belly grow. She is five months along."

"Oh, hell," Dan'l said.

"Sounds like she might need you for a while," Cahill suggested.

"No, she has a maid to help her with everything. And I have an older man who feeds the animals and does some small work around the place. Anyway, this would not be a lengthy project. We could be back here in a week or more."

Dan'l shook his head. "I don't know."

Rivera reached over and put a hand on Dan'l's shoulder. "I have decided, old friend. I will not let you go there with just these men, as good as I know they are. I know the country south of here even better than you. I will also take Fuentes with me."

Dan'l's brow furrowed.

"He works for me too. He served in my command when you were here. He went to fight against Yellow Horse with us."

"I think I remember the name," Dan'l said.

"He is a restless fellow. And he hates One Eye. The Apache killed an uncle of Fuentes a year ago in an attack on a small settlement." He smiled. "He would not let me go without taking him."

Alvarado rose and came around the desk. "The colonel's offer is genuine, Dan'l. I will hate to see him go as much as his young wife, but this cousin of yours must be rescued. Honor demands it."

Cahill liked the way Alvarado put things. And he hoped Rivera would not be dissuaded from going. He liked the looks of him. He looked like a real fighter.

"Well," Dan'l said.

Rivera grinned. "Good. Then it is settled. We will accompany you on your little expedition."

"It'll be a right honor to have you along, Colonel. *Muchas gracias*," Dan'l said with a smile.

"*Por nada*," Rivera assured him. "*Por nada*."

When Dan'l and Cahill left a short time later, Rivera went with them, and he and Dan'l reminisced about Yellow Horse and Running Dog. When Rivera left them at the cantina, Dan'l felt much better about the expedition than he had when the governor had announced his shortage of troops.

McGill and Finney had returned from doing some buying with Dan'l's money, and had stacked food supplies in a downstairs back room of the building. They were just cleaning up in preparation for looking for a place to eat a real meal.

"The owner said we could store anything back there we wanted to," McGill told Dan'l as Dan'l splashed some water onto his rugged face from a pitcher and bowl. Cahill was tidying up his soiled-looking bunk bed, and Finney, sitting on the edge of his bunk, was running a cleaning rod through his pistol.

"Well, we won't be here past tomorrow," Dan'l told McGill. "I can't waste time here in Santa Fe. Molly could be in big trouble. I just can't wait. But at least we got us a couple more recruits today."

McGill eyed him sideways. "A couple?" He and Finney had expected maybe a dozen men from the garrison.

"That's right," Cahill said edgily. "We was lucky to get them."

"One of them is an old friend," Dan'l said. "Used to be commander of the garrison."

Finney looked up darkly from cleaning the gun. "*Used* to be? *Two* more men? What the hell is this, Boone?"

Dan'l was toweling off as he turned to Finney. "It's what is, Finney. It's what we got. There ain't no goddamn soldiers to go with us."

McGill, leaning against a bunk, let out a heavy sigh. "This puts a whole different light on the subject, don't it?"

Finney rose. "It sure as hell does! I didn't join up with you to go on no suicide mission! We need some more men, by God!"

"There ain't no more men, Finney," Dan'l told him sourly. "These people in town had enough of Indian wars. And I can't say I blame them."

"Well, this changes things for me," Finney said. "I got to give this a lot of thought."

"He makes sense, Boone," McGill said. "One

Eye is probably gathering men to him regular now. He might have an army down there by the time we find him."

Cahill turned to them, red-faced. "What the hell's the matter with you two? You forgot what's at stake here? Molly Morgan's life, for God's sake! What do you want to do, turn around and go back to Missouri because things ain't perfect for us?"

The tall mountain man took a deep breath. "Hell, I didn't mean I wouldn't go."

"Well, if I'm going, I want more than you promised us!" Finney said hotly. "This is getting into high-risk work!"

Dan'l put the towel down and came over very close to Finney. Finney was suddenly reminded of the incident between them when he was hired, and he moved back a half-step.

"I just about had enough of you, damn it!" Dan'l growled. "I'm getting to be sorry I ever asked you to come."

"Let him go. He ain't worth nothing anyway," McGill said flatly.

"You think you can talk that way to me just because I served time?" Finney said loudly to McGill.

Dan'l shook his head. "You can't get along with nobody, by Jesus. And I ain't got no more money to offer you. Either get to hell out of here, or shut up about the risk. We got what we got, and you ain't making it no easier by griping about it!"

Finney stood there, absorbing all that for a minute. He shot another look at McGill. "I just don't want to be treated like no convict," he said finally.

"Are you in or out?" Dan'l demanded.

Finney made a face. "Hell. I guess I'm in. I'm hundreds of miles from home, and I don't talk that Mex lingo. What choice do I have?"

Dan'l stuck his Annely revolver into his belt holster, a handmade one he had fashioned out of horsehide. "Fine. Now I'm going to go try to find that crazy Mexican, Zarate."

Finney wrinkled his brow. "Zarate? What the hell for?"

Dan'l sighed. Finney never seemed to learn anything. "Yes, Finney. I been talking to some people. He's good with a gun. Real good. And he hates One Eye's guts. With us having only six men, that makes him a candidate for the expedition."

McGill and Finney both looked surprised. "Are you sure, Boone?" McGill said doubtfully. "He might end up shooting one of us in our sleep."

"It's a dumb idea!" Finney said. "Didn't you hear the way he talked to us last night? He don't like us much more than One Eye!"

Dan'l pointed a thick finger into Finney's face. "Are you finished, damn you?"

Finney hesitated, then looked away.

"I ain't got no choice, by Jesus!" Dan'l said. "If I talk to him right, I think he might come. And he ain't as crazy as he seems. Take my word for it."

"You'll have to keep him sober," McGill said.

"I can handle that," Dan'l told him. He set the black Quaker hat on his head. "Now, I'll see you all later."

"I'm going too," Cahill said.

"Suit yourself," Dan'l muttered.

It was the bartender who directed Dan'l out to the hut of "El Loco" on the edge of town. Dan'l and Cahill arrived there in early afternoon, while Zarate was plucking a chicken inside his hut. He called for the two men to enter, then made a face when he saw who it was.

"Eh? The great Indian fighter? What are you doing at my house?"

Some welcome, Cahill thought.

"There are no Apaches out here, *señores*," Zarate added. "Only dirty *banditos*. When I heard you ride up, I thought you might be them. They robbed two houses in this area."

"Sorry to hear that," Dan'l told him. He looked around the one-room cabin made of brown adobe. There was litter everywhere. An unmade bed sat in the far corner. "They haven't bothered you yet, have they?"

"They think I am poor. And crazy," Zarate answered with a grin. "They do not know about my bank account in Mexico City." He had feathers stuck to his hands and arms. He kept on plucking the dead bird.

Dan'l wondered why anyone with money in a bank would live as Zarate did. Maybe he was crazy after all.

"I didn't come to talk about bandits," Dan'l said. Cahill leaned against the nearby wall, and Zarate watched him carefully. "I want to talk about One Eye."

Zarate looked up and placed the chicken on a small table before him. He stood, wiping his hands on a soiled shirt. "One Eye? Why are you interested in One Eye?"

"He abducted a woman," Dan'l said. "She is of my blood."

"Ah." Understanding flooded into his face. "You wish to retrieve this woman!" He glanced again at Cahill.

"I want a seventh man to go after him," Dan'l said. "I hear you're good with a gun."

A grin crawled slowly onto Zarate's face and showed the hole between his teeth. He pulled at his black mustache for a moment as a feather floated to the floor.

"The great hunter wants me, Crazy Miguel, to go after the Apache with him? My ears must be playing tricks on me."

"I'd pay you. Not much, but I hear business is down for you. You ain't made a trip south for months."

"You talk much about me to others," Zarate said.

Dan'l shrugged. "We're leaving tomorrow plus one. If you're going, I have to know now."

Zarate came over to Dan'l. "I have killed over fifty Apaches without ever wearing a uniform."

"That's why I want you."

Zarate's eyes sparkled crazily. "No one has taken more wagon trains through hostile territory than Miguel Zarate."

"I heard that."

"I am the best Indian fighter in this entire territory!" he announced defiantly in Dan'l's face.

"Then prove it. Come with us when we leave."

Zarate paused and looked over at Cahill. "Where is the other one? With the big mouth?"

Dan'l had to laugh at that. There was nobody more offensive verbally than Zarate himself. "Oh. Finney. He's going too."

"And if I should kill him?" Zarate grinned inanely.

Dan'l met the grin with a straight face. "Then you would have to answer to me," he said carefully.

Zarate stood there, scowling at the Kentuckian. Over at the wall, Cahill smiled slightly, waiting.

"All right. I will go. But if I change my mind on the trail, I will leave you out there, no questions asked. You will be on your own!"

Dan'l marveled at the arrogance of the man. "I been on my own before, Zarate. We'll see you Friday morning at dawn. In back of the cantina. Don't be late."

Zarate slapped his hand to his forehead in a

wild mock salute, a lunatic grin back on his swarthy face. "Yes, *sir!*"

A few minutes later, when they were riding off again, Cahill turned to Dan'l with a sour look. "I wish I could say I'm happy about your choice, Dan'l. Maybe we could have found somebody at the saloon. Now we got two loose cannons in the bunch, and they don't like each other."

"Somebody said once that desperate times require desperate measures," Dan'l said. "Well, these is desperate times, Sam. For Molly Morgan, and for us."

They rode up to a stand of cottonwoods in the dark, neither of them thinking about Zarate's story of area bandits. But, unseen by either of them, shadows lurked in the trees as they approached.

"The main thing is to keep Finney and Zarate from each other's throats," Dan'l said as they rode past the trees. "I'll just have to—"

Suddenly three riders came out of the trees. They came up on the trail in front of Dan'l and Cahill, forcing the two to rein in quickly.

"*Alto! Pare allí!*"

"Oh, hell," Cahill mumbled.

Dan'l looked over the three men. They were dressed like *mestizos*, with serapes and wide-brim hats. Each of them was pointing a pistol at Dan'l and Cahill.

"What is this?" Dan'l said in English. "What do you want?" He was stalling.

134

"Ah, americanos!" the biggest one said with a grin. "I speak English also! It is good, yes?"

Cahill was wearing his gun on his belt, across his belly, and was trying not to look down at it. "We ain't got no money," he lied.

"Money?" the big Mexican said. "Did I speak of money?"

"Just let us go on our way," Cahill said. He was scared. It occurred to him they might not even get to go after One Eye.

The Mexicans were all grinning as the big one translated. "No, we cannot let you go," he said. "We need those horses of yours. And their saddles. Your guns, of course. Maybe your boots." He laughed.

Dan'l was angry, but he did not let it show. He began thinking fast, hoping to save them somehow.

"If you will not take the horses, we might have something better for you," he said to them.

The big Mexican narrowed his eyes. "Better than horses?" he asked suspiciously.

"A family heirloom," Dan'l said, making it up as he went along. "A piece of jewelry. Very valuable."

The *mestizo* translated for his cohorts, and Dan'l could see greed appear in their faces.

"Let us see this jewelry," the big one said, his gun still aimed at Dan'l's heart.

"Is it agreed?" Dan'l said. "Can we go on our way if we give you the jewelry?"

"Let us see the jewelry first," the Mexican said.

"I must dismount," Dan'l said. "All right?"

"Hmmph. Maybe I should just shoot you and look myself!"

Dan'l shrugged. "You won't find it."

The other man hesitated. "All right. Get off your horse. But move carefully."

Dan'l gave Cahill a quick look and let his gaze drop to Cahill's gun for just a split second as he dismounted from the Appaloosa.

"It's back here." He pointed to his bedroll behind the saddle. "I think you'll like it."

Dan'l slowly undid the bedroll. His and Cahill's side arms were ready to shoot, except for cocking. He fumbled with a knot as the three bandits watched eagerly. The two who did not speak English were completely distracted now, guns hanging loose in their hands. The big man was still aiming at Dan'l, but not as accurately. Dan'l opened the bedroll, where he kept an extra skinning knife, a weapon he was very good with. He saw the big bandit move his mount around to see better. But the gun now hung down slightly in his grasp.

Dan'l grabbed the big knife, turned it over in his hand, and hurled it at the big man's chest.

At the last moment the bandit raised the pistol to fire, but the blade hit him hard in the center of his chest, piercing breastbone, heart, and posterior rib.

His eyes opened wide, and the gun went off,

digging up dirt at Dan'l's feet. In the meantime, Cahill had drawn and fired at a second gunman, beating him by half a second. Cahill's lead smacked the bandit in the throat, whiplashing his head and destroying his spine. The third bandit aimed at Dan'l as Dan'l threw himself to the ground beside his rearing horse. The bandit's gun exploded and more dirt flew up just beside Dan'l's head. When Dan'l came back up he had his Annely in a tight grip, and when it roared out its deadly message, the third man was struck in the side as if clubbed. Flying off his horse sideways, he hit the ground hard, tumbling in a somersault.

Dan'l rose to his feet. All three bandits were on the ground now, dead.

Cahill narrowed his gaze on Dan'l. He had always been that tough, even as a boy. It was why he had survived so long when other men had not. It was why the Shawnee called him by a special name and revered it.

Dan'l holstered his weapon and turned back to Cahill. "Now let's get back to town," he said matter-of-factly. "We got some big days ahead of us."

Cahill did not respond to that.

It seemed Dan'l had said it all.

Chapter Seven

At One Eye's remote village, things were going well. A couple dozen young men had flocked to One Eye from other villages because of his suddenly big reputation, and more were on their way. Chief One Eye, as he was now called, was already being compared to the famous Yellow Horse. Some were even saying he had surpassed that earlier chief because he had killed Yellow Horse's killer.

More tipis had been erected, as had a few more lodges with bark-and-skin covers. Hunting was good, and the village was thriving.

There was no hint yet that the great Sheltowee was alive and headed their way.

Molly and Isabel were put to work every day, making rawhide clothing, washing things in the tiny stream that ran through the canyon, and preparing food. One Eye wanted them to know everything an Apache woman knew, and Lone Wolf agreed. The white women just followed orders, hunkering down, waiting, and trying not to let their hope wane. Isabel was expected to perform her wifely duties for Lone Wolf almost every night, but One Eye did not seem to have the same appetite as his brother. Also, One Eye had begun treating Molly like a princess, giving her special clothes and parading her about the village at his side. But Isabel was treated rather badly by Lone Wolf, who yelled at her and beat her regularly.

The Apache women of the village, at least most of them, did not like the presence of the white women, and Nalin was their unofficial spokesperson. She complained often to One Eye about Molly's insubordination and awkwardness, but One Eye paid little attention. He already intended to have a child by Molly, a male child who would one day rule a big Apache clan.

Molly was still slapped occasionally by One Eye if she talked back to him, and with other women treating her like a leper, she was sometimes despondent, but tried not to show that to Isabel. Some Apache women, in fact, had left rather than live in a village with these whiteface females. And with the arrival of more warriors from other places, there were not enough women to go around, and the single ones became communal property.

Molly understood well that if she and Isabel were not "owned" by the chief and his brother, the place would be very dangerous for them. As it was, the new men ogled both women and made remarks to them in Athabaskan that Molly was sure were insulting and salacious.

On the morning after Dan'l and Cahill had narrowly avoided death at the hands of the bandits outside Santa Fe, Molly finished a chore ahead of schedule and took the opportunity to go visit Isabel at Lone Wolf's lodge.

Isabel was sitting outside, grinding beans in a gourd with a wooden pestle. When Molly arrived she immediately saw that Isabel's face was heavily bruised, and her lower lip cut and swollen.

"Oh, God. What happened?" Molly asked.

Isabel looked up pitifully. Her beautiful face looked very different this sunny morning. "*Buenos días*, Molly. I am trying to get some beans prepared."

Molly squatted down beside her. "Oh, Isabel. Did Lone Wolf do this to you?"

Isabel looked around to be sure they would not be overheard. Then she nodded. "Yes. He was in a bad mood last night."

"The bastard!" Molly said heatedly, touching a bruise on Isabel's face.

"I wish I were dead," Isabel said quietly. "I

really do, Molly. I can't do this." Her dark eyes watered.

"Don't say that. We have to keep going. We have to survive until somebody comes to help us."

"Somebody?" Isabel said. "Who, your cousin? Who may be dead?"

Molly sighed. "Have courage, Isabel. Please. I have this feeling that everything will come out all right."

"I must admit, I do not have such a feeling."

"There are herbs I can apply to your face," Molly said. "To make it heal faster. Three Tongues taught me."

Isabel smiled past her swollen lip. "You are a friend, Molly. I can never repay you for your kindness."

"Just don't give up. That's all I want from you."

Molly heard her name called. She stood and turned to see One Eye coming toward her. He had been brushing up on his Spanish, so they could communicate while Molly learned his language.

"Molly," he said in a deep voice. "Your work is finished?"

Molly nodded as he came up beside her. "Yes."

He glanced at Isabel and saw the bruises. "Good. I will speak with you. Come."

Molly pointed at Isabel. "Look. Your brother did this."

One Eye understood, but shrugged. "Yes?"

"He must stop!" Molly said excitedly. "He will hurt her badly!"

"He is my brother. She is nothing to me."

"Please speak to him," Molly said, realizing she was asking a favor, the last thing she wanted to do.

One Eye looked down at Isabel, then smiled slightly at Molly. "We will see, woman. If you are good, perhaps."

Molly had trouble with some of the Spanish.

"He says maybe," Isabel said.

Molly looked at her and nodded.

"Come," One Eye commanded again.

Molly followed him to their lodge, and he unrolled an antelope-skin map of the immediate area on the floor. She had never seen anything like it.

"You look," One Eye told her. He put his finger on the skin. "There. That is Mexican place. One day's ride."

She looked at him quizzically.

"Your father was here. At that place."

"What?"

"Your father, Pale Dove." That is what he had begun calling her. Isabel had not been renamed. "Sheltowee, the one you call Boone. The one I killed in Missouri."

"Dan'l Boone was there?" she said, looking at the map.

He nodded. "Your father." He looked somber. "He killed many Apaches."

Molly looked into his scarred face. "One Eye, Dan'l Boone is not my father."

He furrowed his brow, thinking he had not understood. "What did you say?"

"Mi padre no es Boone," she repeated. *"El es primo. Comprende?"*

"Primo?" he said.

"Como usted y Running Dog."

Understanding flooded into his long, scarred face. *"Primo?"*

"Sí."

One Eye stared at her with a look that chilled her. "Cousin!" he repeated. He turned, picked up a nearby bench, and hurled it through the open front entrance of the lodge.

Molly jumped in fear. One Eye turned back to her, his eyes full of rage. *"Cousin!"*

"I'm . . . sorry," she said in a half-whisper. Already she regretted telling him.

He pulled his long war knife from his belt and held it in front of her face. They were both standing now. "Look at this, whiteface! I would kill you with it in Missouri if I know!"

Molly swallowed back her fear and stuck her chin out. "A cousin is just as good. Dan'l won't forget me."

He did not understand. "You will say nothing of this! Understand?"

She shrugged. "Yes." She had already told Isabel, but would not admit that to him.

"Never say it!" he repeated. He bent and yanked the skin map from the floor.

"At this place, defiled by Sheltowee," he said in his own language, "there is another settlement of whites. We go there tomorrow and kill everybody. Everybody!"

Molly did not get the words, but she understood the fire in his eyes. She stood there silent as he rolled the skin up, gave her a hard look, and strode angrily from the lodge.

Molly heaved herself onto a bench. She had had no idea he would react so violently to her revelation that she was not Dan'l's daughter. Now her future with him might be even less secure. She would find Isabel immediately and urge her to keep quiet about the whole matter.

Later that morning, the warriors of One Eye's clan rode out to the northeast, to a tiny settlement made up of a couple dozen families of Mexican and American settlers. It was on the stage trail between Santa Fe and Soccoro. One Eye and his men arrived there an hour after noon, and when they reined up on a rise of ground before the village, Gray Hawk came up beside One Eye and his brother Lone Wolf. Gray Hawk looked very ferocious in his heavy war paint.

"I wish a white woman," he said to One Eye.

One Eye regarded him coolly. "What?"

"You and your brother are royalty, I know. But I have served you well and without question. I stand high among your *akacitas*. I ask it as a reward for my unwavering loyalty to your cause."

"You are impudent!" Lone Wolf snarled. He considered the white women of him and his brother a mark of their privilege as leaders of the clan. For a mere warrior to have one would demean the symbol.

But both he and Gray Hawk were surprised by One Eye's reaction.

He stroked his chin and nodded. "I have thought on this," he said seriously. "There is no reason why a few select warriors of high standing should not have a white woman if that is their preference. Imitation of our life choices gives praise to our own judgment and strengthens the validity of our new custom."

Lone Wolf frowned heavily at his brother but did not dare to oppose him in the matter. He turned and glared at Gray Hawk.

"Your wish is granted," One Eye told Gray Hawk. "If you find a suitable woman today, you may take her back."

Little Crow came up beside them, looking blocky and dangerous. He pointed to the village, only a hundred yards away. "They have seen us."

One Eye looked and saw a young man waving his arms and running into the village of white adobe houses, spreading the alarm.

One Eye nodded and raised his arm skyward. "It is time. *Attack! Attack!*"

Moments later the fifty Apaches swarmed into the small village, firing guns and arrows and yelling. The Mexican and American men who ran into the street to defend the village were quickly cut down, overwhelmed by the sheer number of the attackers. The Apaches ran wildly into huts and houses, lopping off the heads of women and children with long knives and stolen sabers, and impaling others to walls with gaily decorated lances. A middle-aged American man from Boston was tied to a hitching post outside the small cantina, and warriors began gathering wood and piling it around him at his feet.

Several rapes took place in the next hour, after which the victims were killed. One woman was shot with so many arrows that she resembled a large pincushion. The Indians found liquor, and were swilling it eagerly.

Gray Hawk had rushed into a small house and found a small, petite blond woman bending over her dying husband. Her name was Rachel Avery, and she and her husband had come there from a more civilized area of eastern Texas only a month ago. She was terrified when she saw Gray Hawk enter the house. Gray Hawk looked down at her fiercely; then his face changed. He liked the looks of her. He liked her blond hair, different from that of both Molly and Isabel. She was not quite as pretty as Molly, but she whetted Gray Hawk's appetite.

Gray Hawk, not having the sensitive nature of either of the brothers, jerked Rachel away from her dying husband and casually shot him in the head with his Mortimer pistol.

Rachel jumped visibly, then began screaming uncontrollably. Gray Hawk slapped her hard across her face, and the screaming stopped as if a door had been closed. Without even allowing her a last look at her dead husband, he dragged her outside, waving his arm above his head and displaying her proudly to the other warriors.

At the hitching post, the middle-aged fellow from Boston was getting his first taste of life in Apache country. He had been in tiny Estacion Tres just ninety days, and had seen no trouble with the local Indians.

But now the fire had been lighted at his feet, the flames were licking up around his hips, and he was yelling in panic. He had no way of knowing, but the Apaches had chosen him as the subject of an age-old ritual, to thank their ancient gods for victory in battle. As his screams rent the morning air and his flesh began darkening in the heat of the fire, several of the Apaches began shooting arrows into his torso, one after the other, thus ending the victim's misery in a burst of excitement. Crooked Leg stepped in when the fire had burned itself out, cut open the chest of the dead man, yanked the heart out, chewed off a chunk of it, and ate it. Other warriors of higher rank followed suit until there was none of it left.

Rachel Avery saw some of that and fainted, slipping from Gray Hawk's grasp. He frowned down on her and kicked her in the thigh angrily.

Then he picked her up, loaded her onto his pony, and rode out with the others, leaving Estacion Tres a burning, bloody butcher's ground.

One Eye turned and took a last look, with a slight smile on his long face. He had lost some self-respect on learning Molly's true relationship to Dan'l Boone, but now some of that had been restored.

There was no real shame in mistaking Molly for Sheltowee's daughter. The clan could be told the truth later on, when it would not seem so important.

When he was ruler of this entire territory.

In Santa Fe, Dan'l was busy preparing to leave for the south. The afternoon of One Eye's raid, though, Governor Alvarado sent a messenger to Dan'l, asking to see him.

This time Dan'l went alone.

It was an overcast day in Santa Fe, a rarity there, when Dan'l arrived at the governor's private offices. There was so little light coming in through the big windows behind Alvarado's desk that he had lighted oil lamps all around the room. The governor greeted Dan'l warmly before they seated themselves at Alvarado's desk. Dan'l held his black Quaker hat on his knees. His wild hair was slicked back, his graying beard was combed, and he looked almost civilized. But not quite.

"It looks like we might get some rain," Alvarado said, looking dapper in a dark suit, his silver hair reflecting the soft light from the lamps. "The gods appear to be smiling on us this season."

Dan'l smiled through his beard. "The Indians probably did a dance," he suggested. "The Taos people are good at scaring up rain." He was referring to the local Indians just outside of Santa Fe to the north. Some of them had been with Dan'l on his campaign against Yellow Horse.

"Sometimes I am convinced that they can influence the elements," Alvarado said, his face serious. "And the events of men. For good or bad."

Dan'l grunted. "When they start shaking them buffalo-scrotum rattles, I don't want to be nowhere near."

"I think the Indians take their religion much more seriously than we do," Alvarado said. "And because they believe, they are fierce warriors."

Dan'l nodded his agreement. "I can vouch for that part, Governor."

"You know, some of them still believe that you are the incarnation of an ancient god, Dan'l. Because you fit his physical description."

Dan'l shook his head slowly. "I'd give my house in Missouri to put an end to that. But I ain't got no control over it." He still had the small bear stitched to his shirt, however.

Alvarado leaned forward over his desk. "I hope you understand that your legend can work against you as well as in your favor. One Eye hates the very idea that a white man could em-

body an ancient god of the proud Apache. As
Yellow Horse and Running Dog hated it. He will
do anything to discredit the legend. That is why
he went all the way to Missouri to kill you."

"I know."

"Can you imagine his fury when he learns
that you survived? If he does not already know
you are here, he will learn of it soon. He will be
ready for you."

Dan'l sighed. "If he didn't take Molly, I probably wouldn't come. But he stepped over a line,
Governor. The Shawnee learned to leave our
women alone, generally. One Eye's got to get
the same message, him and Apaches like him.
Even if he's killed Molly, I won't quit till that
message is delivered."

"I understand," Alvarado told him. "But listen
carefully to what I will tell you, *amigo*. I can
send a message to Soccoro. I was thinking
about it last night in bed. The colonel there
owes me a favor. I will ask him to send a small
detachment here temporarily, to bolster my
own defenses. Then I will give you a few of my
own men to go with you. You cannot hope to
have much success in your enterprise with this
handful of men you are taking with you."

Dan'l thought about that for a long moment.
Then he said, "Governor, you're a good friend.
A man can count on you when he has to. But I
can't wait for help from Soccoro. If I got to
Molly a day late, or an hour late, I'd never for-
give myself. Maybe One Eye plans to make her

his permanent woman, I don't know. But maybe he's right on the edge with her, thinking he don't want her around no more. Her life might be hanging on the line right now, Governor. I just can't wait."

Alvarado nodded gravely. "I understand your position."

Dan'l rose from his chair, and so did Alvarado.

"I got some things to do yet today," Dan'l said, "so I reckon I'll be moving my freight. I'll tell Colonel Rivera you wish us well."

Alvarado extended his hand. Dan'l took it, and the governor was again surprised by the iron strength in Dan'l's grip. *"Vaya con Dios,"* he said to the Kentuckian.

"Thanks."

The same day, Dan'l took Zarate and Finney down to a nearby hostlery to pick out a supply wagon for the trip south. They needed a wagon for supplies and equipment for seven men. It would slow them down some, but it was a necessity. He asked Zarate to pick out two team horses while he and Finney paid the hostler for the wagon and animals.

When Dan'l came back out of the livery stable, Finney was already there with Zarate, giving the Mexican some trouble.

"I'm telling you, that mare ain't worth the money!" Finney was saying loudly. "Go pick another one out, greaser! We ain't got all day!"

"There is nothing wrong with this animal!"

Zarate replied hotly. "Only with your eyesight!"

"It ain't a matter of eyes," Finney said. "It's your goddamn head. If your brains was dynamite, you couldn't blow your eardrums out!"

Zarate realized that Finney was harboring a grudge from the night at the saloon and had been baiting him ever since. Zarate had just ignored him, but now that seemed as if it might be impossible.

Zarate drew a knife from his belt and held it out in front of him ominously. "Brains, heh? Maybe you are smart enough to talk this blade back into its leather, Irish!"

Finney was enjoying this. He drew the well-oiled Mortimer at his hip and aimed it at Zarate. It needed only cocking.

"Boone kept me from killing you once, Mexican. But that ain't going to work this time!"

"If you cock that piece, I will plunge this into your Irish heart before you can pull the trigger!" Zarate warned him.

Dan'l had come up behind them, shaking his shaggy head slowly. He had begun to wonder why he had recruited Finney back in Missouri.

"I think he can probably make good on that," Dan'l said casually from over Finney's shoulder.

The arrogant ex-convict turned slightly and saw Dan'l. "You trying to save this Mexican's ass again?"

"I'm trying to save yours," Dan'l said evenly. He walked past both of them and looked the mare over. Finney stood there hesitantly.

"You're right, Finney," Dan'l said after a moment. "This horse wouldn't be good for a saddle horse. But there ain't nothing wrong with her for pulling a wagon."

Finney looked from Zarate to Dan'l. Dan'l's acknowledgment that the mare was not riding quality cooled him down some. "She'd be in a glue pot back home," he said quietly.

"That mare will pull that wagon to hell and back!" Zarate said loudly.

Dan'l nodded. "She'll do fine, Zarate. Why don't you come over here and help me get her hitched up?"

Zarate hesitated, then slid the wicked-looking knife back into its sheath. Finney lowered the muzzle of the pistol as Zarate gave him a look, and went off with Dan'l.

"Finney, get that other animal over here," Dan'l said casually. "Then we'll go get our supplies onboard."

Finney felt foolish, standing there with his gun out. He holstered it and shot a hard look at Zarate as he walked toward the stocky gelding that would be the mate on the team.

"This is a lot better animal," Finney said over his shoulder.

Zarate caught Dan'l's eye and gave him a sly, slightly crazy grin. "I would have cut his heart out."

Dan'l regarded him sideways. "Listen to me, Zarate. I don't want no trouble once we're gone. Not from my own people."

"The Irishman wants trouble," Zarate said.

"Just remember what I said. If I have to get between you two again, neither one of you is going to like it much."

Zarate grinned wildly at him. "You are such a sweet fellow, *compadre!*" he said. "Always thinking of your people."

Then he walked off across the stable yard to get a harness for the mare.

Chapter Eight

The land of the Apache was not coveted by many white men, Mexican or American. It was a hard land, arid and barren, dotted with sagebrush, Spanish dagger, and prickly pear cactus. The soil was gray and brown, with little moisture in it, and even the rivers were just dry washes much of the year. The shamans prayed to their gods for rain that rarely came and picked wild berries and fruits when they were available, and the warriors depended on hunting buffalo and small game for survival.

That was the terrain that Dan'l headed into the next morning with his six picked gunmen. It was a country that Dan'l knew somewhat since his war against Yellow Horse, but he would never come to like it. It was a place of

Gila monsters, sidewinders, and scorpions, a land where survival was a day-to-day matter, where you could not turn your back on the country for a moment without inviting some disaster.

By midday, the small party with its lone Conestoga wagon was well into Apache country. Six months before, there would have been little danger in traversing this area, because the Apache had been quiet, like a dangerous, sleeping dog. But now there was One Eye, and the Apaches who were joining him; and other chiefs, seeing One Eye's success in opposing white settlement, might decide to go on the warpath again too.

Dan'l's party moved quickly but cautiously. Zarate's judgment about the mare had been correct. The two horses pulled together well in harness, and ably moved the light wagon along the trail that eventually led to Mexico City.

But Dan'l knew they would have to leave the trail in the afternoon and head off to the southwest to find One Eye's village. When they rested at midday for a brief meal, he reminded them of that.

"In another couple of hours we'll turn off at that red butte," he said after they had eaten and were sitting in a loose circle drinking coffee.

Fuentes took a pot of coffee around to the others. After Rivera and Cahill, Fuentes was the most dependable man he had with him, Dan'l figured. He was accustomed to taking orders, most of them from Rivera, and he had a reputation as a skillful Indian fighter.

"Muchas gracias, peón." Zarate grinned up at Fuentes after taking more coffee. He had used a word that was a small insult to Fuentes.

Fuentes looked at him but did not respond.

Pedro Rivera, the ex-colonel with the military bearing, sat beside Dan'l on a flat boulder. He caught Zarate's eye with a cool glance. "Just drink your coffee without comment, *por favor,"* he suggested.

Zarate grinned at Rivera. *"Sí, Coronel."* Rivera had been named Dan'l's second in command, and Zarate was aware of it. But he had no great respect for authority. He respected only Apaches. He had killed them, raped them, and stolen from them. But he held them in higher regard than the Mexicans who ruled this territory. He felt that politicians and military officers like Rivera were generally arrogant buffoons who could not hold a candle to men like Yellow Horse and even One Eye.

Finney sat across the circle from Zarate, beside the mountain man McGill, and fixed Zarate with a brittle stare. If Dan'l had kept out of it, they would be rid of the one called El Loco now. Finney resented Dan'l's interference, and still was not convinced of Dan'l's ability to lead other men.

"There is a small trail that leads off at the butte," Rivera told Dan'l. "If Apaches were looking for trouble, they might watch that trail.

Maybe we should make our turn west farther along, Dan'l. Through unmarked terrain."

Dan'l nodded. "That sounds right, Colonel. Cahill, you just looked at that map. Any big terrain problems south of the butte?"

Cahill took off his felt hat and ran a hand through his thinning hair. He looked older than he had when he had started out in Missouri. "I didn't see none, Dan'l."

The tall, slim McGill sipped some coffee and turned to Dan'l. "The rougher the country we ride through, the less chance they got of finding us. I say go the worst route we can navigate. We'll still get there."

Dan'l nodded. "Good thinking. Except there's a matter of time, McGill. Molly might still be alive."

Cyrus Finney grunted, and Dan'l looked over at him.

Zarate caught the meaning of Finney's reaction. "She is still alive," he said deliberately.

"Is that just one of your gut feelings, Crazy Man?" Finney said with an easy grin.

Zarate ignored him, staring at the coals of the fire. Overhead, the sun was hot on their backs.

"The girl is an important trophy for One Eye," Zarate said after a moment. "She is related by blood, yes?"

"That's right," Dan'l said.

"He will keep her until she no longer gives him power. She is considered strong medicine now. When that changes, he will kill her in an unpleasant way."

A heavy silence fell over the group. Dan'l threw some coffee dregs into the fire, and they sizzled there.

"What makes you the expert on One Eye?" Finney finally asked. "She could be dead now."

Cahill scowled at Finney. He was sorry he had suggested the ex-convict to Dan'l. "Why don't you just shut your mouth, Finney!" he said rather loudly. "Every man here knows more about the Apache than you do! Just shut your damn mouth!"

"That is good advice," Rivera said darkly to Finney.

Across the circle, Zarate was grinning happily.

"For Christ's sake!" Finney said. "I was just talking, like the rest of you!"

"Except you have nothing to say, *amigo!*" Zarate said.

Finney glared at Zarate in stony silence.

"It don't matter what's said or ain't said," Dan'l intervened. "We'll find out soon enough what's happened to her. Either way, I got a score to settle."

They sat there absorbing that, and Rivera found himself wondering what it would be like to have Dan'l Boone coming after you to settle a score. It would have to be unnerving. Dan'l was not a man you crossed without killing him.

He would not give up on this, Rivera figured, until either he or One Eye was dead and buried.

That was the way he was.

Dan'l got up and walked over to a nearby gnarled tree and stood in its shade by himself. After a moment, Rivera joined him. Not far away, one of the team horses whinnied softly. The mounts were picketed in a clump of junipers not far from the wagon.

"This was a very unusual thing One Eye did, you know," Rivera said to Dan'l over his shoulder.

Dan'l turned to him, and his square, lined face showed the strain he had been under.

"Apaches rarely leave their own territory. What he did, coming after you like that, is without precedent. It is powerful medicine."

"I know," Dan'l said.

"It also shows the depth of One Eye's hatred for you. It cannot be underestimated by us."

"I ain't about to do that, Colonel," Dan'l assured him.

"On the other hand, when it is learned that he failed," Rivera said, "and that is likely to happen very soon now, that can work to your advantage."

"He might lose some of them new recruits."

"It is more than that. Some of them will think he failed because you are unkillable. Because you really are an ancient Apache god."

"The Ancient Bear thing?" Dan'l said. "Well, if that will help me get Molly back alive, I won't

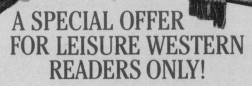

GET YOUR 4 FREE BOOKS NOW—
A VALUE BETWEEN $16 AND $20

Mail the Free Book Certificate Today!

FREE BOOKS CERTIFICATE!

YES! I want to subscribe to the Leisure Western Book Club. Please send my 4 FREE BOOKS. Then, each month, I'll receive the four newest Leisure Western Selections to preview FREE for 10 days. If I decide to keep them, I will pay the Special Members Only discounted price of just $3.36 each, a total of $13.44. This saves me between $3 and $6 off the bookstore price. There are no shipping, handling or other charges. There is no minimum number of books I must buy and I may cancel the program at any time. In any case, the 4 FREE BOOKS are mine to keep—at a value of between $17 and $20! Offer valid only in the USA.

Name_____

Address_____

City_____ State_____

Zip_____ Phone_____

Biggest Savings Offer!

For those of you who would like to pay us in advance by check or credit card—we've got an even bigger savings in mind. Interested? Check here. ☐

If under 18, parent or guardian must sign.
Terms, prices and conditions subject to change. Subscription subject to acceptance. Leisure Books reserves the right to reject any order or cancel any subscription.

PLEASE RUSH
MY FOUR FREE
BOOKS TO ME
RIGHT AWAY!

Leisure Western Book Club
P.O. Box 6613
Edison, NJ 08818-6613

AFFIX
STAMP
HERE

turn my back on it. Anything that works, Colonel."

"I am glad to hear that, Dan'l. We should use every weapon in our arsenal, yes?"

Dan'l nodded. "Sure. Now, let's get moving. We got a lot of ground to cover before the day is over."

A few minutes later, they were under way again.

One Eye's demeanor toward Molly had cooled off considerably, but he had not abused her in any way. At the first opportunity, Molly went to Isabel and told her to keep secret the fact that Molly was not Dan'l's daughter, and Isabel promised she would.

They had both been shocked when Gray Hawk rode in the previous day with Rachel Avery and threw her unceremoniously into his hide tipi. While the warriors drank and danced to their victory that evening, they had gone to Rachel and comforted her, and Rachel took solace in the fact that there were other white women in the village. She was still in shock over the death of her husband and what she had seen at Estacion Tres, but at least Gray Hawk had not physically abused her yet.

Now, on this day after the battle, the shaman Eagle Spirit came to One Eye and requested a formal palaver with him.

Eagle Spirit had come from another clan and was considered a second-rate shaman, and One

Eye merely tolerated him in his village. One Eye put little stock in the basic religion of the tribe anyway, and this feeling was heightened by his disdain for the Ancient Bear legend and its more recent interpretation involving the whiteface called Sheltowee. One Eye felt that the warrior class was the only important one in any clan, and that leadership should come from them, with little interference from shamans.

One Eye met with Eagle Spirit in the Great Lodge, his brother Lone Wolf with him. Neither he nor Lone Wolf wore any special clothing, and this in itself was a sign of disrespect to Eagle Spirit, who was outfitted in a skirt blanket of intricate design, with an ornate cross-shaped headpiece and a painted face. Before he began his palaver the shaman threw powder onto a low fire, making white smoke rise to a hole in the ceiling, and chanted some prayers in ancient Athabaskan.

Sitting beside One Eye, Lone Wolf wore a simple breechcloth and a red-dyed elkskin sash at the waist, a symbol of the society of Dog Soldiers, and a reminder to Eagle Spirit of Lone Wolf's high standing in the clan.

"Let this smoke show my fealty to you, my chief," Eagle Spirit began slowly. His middle-age paunch made a sharp contrast to the muscular, athletic figures of the younger men who sat across from him.

"Yes, yes," One Eye said impatiently.

"News has come to my ear, my chief, that rests heavy on my aging heart."

One Eye frowned. "Yes?"

"Gray Hawk has brought a third white woman into our village. Is it not so?"

"Yes. I gave him permission."

Eagle Spirit looked into the fire. "There is much talk about this, highest one. There seems to be much discontent, especially among the women of our people."

Lone Wolf smiled slightly. He knew that One Eye considered this none of Eagle Spirit's business.

"I know all this, shaman."

"It has also come to my ear that the other clans in this area have given a name to our village. They call it The Place of White Women."

One Eye frowned, and Lone Wolf looked over at him.

"This is true?" Lone Wolf said to the shaman.

"I am afraid it is, my chief. And the name is said in derision by the others of our tribe."

"Derision?" One Eye said darkly.

Eagle Spirit nodded. "It is a great burden that has descended on us," he said quietly. "There is no suggestion of criticism of our great leader One Eye, of course. He may have any woman he pleases. And, of course, his brother, who is also of noble blood. The question becomes, how far will this be taken, my chief? Will the white-face females replace our own fine women in this clan and bear mixed offspring? Such questions are being raised now."

"Raised by whom?" One Eye demanded.

Eagle Spirit noted the tone of One Eye's question and averted his eyes. "The outcry is general, my chief. There is a definite undercurrent of discontent."

One Eye was furious. It was not the place of a shaman to report discontent to a great chief like himself. "Is this all, Eagle Spirit? Is this why you called my brother and me to this meeting, interrupting our day?"

Eagle Spirit hesitated. "There is another thing, my chief. Some of the men are saying that the white women shed no dishonor on the clan if it is clear that their stay here is temporary. It is suggested that when our great chief and his brother are finished with satiating their appetites with these foreigners, these women of hated enemies, that they be executed publicly, and as soon as is reasonable, to show our chief's true feelings toward these blasphemers of our religion, these pallid-faced infidels."

Lone Wolf screwed up his handsome face in surprise. "What is this? Some kind of bad joke? Does the shaman deign to advise the chief of this clan how to conduct his personal life?"

Eagle Spirit wondered if he had gone too far. "Excuse me, my chief. You must understand it is not I who speaks these things. I merely report them to the great chief and his brother. They are the thoughts of others."

"Well, the report is ill-advised!" Lone Wolf told him.

Eagle Spirit took courage from One Eye's silence. He shrugged. "I saw a vision in the night. A great storm cloud hung over the village, and the faces of these women were in the cloud. It is not a thing that may be ignored."

Suddenly One Eye rose to his feet, which was a violation of protocol and an insult to Eagle Spirit. Lone Wolf rose, too, scowling at the shaman.

"Are you finished now?" One Eye said coldly.

Eagle Spirit swallowed hard. He rose to his feet and bowed his head to One Eye. "That is everything, my chief."

One Eye came nose to nose with him. "It is always difficult to know," he said easily, "how much of a report like this originates in the head of the adviser."

Eagle Spirit's eyes widened slightly. "My chief, I would never—"

One Eye drew a long knife from his belt and held it up in the shaman's face. "It is really you who wants the white women gone, shaman. Is it not so?"

"My chief!"

"I have had a vision too, Eagle Spirit," One Eye said casually. "In my vision, the shaman of this village is killed by the chief, and there is nobody to mourn his passing in The Place of White Women."

"My chief—"

One Eye's next move surprised even Lone Wolf. One Eye sank the blade of the knife into Eagle Spirit's belly as the shaman's eyes widened, and then he drew the knife upward. At the top of the incision, he left the knife in place.

Eagle Spirit grabbed the knife handle with both hands and stood there for a long moment, staring at One Eye as if he had gone crazy. Then he collapsed into the low fire, making sparks rise into the room.

One Eye turned to his brother. "Bury him well away from the village," he said evenly.

Lone Wolf nodded. "But you have killed a shaman. What will I tell the people?"

"Tell them that the great One Eye has no need for shaking of bones and chanting to ancient gods. Tell them that I make my own rules, and that I am my own adviser. If they do not like it, tell them they may leave."

Lone Wolf thought about that for a moment. "Very well, my brother."

"And tell them that the women stay. For as long as it pleases me to have them here."

Lone Wolf nodded. "It shall be done."

Later that day, Gray Hawk and Crooked Leg came upon Dan'l's camp, which had just been set up on the bank of a dry riverbed.

Dan'l had picked the spot because a high plateau rose between it and the area where One Eye's village lay, and Dan'l figured the site would afford the most secrecy for them.

But the two warriors who had been with One Eye at Dan'l's house in Missouri had been out hunting farther north than usual, and when they crested the edge of an escarpment looking down over a wide area to the south, they saw the riverbed and Dan'l's wagon, only a mile away, in fading sunlight.

"White men," Crooked Leg said quietly, as if those below might somehow hear. He had been opposed to One Eye's taking Molly from Missouri, and was one of those now speaking about their village becoming a haven for white women.

"It looks like several of them," Gray Hawk added, peering out into the dusk. "There might be too many guns. But there are many horses." He had not forced himself on Rachel yet. He did not like hysterics in women, and Rachel yelled every time he came near her. He would give her a couple of days. Then she would become his woman.

Crooked Leg nodded, holding the reins of his mount loosely. "They must be traveling south, though. They may ride right into our rifles tomorrow or the next day."

"Maybe we should take a closer look," Gray Hawk offered. "And report this back to One Eye."

"Very well. We will go on foot."

They picketed their mustang ponies to a low, gnarled juniper and headed out down the escarpment trail. When they reached level ground, they tried to keep to cover as much as possible. Within a half hour they were within a hundred yards of Dan'l's camp, and decided it was not safe to go farther.

They squatted behind a reddish boulder, staring at the campsite. A low fire was visible, with several men moving about near it. Riding horses and the wagon team were picketed back by the wagon. Crooked Leg reached into a buffalo udder pouch and retrieved a beat-up pair of binoculars, stolen from a Mexican expedition.

"I will use the glass," he said.

The binoculars were considered clan property, but One Eye usually allowed Crooked Leg the use of them, and Crooked Leg had come to look on them as his. They gave him a certain standing among the *akacita*, the Dog Soldiers of the clan, and he guarded them fiercely.

Gray Hawk watched Crooked Leg put the glasses to his eyes.

"There are seven of them," he reported to his companion. "Mexicans and maybe a few whites from the east. I can't see all their faces."

"Let me take a look," Gray Hawk said testily.

"No, wait. I am looking at the horses. There are nine, it appears. A saddle horse for each man, even though one must drive the vehicle." His eyes widened. *"Aaiieh!"*

"What is it?"

"Colonel Rivera is with them. I know him by sight."

"Alvarado's retired commander?"

"The same."

"It is a military expedition!" Gray Hawk said.

"I see guns. Many guns," Crooked Leg said softly.

Gray Hawk yanked the binoculars away from the other man. "You do not own the glass! Let me see!"

Crooked Leg scowled at him as Gray Hawk put the glasses to his face. He focused, and the campsite came into view. He saw Rivera speaking to Fuentes near the fire. He saw Finney and Cahill at the wagon, gathering utensils for eating. McGill was piling small pieces of wood onto the fire, and Miguel Zarate was erecting a support over the fire.

"That bastard Zarate is there too!" Gray Hawk whispered harshly. "The murderer of Apache children!"

Crooked Leg made a snarling sound. Most of the stories about Zarate were untrue, but all the Apaches hated him.

"There is a bearded whiteface coming out of the wagon, carrying a sack," Gray Hawk said. Then he sucked in his breath.

"What is it?" Crooked Leg asked in a hiss.

"By the White-Painted Woman!" Gray Hawk muttered, invoking the power of an ancient god. "It is the spirit of Sheltowee!"

Crooked Leg looked over at him as if he had gone insane. Then he yanked the glasses back and put them to his own eyes. He clearly saw

Dan'l walking toward the fire, looking very much alive and dangerous.

"It is not his spirit!" he said in a choking voice. "It is Boone himself!"

Gray Hawk turned away, as if the scene might disappear entirely if he could not view it.

"How can this be?" he asked. "We saw him dead!"

"Did we?" Crooked Leg said hollowly, taking the glasses down. "One Eye should have put another bullet in him. I thought so at the time."

Gray Hawk looked at him, fear in his face. "Is it possible he does have the spirit of Ancient Bear in him?"

Crooked Leg grabbed Gray Hawk's bead necklace and drew the bigger man to him fiercely. "If you ever voice that opinion in the presence of One Eye, you are a dead man!"

Gray Hawk's head was spinning. "Maybe it is the glass," he said. "And the bad light."

"It is not the light," Crooked Leg said heavily. "It is obvious that Sheltowee survived our attack on his family and is on his way to rescue the white woman! I knew no good would come of this blasphemy! The gods do not allow intimacy with the whitefaces!"

Gray Hawk was breathing shallowly. "We must get back to One Eye quickly and warn him. Preparations must be made!"

"Come. We have stayed long enough," his companion said.

* * *

In Dan'l's camp, they all had a light meal of antelope stew and hardtack. Zarate had done the cooking, and he was good at it. Everybody seemed to like the meal except Finney, who threw half of his stew on the ground, swearing under his breath about the taste. Dan'l could see clearly that the thing between Finney and Zarate was not abating, and he had decided there was only so much he could do to avoid real trouble between them. Some things just had to resolve themselves, he figured, and this might be one of them.

Zarate had seen Finney's rejection of the stew but had made no comment about it. He realized that the Missourian was making a fool of himself before the others, and that pleased Zarate. He was much better at playing these games than Finney, and he was enjoying his success.

McGill was not much better than Finney. He did not invite arguments or bait anybody about anything, but he was a too-quiet, surly fellow who did not really know how to act around other people. He had been out alone in the mountains and wilderness for too long. He also seemed to resent Rivera's preferential position of authority and Dan'l's close personal relationship with Sam Cahill. McGill, for reasons of his own, had felt like an outsider all the way from Missouri, and now that the Mexicans had joined the party, he felt even more so.

After they had eaten, and while Fuentes and Cahill were cleaning up, Dan'l took Rivera aside to speak with him privately again. Rivera had fought bravely and well against Yellow Horse, and Dan'l respected his judgment greatly.

"I hear One Eye has people flocking to him in numbers now," Dan'l said quietly.

"Yes, that is the report," Rivera told him. "This reminds me of the days when Yellow Horse was building his power in the area. Apaches who would ordinarily try to get along with us will be drawn into the evil vortex of One Eye's mania. It will start all over again."

Rivera had just sent McGill out on the perimeter to stand sentry duty on the first watch. If McGill had gone fifteen minutes sooner, he would have discovered Gray Hawk and Crooked Leg out there, and Dan'l would be aware that he had been discovered.

"How many able warriors do you think he might have?" Dan'l asked Rivera.

Rivera shrugged. He was just as fit-looking as ever, in his dark suit and silver-studded boots. But his face was more worn now, and the graying in his hair showed his advancing years. He ran his fingers through a thick mustache.

"We don't have any hard intelligence, *compadre*. But I would guess he can muster dozens of untrained soldiers if he has to. Probably fifty experienced ones."

Dan'l nodded. "With our seven guns, sounds like the odds is just about right," he said with a grin.

"It is clear we cannot defeat them in open battle," Rivera replied seriously. "I hope you understand, *amigo*, that when One Eye learns that you are alive and coming for the girl, he may execute her immediately to keep you from rescuing her."

Dan'l looked out into the night. "I been thinking about that. That's why we can't give him too much time to think on it."

"The trader we met on the trail earlier. He mentioned a rumor to me about One Eye's village. That they have a second white woman there now."

Dan'l grunted. "Ain't that kind of unusual?"

"The Apaches do not ordinarily think much of white women. But who knows? This may become a custom with One Eye's people. Maybe it is good for your cousin that there is a second one there."

"If Molly is still alive," Dan'l reminded him.

"*Exactamente.*"

Over at the fire, there was some loud talking. Dan'l turned and saw Finney and Zarate face-to-face again.

"Oh, damn!" Rivera said. "Nobody can get along with El Loco. I will put a stop to this."

"No, wait," Dan'l said, his face somber. "I've had enough of them two. Let them go at it, and we'll deal with what happens. I don't need this going on."

They moved over near the fire.

"I'm telling you, you damn greaser!" Finney

was saying loudly. "If you can't shoot no better than you can cook, you might as well go back to Santa Fe right now! You won't be no good to us!"

"What?" Zarate said happily. "You don't like my stew? But I got the recipe from your unwed mother, *cabron!*"

Finney became red-faced very quickly. Sam Cahill, standing nearby, stepped up beside him. "For Christ's sake, Finney! We wouldn't brung you on this if we knowed you'd cause trouble every chance! Just let it go!"

Finney turned hotly to Cahill. "Didn't you hear what he said? A damn bean-eater insulting my own mother!" He drew the pistol at his belt and aimed it at Zarate's chest. "Nobody ain't stopping me this time! I'll blow his liver out of his yellow back!"

Zarate glanced at the side arm and saw that it was not primed. Finney was usually very careful about that, but he had shot at an antelope earlier and had put off repriming. Now, in the heat of the argument, he had forgotten.

Zarate's own gun was primed and ready to fire. But as with the last confrontation with Finney, he chose not to draw the weapon. Zarate prefered cutting if the situation allowed it. He had stabbed and scalped more Apaches than he could remember. Now he pulled his long knife from its sheath at his belt.

"You cannot kill me with that, farmer boy!" he said with a laugh.

174

"Oh, no?" Finney replied. He cocked the thick gun and re-aimed.

"Stop this!" Fuentes cried out from nearby.

But Finney was not listening. With them all watching, he squeezed the trigger of the pistol.

The hammer clicked hard on the cradle, but there was no explosion.

Finney looked down at the gun, dumbfounded. Then he remembered. Finney, the gunsmith. Finney, the gun lover. Finney, who oiled the side arm every night and handled it like a baby, had forgotten he had left it unprimed.

Dan'l and Rivera saw the fury mount in his Irish face, and then he was hurling himself at Zarate, to club him to death with the pistol.

Zarate ducked under the attack, and the gun careened off the side of his head, just hitting him a glancing blow. In the same instant, Zarate grabbed Finney's gun hand, and then they went down together, hitting the ground hard. Zarate rolled on top of Finney, pulled his right arm free for just a moment, and drew the blade of the knife across Finney's throat, from ear to ear.

Bright red blood spurted up into the Mexican's face and onto his tunic. Finney's jaw was working, but his eyes were glazing over.

Zarate rose and stood over Finney, a hard grin etching itself onto his stubbled face.

"Now how do you like the stew, *cabron?*" he said between his teeth.

Rivera was very angry. "Damn that man!"

Finney was already dead, his blood forming a pool around his head and shoulders. As Zarate stepped away from the corpse, Dan'l walked over to him and slugged him across the face so hard that everyone present heard bone crack in Zarate's nose.

Zarate fell heavily onto his back, not far from the fallen Finney. Dan'l stood over him, fire flashing in his Quaker eyes.

Zarate lay there stunned, pain rocketing through his face and head. He had lost the knife in the fall. He stared up at Dan'l fiercely.

"Madre mía!" he spat out.

Dan'l pointed a thick finger at him. "I told you!" he said quietly. "It wasn't just Finney, and you damn well know it. Now we're a gun short going against One Eye! You think this is some damn *game?*"

Zarate saw Dan'l's eyes and decided not to respond. He sat up and felt his nose. Blood ran down onto the lower part of his face.

"You start anything with anybody else, by Jesus," Dan'l said carefully, "and I'll take care of you myself. You understand me?"

Zarate rose unsteadily to his feet, and despite the fear inside his gut, managed an imitation of that crazy grin of his.

"You are the boss, *Señor* Boone!"

Dan'l nodded. "Don't you ever forget it, you son of a bitch!" He turned to Cahill. "Help this crazy man bury Finney. Then let's all try to get some sleep. We might just run into One Eye to-morrow."

Dan'l walked stiff-backed to the wagon, with Rivera and the others staring after him. Rivera let out a long breath. If he had ever doubted Dan'l's ability to lead, those doubts were long ago resolved.

The matter was beyond debate.

Chapter Nine

At One Eye's village that evening, there was discontent among the Apache women.

The arrival of Rachel had made them wonder about their future in the clan. Would there be other white women brought there, and would this become a clan custom, to take whiteface females to the beds of warriors? It was all very unnerving, and it was Nalin and a few others who had complained most loudly to Eagle Spirit, encouraging him to speak to One Eye about it. Now that Eagle Spirit was newly buried, most of them resolved to keep their silence, lest One Eye's wrath should fall also upon them. That group included Three Tongues, who had become Molly's unofficial interpreter. But the rejected Nalin led a small knot of females who only became angrier after Eagle Spirit's death, and more resolved than ever to rid themselves of these paleface women who had disrupted the serenity of the clan and created uncertainty in its future.

Bones were shaken secretly in the night, and portents were read into cloud configurations. Earlier that day, Nalin had had an argument with Molly when Molly refused to perform an assigned task. One Eye had intervened, and when Nalin had spoken harshly to him, defending her position, One Eye had struck her, knocking her down in front of several clan women.

That loss of face had been so traumatic for Nalin that she had gone a little crazy and decided that Molly had to die for Nalin to regain her status in the clan. Even if One Eye later executed her for her deed.

That evening, as Crooked Leg and Gray Hawk were on their way back from Dan'l's camp, intending to ride all night to deliver their explosive news, Molly went out into the compound after eating an evening meal with One Eye. Now he was in the Great Lodge, meeting with Lone Wolf, a few top warriors such as Little Crow, and other high-ranking soldiers, to discuss future plans for raids.

Molly had just placed a pot on the communal fire when Nalin found her there. Nalin, with a short, slim knife in her decorated belt, came up to Molly from behind.

179

"You dare show your white face out here?" she demanded in Spanish.

Molly turned quickly, surprised. "Oh. You."

"Do you know what you did today?"

Molly turned back to the fire. "I do not take orders from you. You caused the trouble."

Nalin's Spanish was not good, but she knew the meaning. Suddenly the knife was in her hand. "You do not belong here!" she declared in Athabaskan. "None of you belongs here!"

At that moment, Rachel Avery emerged from Gray Hawk's tipi not far away. Her blond hair was disheveled and her clothing was wrinkled, but she looked much better than she had when she was brought back from the raid. She saw Nalin holding the knife, and sucked her breath in audibly.

"By the ancient gods, you must die!" Nalin said in her own language.

Molly was staring incredulously at the knife. She could not believe Nalin would attack the woman of One Eye. But Nalin had lost all reason.

Molly had thought upon her arrival at the Apache settlement that she did not care if she died. But now she had resolved to somehow survive this ugliness, whether or not Dan'l showed up. It was not in her nature to give up.

But she was scared. "No, wait! We will talk."

"No more talk!" Nalin hissed. She thrust the knife toward Molly's torso.

Molly grabbed at the knife involuntarily, and

the blade sliced a cut along her palm; then she gripped Nalin's wrist with all her strength. They struggled, Molly trying to keep control of the knife.

"*Stop!*" Rachel yelled. She ran to them and threw herself onto Nalin's back. "Isabel! We need help!"

Nalin was taken by surprise, and was now fighting both Molly and Rachel. Because of her fury, she was very strong, and she quickly threw Rachel off her back and to the ground. Then she wrested her wrist from Molly's grasp and faced her again, her face screwed up with hatred, the knife out in front of her.

But now Isabel was outside, and she ran at them without hesitation. "Nalin! *Alto!*"

Just as Nalin thrust again with the knife, Isabel arrived, her dark hair flying behind her. The blade grazed Molly's side, and Nalin was knocked off her feet by the force of Isabel's charge. They went down together, and Nalin lost the knife as the two began hitting and scratching at each other. Molly grabbed Nalin and pulled her away from Isabel, and Rachel stood between Isabel and Nalin.

They were all breathless. Molly had a shallow cut on her hand and a scratch at her waist. Little Crow came out of the Great Lodge not far away and walked over to them.

"What is this?"

"None of your business!" Nalin spat out.

He saw the knife on the ground and the small

amount of blood on Molly's hand. He shook his head slowly. "White women!"

"I will kill them! One at a time!" Nalin said harshly.

"You will leave them alone!" the broad-shouldered Little Crow shouted at her. "Or you will join Eagle Spirit with your ancestors! Believe me, I know One Eye's mood!"

"She was going to kill Molly!" Rachel blurted out, her blond hair wild-looking.

"The damned Apache whore!" Isabel muttered.

"She must be insane!" Molly said breathlessly. "When One Eye hears of this—"

Little Crow recognized his chief's name and turned to Isabel. He knew a few words of Spanish. "One Eye. Must not know. Bad for all. You understand?"

"He says do not tell One Eye," Isabel said to Molly in English, so Rachel would also understand.

"Tell him!" Nalin said in Spanish, picking up on the meaning. "I want you to!"

Molly understood Little Crow very well, though. A full report to One Eye could cause big trouble not only for Nalin, but for all of them.

Molly nodded to Little Crow. *"Comprendo."* Then she turned belligerently to Nalin and said in heated English, "If you use that thing on me again, you better finish the job!"

Nalin spat onto the ground between them, then strode away from the fire toward her tipi, where she lived with her elderly mother.

The three white women went to their own places, and Molly cleaned her hand. When One Eye arrived back a little while later, she told him she had cut it on an iron pot.

At bedtime, One Eye had sex with Molly. She no longer offered any resistance. It was pointless; she was his legal spouse under Apache law, and he did not abuse her in the coupling. But she never really participated, and she could see that that was beginning to bother him. A time would come, she knew, when the resentment would build in him, and he would be done with her. At that point, the danger would be extreme.

When they were lying there afterward, side by side, Molly heard some yelling from Lone Wolf's lodge, and knew that Isabel was fighting One Eye's brother off once again. Rachel had no such problem that night, because Gray Hawk was still out there in the night, traveling back with Crooked Leg to deliver world-shaking news to One Eye.

One Eye lay awake beside Molly for some time and began telling her of his grand plans to rule the entire area, to band all Apaches together into a powerful nation, like the Sioux to the north. He began in halting Spanish, then slipped into his own language, and Molly lost the meaning. He was explaining to her that his empire would be greater than that of Yellow Horse, and he would form an army that would drive all white men from New Mexico.

Finally he fell asleep beside her. She watched his muscular chest heave deeply in sleep, and wondered what would happen to the clan if she found his dagger and drove it into his eyeball while he slept. She would be doing the Mexicans a great favor, she realized, and maybe even save hundreds of innocent people from death at One Eye's hands.

But even if she had the courage to accept the consequences of such a murder, she knew she would still not be able to do it. First of all, she was not certain she was skillful enough to accomplish it. One Eye slept like a cougar, always alert on some level. But secondly, she did not think she could bring herself to even attempt to kill this man in his sleep. As fierce an enemy to her people as he was, he was a human being, he was her husband under his law, and he trusted her now, enough to sleep beside her without fear. To kill him under such circumstances went against Molly's most basic feelings.

Finally Molly fell asleep too. And suddenly she was back in Missouri at Dan'l's house, and they were all there, just as they had been on that fateful day. They were all laughing and having a great time, and her fiancé Jock Parrish was leaning over her and placing a kiss on her cheek. Molly looked up into his rough-hewn face and was very happy they were about to be wed. Uriah Gabriel was telling a quick joke, and then Dan'l was offering them all a refill for their wineglasses. It was all very idyllic.

Then the peace was disturbed by the crashing of the big door, and the Apaches were there, looking like wild bandits. The room was filled with the explosions of gunshots, and she saw Jock Parrish hit and falling to the floor, and then she could hear only the sounds of her own screaming.

Molly twisted and turned beside One Eye, and moaned slightly in her sleep. He moved but did not wake. Then she was dreaming again. She was unconscious on the back of a horse, galloping away from the house, an Indian holding her up. But her spirit was still back at the place of death, and as it hovered in the background, seeing Parrish dead, and the other man, Gabriel, she saw Rebecca and Jemima return and revive Dan'l, and she saw that he was still alive. Then time jumped ahead, and she saw Dan'l boarding a mottled Appaloosa stallion and riding west with some other men to go after her.

Suddenly she sat straight up on the ground robe, not knowing where she was for a brief moment. She looked over and saw One Eye sleeping peacefully beside her.

The dream had been very real. And as she sat there staring into the darkness of the lodge, she got the feeling, deep inside of her, that this had been more than a dream. Maybe the feeling came from living with the Apaches, but she saw the dream suddenly as a vision, as a kind of mystical experience like those the shamans were always reporting. She believed that Dan'l was definitely alive and coming to rescue her, just as she had hoped all along, and that he had somehow sent her that message in her sleep.

"Oh, God, Dan'l," she whispered into the darkness. "I hear you. I know you're out there. Please come quickly and end all this for me. Please!"

"Huh?" One Eye said sleepily beside her.

His eyelids fluttered open and he focused on her. She reached over and touched his bronze, muscular arm.

"It is all right. Sleep."

One Eye grunted and went back to sleep. Molly lay back down, stared at the black ceiling of the lodge, and hoped she was not fooling herself, that this was not just some kind of vain hope to enable her to survive.

It was much later that she fell again into a restless sleep.

One Eye slept later than usual the following morning, and Molly was up well ahead of him, just as light was flooding into the eastern sky. She filled a pot with water, took it out to the guttering fire, got the fire going again with some kindling wood, and put the pot over it. Hot water would be needed for several purposes in the next hour or so.

There were three Indian women up and about, and they all avoided contact with Molly. Nalin came out shortly, glared just once toward Molly, then went about grinding some wild maize into a mash over by her own tipi.

Rachel was still asleep, but Isabel showed up shortly, while Molly was stirring some mash into her pot. Isabel saw Molly immediately and walked over to her, casting a sour look toward Nalin on the way.

"That little bitch!" Isabel muttered in Spanish. "*Buenos días*, Molly. How is your hand?"

Molly smiled. "It's nothing. It's already healing."

Isabel sat on a stool made of sticks and antelope skin. She gestured toward Lone Wolf's lodge. "He came to me again last night, Molly. I could not defend myself, he is so brutally strong. I feel dirty and ashamed."

Molly sighed and touched Isabel's shoulder. "Just look at it as you would a beating from him. A physical assault that you can endure and heal from. You're clean inside."

Isabel shrugged. "I suppose so."

"There are forced marriages in Europe, Isabel. Aren't there?"

Isabel looked at her. Her chiseled face was very pretty. "Yes, I think so."

"Arranged marriages, where the girl has no love for her husband but must accept intimacy with him. Think of this as a similar situation. These men are our husbands in this world."

"He takes me, even though I don't want it."

"I know."

"He beats me if I refuse."

Molly nodded. "They do the same to their

own women. It's their way. It's our way, too,
until this is all over."

Isabel looked toward Nalin. "It's becoming
dangerous, Molly. It is a bad situation for us.
Other women are almost as crazy as Nalin
about this. There will be more trouble."

"I had a dream, Isabel. In my dream, I saw
my cousin, Dan'l Boone. He was alive."

"But I thought you saw them kill him."

"In the dream, he survived. In the dream, he
is coming for me."

Isabel touched Molly's hand, and Molly
grasped it tightly.

"Don't you see, Isabel? He will rescue all of
us! He's coming; it's just a matter of time. We
have to hold on till then!"

Isabel looked into Molly's green eyes and
touched her long, auburn hair with her free
hand. "Molly. It was only a dream. Your cousin
is probably dead."

Molly frowned. "No, you don't understand.
This wasn't just a dream. It was a thing like the
shamans have. It was a vision, Isabel. A vision
of the future. Of reality."

Isabel smiled at her. "Maybe you are becoming an Apache," she joked. "Maybe the physical
contact with these brutes will turn us all into
Indians!"

Molly took in a deep breath. "I don't know.
Maybe you're right. But I believe in the dream,
Isabel. I have to. I want you and Rachel to be-
lieve in it too."

Isabel shrugged. "What can it hurt to believe? Your Dan'l Boone is on his way here at this very moment, to rescue us all from our torment, and we will all live happily ever after!"

Molly laughed softly. "That's exactly right. Now, don't forget it."

Isabel looked into Molly's pretty eyes. "I have known you for such a short time, *amiga*. But I feel as if we are lifetime friends. I feel closer to you than almost anybody I have ever met."

"I feel the same, Isabel."

"If we come through this alive, we will be friends forever. All three of us," Isabel offered.

"Absolutemente!" Molly agreed.

Across the compound, one of the Apache women stood, looked toward the edge of the village, and began gesturing and talking loudly to a second woman.

Isabel looked toward the horizon, beyond the village, and saw two riders coming, kicking up dust. They had arrived just after the sun. It was Crooked Leg and Gray Hawk.

"Two warriors," Isabel said glumly to Molly. "Back from hunting, I suspect. But they have no animals."

Molly watched as the two riders came dusting to a halt in the center of the compound and dismounted. Surprisingly, they both looked very agitated.

"Where is One Eye?" Crooked Leg asked breathlessly. Both his horse and Gray Hawk's were frothy from the long, fast ride.

The woman he asked indicated One Eye's lodge, from which he was just emerging, stretching in the morning sun.

"There! He has just come awake."

Crooked Leg and Gray Hawk exchanged a long look, then walked over to One Eye, out of earshot of Molly and Isabel. When they got there, One Eye regarded them with surprise on his scarred face.

"What is this? You were going after antelope. Why are you back here this morning, and without any game?"

They exchanged another dark look, neither wanting to be the bearer of bad news.

"We came upon a whiteface camp," Crooked Leg began.

One Eye frowned heavily at them. "Yes?"

"There were seven men, and they are coming this way," Gray Hawk added.

"Good," One Eye said. "They should be easy pickings for us if they come near here. We will take their horses and their lives. But why did you return early just because you saw white-faces?"

Both men looked very uncomfortable. "Two of these men . . . well, actually, three . . . are known to us," Crooked Leg said heavily. "There is the white Apache, Zarate."

Some of them called Zarate that because he acted more like them than any white man they had ever known, and many thought he had Apache blood in him.

"Ah, the baby murderer," One Eye said. "If he comes within my lance's range, it will be my personal pleasure to cut his liver out."

Crooked Leg nodded, and Gray Hawk gently prodded him with an elbow.

"The second man is Colonel Rivera," Crooked Leg said, shifting his weight off his gimpy limb.

One Eye became somber. "Interesting. How many did you say there are?"

"Just seven, my chief. But they are heavily armed."

One Eye stared off into the brightening sky. "Rivera is a brave soldier."

Gray Hawk turned to Crooked Leg now impatiently. "Tell him!" he hissed.

At that moment, Molly came over to the lodge, set the boiled mash down, and stood at the entrance. She was suddenly within earshot. One Eye saw her but paid her no heed.

"Tell me what?" he said to Crooked Leg.

Crooked Leg's upper lip was sweating. "*He* is with them!" he said unsteadily.

Molly glanced toward them, listening.

"He?" One Eye said harshly.

"Sheltowee!" Gray Hawk blurted out.

One Eye's face was suddenly charged with several emotions, flickering across its bronze surface like a hot aurora. Nearby, Molly looked thunderstruck. She knew Dan'l's Shawnee name well. She cried out involuntarily, and One Eye whirled on her.

"*Get inside, woman!*" he yelled.

She hesitated, then hurried through the lodge entrance and out of sight, still stunned by the fact that it seemed her dream really was coming true.

One Eye turned back to Gray Hawk with a fierce scowl. "What are you saying? I killed Boone with my own hands in Missouri!"

"We are telling you only what we saw!" Gray Hawk said in a tight undertone. "He was there."

One Eye turned away, his cheeks feeling hot. He paced back and forth for a moment, then came and shouted into Crooked Leg's face, *"I saw him dead! At my feet!"*

Gray Hawk, fear in his face, forgot for a moment to whom he was speaking. He muttered almost inaudibly, "Legend says he cannot be killed."

One Eye heard him, though. He whirled on Gray Hawk and shouted, *"What! What did you say?"*

Gray Hawk saw his mistake. He cowered before One Eye. "I . . . was just thinking aloud, my chief."

One Eye swung his hard fist into Gray Hawk's head, smacking him audibly across the ear, and Gray Hawk flew off his feet and hit the ground.

"You fool! If you mention the legend again, you will die!"

Gray Hawk, holding the side of his head, nodded numbly. "Yes, my chief."

One Eye turned to Crooked Leg. "Any man,

woman, or child who mentions this thing in my presence will be executed!"

"Yes, One Eye," Crooked Leg said. He had warned Gray Hawk not to talk about the Ancient Bear legend, but the other Apache had been too gripped with fear to remember.

One Eye paced some more. "One more bullet," he said, echoing the thoughts of Crooked Leg. "One more bullet and it would have been certain."

"There is no magic in it," Crooked Leg said hastily as Gray Hawk rose to his feet, keeping his distance from One Eye. "Many of our warriors have recovered from wounds that should have killed them. He is mortal, like the rest of us."

Those were the words One Eye wanted to hear. But they did not quiet the unrest inside him. "So. Our mission failed, after all."

"There is no way to keep this from the people," Crooked Leg told him.

One Eye glanced at him. "I know that."

"He is obviously coming for the girl," Crooked Leg added.

"With only seven guns," Gray Hawk said, trying to get back into One Eye's favor. "We will annihilate them!"

One Eye walked in a tight circle and stopped. His face brightened. "The gods continue to smile on us!" he said.

"What?" Gray Hawk said.

"Don't you see? He has given us a second

chance! Let him come, because we will be ready for him! In fact, *we* will take the fight to *him!* But there must be preparations! Call a meeting of the entire society of Dog Soldiers. We will plan our attack on Sheltowee and his murderers, and we will do it right this time!"

Crooked Leg nodded doubtfully. "I will gather them immediately, my chief," he said with a lowering of his head.

"He will rue the day that he returned to our proud land!" Gray Hawk said loudly.

But One Eye noticed that there was a hollowness in his voice.

Chapter Ten

About fifty miles north of One Eye's village, on that same sunny morning, Dan'l Boone and Pedro Rivera rode out in front of the others almost a mile, scouting the terrain and watching for trouble. Even though they had seen no Indians since leaving Santa Fe, Dan'l was certain that by now One Eye must know of his presence in the area. Dan'l knew One Eye would be shocked and furious, and might attack at any time, once he knew Dan'l was coming. Dan'l knew also that that knowledge would place Molly in even graver danger, if she was still alive.

They were in the hot country now, and even though it was just after sunrise, the air was warm. High buttes rose around them on all sides, and it was primarily sagebrush that dotted the landscape now, except for an occasional gnarled, dwarfed tree.

Dan'l had sent McGill off to the west of the slow-moving wagon to a spot where they had seen antelope the previous day, in the hope that McGill would bring back some camp meat. Cahill was riding out in front of the wagon a hundred yards, and Zarate had been directed to ride behind it. Fuentes was driving the vehicle, with two mounts tethered to its back end.

Of all the men Dan'l was left with on the expedition, Sam Cahill and Pedro Rivera were the ones he would trust his life to. Cahill went back almost to boyhood with Dan'l, back to Carolina and the French and Indian War, and Rivera had proved his loyalty to his comrades-in-arms in the fight against Yellow Horse. It seemed that you always were closest to men you had soldiered with, Dan'l thought as he rode along.

They had just created a small expanse of high ground when Dan'l dismounted and studied the ground carefully. Rivera watched him with admiration. Dan'l could track better than a lot of Apaches, and the Apaches knew it. He ran his fingers through the dust where he knelt.

"Apaches," he said to Rivera. "They passed this way within the past few hours, and there was a dozen of them."

Rivera shook his head slowly. He had not even seen the tracks, they were so faint.

"I don't know how you do it, *amigo,*" he said with a grin.

Dan'l rose and looked off into the distance. "They was headed east. I don't think they was One Eye's people."

Back in Kentucky, the Shawnee had known him as a hunter who could track the smallest game over bare rock, and smell a bear a mile away.

"They could be dangerous anyway," Rivera told him. "Since One Eye's rise to power, even clans who have not joined him are becoming more aggressive again. Attacking traders and travelers. We must be very watchful."

Dan'l remounted and looked over at Rivera. It was good to have him along. He knew Apaches, and he knew the latest developments among them. And just as important, he was an excellent soldier.

"Reminds me of our Yellow Horse campaign," Dan'l said quietly. "With the Polack, and the refugees at Spanish Wells."

They headed on out again, riding side by side.

"I heard Running Dog killed the Pole," Rivera said. "After you and he started back to Missouri."

"Burned him alive," Dan'l said grimly. He had had to watch the whole terrible death, and the scene had been etched on his memory forever. That was why he wanted to get Molly back before they tired of her. There was no telling how they would kill her, once they took a notion.

Rivera sighed. "I feel responsible for getting you involved in all of this," he said. "If you had not volunteered to help go after Yellow Horse, One Eye would not have come after you in Missouri three years later."

"Hell, didn't nobody twist my arm, Colonel. You know how hard it is to keep me out of a good fight."

"You made some good decisions for us," Rivera said, recalling the campaign. "Attacking Yellow Horse in the middle of that storm to catch him off guard. That won the day for us. And saved a lot of lives. I will always be indebted to you, old friend."

Dan'l was embarrassed. "You was in charge, Colonel. The credit goes to you. I wouldn't even knowed where to find Yellow Horse. But I think you know how much I appreciate you coming along this time. You being with us will give old One Eye something to think about."

Rivera smiled. "No, it is the coming of Ancient Bear that will stir things up. I would like to be in One Eye's camp when they find out about you. They may run in all directions. You could ruin One Eye's dream of power just by appearing out here, without ever firing a shot."

Dan'l sighed. "I don't know how the others will react, but One Eye will come to do his unfinished work, I think. And he'll know we're outgunned."

"We will hope to avoid an open fight," Rivera said. "He will come in large numbers if he can. At some point we may have to abandon the wagon and play hide-and-seek with him."

"Whatever it takes," Dan'l said. "But I have to get Molly."

With that they fell silent again.

Half a mile behind them, the Boone wagon moved along at a steady pace, with Fuentes driving. McGill had returned with the carcasses of an antelope and a jackrabbit, and they all stopped for a short break to skin the animals and bleed them. Fuentes made some coffee over a small fire, and the team horses got a needed rest.

Sam Cahill tended the horses, asked Zarate to check a squeaking wagon wheel, and told the others to be ready to leave in fifteen minutes. He had a big pocket watch, but Zarate kept pulling out a pocket sundial that he insisted was more accurate than Cahill's watch. It had a built-in compass, and a sun indicator that hinged to lie flat when the brass case was closed.

"What is the hurry, *amigo?*" Zarate asked Cahill.

"Yeah," McGill said. "You trying to be Boone while he ain't here?"

Cahill's face colored slightly. "Somebody's got to keep track of things. This ain't no Sunday picnic in St. Louis, McGill."

Fuentes came over to the fire, swigging a tin cup of coffee. "Cahill is right. We cannot delay. *Señor* Boone does not even know we have stopped."

"*Señor* Boone," McGill said, shaking his head. He had not had much to do with Mexicans in his isolated life of trapping, and did not like them much better than Finney had. "What a time we're a-having, heh?"

Fuentes gave him a sober look and turned back to Cahill. "You have known Boone for a very long time, yes?"

Cahill nodded. They were all standing around the low fire, holding their cups. "Him and me drove wagons together in the Frenchie war. Now, that was a real fight. Dan'l saved my skin a couple of times. I owe him."

There was a brief silence among them.

"Is that why you come out here?" McGill finally said. "For a payback?"

Cahill scowled at the lean mountain man. "I come out here because Dan'l's family is my family," he said quietly. "I come out here to get Molly back. Not for money, like some."

McGill eyed him narrowly. "You saying I shouldn't took no money for this?"

"No, I ain't. I'm saying we got different reasons for bringing our guns out here."

McGill grunted. "I guess Boone's got his own reasons, too."

"What the hell does that mean?" Cahill said.

McGill shrugged. "He's got a big reputation back there. It must be kind of embarrassing to let a handful of Apaches sneak in and steal your cousin like he done. He'd have to do something, wouldn't he? No matter what he thinks of the girl."

"You son of a bitch, you don't know Dan'l at all!" Cahill said hotly, his eyes blazing.

McGill casually threw his coffee into the fire. "Careful who you're riling, old-timer. I don't cotton to being called cute names. You ain't saw me mad yet, and I don't think you want to."

"Now, boys," Fuentes said quickly. "Drink your coffee and then we will leave, *sí?*"

But Zarate was enjoying the exchange. "No, Cahill is right, *compadres*. We must not insult the name of the great Boone, yes? He is *un santo*, a saint, in Santa Fe. If he kills One Eye, we will all be put to work erecting a statue of him in the grand plaza! And we will be required to mention his name only in whispers!"

"Shut up, damn it!" Cahill ordered Zarate. "It's time to head out! Get the wagon ready!"

In late morning, Dan'l and Rivera saw a lone Apache on a high butte less than a mile away. Not long afterward, they rode back to the wagon for a midday break and reported the sighting to the others.

"Maybe One Eye spotted us," Cahill said to Dan'l. They were all standing around the fire again, chewing on roasted rabbit and hard bread.

"He probably has," Dan'l told them. "But I think these Indians was from off to the east.

They might be planning something. They know we got guns and horses to steal."

"They may also know about One Eye's abduction of Dan'l's cousin," Rivera offered. "If they are a rival clan, they may need the prestige of a successful raid on a wagon. They may also have heard that Dan'l is among us. If so, they might want to see him for themselves."

"Because of the legend?" Cahill said.

"That is right," Rivera said.

"Maybe you put more importance on it than the Indians," Zarate suggested with a grin.

McGill grunted his agreement and laughed in his throat. Rivera eyed him. "You can take my word for it, Mr. McGill," he said. "The Apaches do not take the Ancient Bear legend lightly. Many still believe that Dan'l Boone is the reincarnation of that tribal god, come to destroy its leadership and take charge of the entire Apache nation. When it is generally known that he is back, there will be confusion and dissension among the Apaches. It is an advantage we must not ignore."

"There ain't no accounting for what Indians will believe," Dan'l put in. "But whatever they think about me, they won't just turn Molly over to us on a silver platter. We'll have to go get her."

Fuentes came over to Dan'l. "Maybe I should picket the animals behind those rocks over there," he suggested. "I have this funny feeling, *amigo*. On the back of my neck."

Dan'l grinned slightly. "I got it too." He looked

out at the horizon. "We're in a pretty good position here among these rocks. Maybe we better just set tight for a little."

"I'll help Fuentes move the animals," Cahill said.

While the horses were being moved, Dan'l heard the distant cry of a coyote, but in his gut he did not think it was a coyote. He did not mention it to the others, but let them finish their meal. The horses were well-hidden now, including the team animals, behind a rock outcropping a short distance away. The wagon itself sat in front of those rocks, close enough so that riders could not really get behind it. If they moved on out just to make time, that defensive position would be lost to them. So Dan'l bided his time. And waited.

All of the rifles were taken out of the wagon and off the saddles, and stacked together near the fire. Dan'l asked all of the men to procure a side arm and load and prime it.

After that was done, and while Fuentes was putting the fire out with loose sand, the coyote call came again. They all heard it this time.

"They are out there, aren't they?" Fuentes said.

"I suspect so," Rivera replied.

"Maybe we could lead Finney's mount out and offer it to them," Zarate said. "He will not need it anyway," he said with a grin.

"That wouldn't do it," Dan'l said, eyeing the high rocks and the flat plain leading into them.

"They don't want tribute. They want us."

The coyote call came a third time. It was closer.

McGill walked over to the rifles, picked out his Jaeger, and primed it. One by one, without having to talk it over, each of them went and retrieved a rifle, including Dan'l.

Then, about a hundred yards out at the entrance to the rocks, they appeared.

There were a dozen of them, and Dan'l figured they were the same party whose tracks he had discovered earlier.

"There!" Rivera said excitedly.

"Get behind the wagon and them rocks!" Dan'l ordered.

They all took cover, facing the assembled attackers. The war party was led by a thin fellow wearing several golden eagle feathers and a lot of war paint.

"Well, I'll be damned!" McGill said from behind the wagon. They had taken the canvas cover off so they would all have a clear view of the Apaches. "There *is* Apaches out there!"

Zarate held his Charleville tightly at the ready, his face full of excitement. There was nothing he enjoyed more than killing Apaches.

"*Sí*, they are out there," he said darkly. "And soon they will be here. In your arms, *compadres!*"

"It is not One Eye," Rivera confirmed, looking them over. "I know this renegade. Some of his people have already joined One Eye. He wants to keep those who are still with him. A victory here would give him stature."

"Hell," McGill said with disdain, "we can drop most of them before they get here."

"Don't be so sure," Fuentes warned him, hiding behind a large boulder near the wagon.

"Here they come!" Dan'l announced. *"Let them come in close! Make sure of your target!"*

Unlike One Eye's warriors, who were all armed with rifles and muskets, this group had just a few long guns, and the rest were using the familiar short bow and lances. They came at a gallop, the feared horse warriors of the southwest, each pony and rider looking like one animal. They leaned far over their horses' necks, low and horizontal, yielding only small targets to their enemy. As they closed in, they began uttering staccato yelps, like excited coyotes.

Dan'l and McGill, accustomed to long-range shooting, both fired when the Indians were just halfway there, and each took an Apache off his mount. The other defenders waited until the Apaches were almost on top of them, then issued a fusillade of heavy gunfire. By that time Dan'l was reloaded and primed, and hit a second Indian as they swarmed onto the wagon. Then he had the Annely pistol out and was priming it.

Two other Apaches had been hit, and their mounts had run off at an angle to get away from the chaos. Zarate had hit one of them, and Rivera also. Cahill and Fuentes had both missed on their first shot, and now were desperately trying to get their side arms ready.

Now the fighting was close in, with arrows flying wildly at the defenders but hitting little. The warrior with all the war paint hurled a long lance that missed Rivera's head by an inch and caromed off a boulder behind the wagon.

The Indians could not circle the wagon to release their arrows, so there was some confusion among them after their arrival. They turned and wheeled their mounts before the defenders and presented better targets. McGill killed another one, and so did Dan'l. Rivera hit a big warrior in the head, and there was a spraying of blood and matter. Sam Cahill finally hit his first Indian, and the Apache fell from his pony, lifeless. Fuentes fired again and again, and only wounded one Indian.

Suddenly the Apache leader looked around and saw to his surprise that his force had been decimated. But he was so angry about his quick losses that he lost all reason and resolved to fight to the last man.

Then he saw Dan'l close up for the first time.

In a moment that seemed to stand still in eternity, he reined his mount in and just stared at Dan'l, eyes wide.

"Ancient Bear!" he muttered.

Despite the gunfire and yelping, Dan'l heard the exclamation clearly, and so did Rivera, beside him.

The Apache suddenly raised his arm and

shouted something in Athabaskan, and the other Indians held their fire and stared hard toward Dan'l.

"Cease firing!" Dan'l shouted at his people.

The Apaches just sat on their steadied mounts, confronting the defenders head-on, presenting easy targets, but they were not firing.

Zarate ignored Dan'l's command and fired and killed one of the few surviving Apaches. The Indian fell slowly off his pony, and Zarate grinned.

"Stop it, damn you!" Dan'l shouted again, and turned his Annely on Zarate.

Zarate and McGill just stared at Dan'l as if he had gone insane.

"Qué pasa?" Zarate said throatily. "We will kill them all!"

"Fire again, and I'll kill you!" Dan'l warned him.

There was sudden silence between the two groups. There were just three Apaches mounted now, and a couple of wounded ones on the ground. The thin leader moved his mount forward and stared even harder at Dan'l.

"Ancient Bear!" he said hollowly. "You have arisen again! After One Eye killed you!"

Dan'l said nothing. McGill lowered his side arm and frowned quizzically at the Indians. Zarate looked very angry.

Rivera stepped forward, out in front of the wagon.

"Ancient Bear cannot be killed," he said slowly.

The Apache leader dismounted, to everyone's surprise, and knelt on one knee beside his pony.

"We did not know. Take our lives, my chief, in payment for our foolishness." He had now seen the bear on Dan'l's shirt.

This was all said in his own language, but Rivera understood most of it and translated for Dan'l.

"Kill them!" Zarate hissed.

"Oh, hell," Dan'l said with a sigh, holstering his weapon. Cahill came over beside him, looking confused.

"What is it, Dan'l?"

"It's that ancient god thing again," Dan'l said as if he had a bad taste in his mouth. "I hate this stuff. It ain't fair to them."

The other Apaches had remained mounted, but their shoulders drooped now and they averted their eyes.

"They await their execution," Rivera explained to the others.

"Good. Kill them," Zarate said.

Dan'l sighed heavily. He had to play a part now. For Molly's sake.

"Ask him about Molly," he said to Rivera. He took his dark hat off, revealing his shaggy head, and one of the Apaches sucked in his breath.

Rivera used his halting Athabaskan and received an answer. He turned to Dan'l. "She has been taken as One Eye's woman. He thinks she is alive. There are two other white women in his village now."

Dan'l stood there absorbing all of that. Then he went forward, touched the Apache's shoulder, and motioned for him to rise. The warrior averted his eyes.

"Tell him Ancient Bear spares his life. To go spread the word. I'm coming for Molly. If she's harmed, the hand of death will touch all who let it happen."

Rivera repeated the message, and the thin Apache began breathing rapidly and shallowly, thanking Dan'l for his godly beneficence. Rivera told him to take his wounded with him when he left, and moments later they were riding off, subdued and silent.

Zarate came over and yelled into Dan'l's face, *"You call me crazy, man from Kentucky?"*

"I don't kill a man that disarms hisself," Dan'l said evenly to him. "And nobody under my command does, neither."

Rivera stepped up beside Dan'l. "Do not forget your place, Zarate."

"Hell, I'm with the crazy Mexican," McGill said, shaking his shaggy head slowly.

Rivera turned to him. "Dan'l decided to use the legend to his advantage," he explained impatiently. "It was the smart thing to do. And he should not have to spell it out for you."

"Dan'l was outfoxing old Chief Blackfish, back in Kentucky, when you was in diapers, mountain man," Sam Cahill said easily to McGill as he reholstered his weapon.

"Now we must move on," Rivera told them. "We don't want One Eye to know our exact location. Fuentes, let's get the team animals over here and—"

He had walked over to the boulder where Fuentes had been firing from. When he stopped suddenly, they all looked in that direction.

Fuentes lay stone-lifeless on the dusty ground, a lance impaling his head to the dirt through the left eyeball.

"Oh, damn!" Dan'l said heavily.

Rivera knelt over his manservant, who had fought with him and Dan'l in the war against Yellow Horse. Fuentes had been one of the best soldiers Rivera had ever commanded.

"He died instantly," Rivera reported to them.

"I'm sorry, Colonel," Dan'l said.

"Now maybe you don't think it was so smart," McGill snorted, "letting them dirty Indians ride off without a scratch."

Dan'l walked over to him. "You're beginning to get under my skin, McGill. Almost as much as Finney."

McGill grunted, and held Dan'l's look with a stony, cold one. "Pay me off and send me on my way anytime, Kentucky man. It's all money to me."

Zarate stood nearby, grinning. He loved to watch conflict between other men. And he was angry at Dan'l.

"I'll tell you when I can't stand you no more," Dan'l said to McGill. "In the meantime, hunter, you can help Cahill harness up them team animals."

"Anything you say," McGill answered with a smirk. He moved off with Cahill to get the two horses, still safe with the mounts behind the wagon in the rocks.

Zarate pulled some arrows out of the wooden sides of the wagon, and Rivera turned to Dan'l. "Do you think One Eye will heed your warning?"

Dan'l gazed off toward the south. "I don't think One Eye believes in the Ancient Bear thing any more than I do. He wouldn't come to Missouri if he had any fear of me. I reckon at this point he'll use Molly as a chess piece, and kill her in a minute if it's to his advantage."

Rivera nodded. "I would have to agree."

"Well," Dan'l said. "Let's get your friend buried."

"Yes," Rivera said tiredly. "The vultures are already gathering."

Chapter Eleven

Disruptive forces were reshaping reality with every hour that passed at The Place of White Women.

As soon as the word spread that Dan'l Boone was alive and heading for their village, most of the recent converts disappeared into the desert.

They just scattered to the winds, returning to their old villages or hiding out in the buttes. Anything to get away from the source of Ancient Bear's displeasure—One Eye.

Not all of them believed in the resurrection of the age-old leader of the Apaches, the god-chief who had turned into a bear to guide the tribe from above, and pledged to return as a bearded man to take control of the people if their leadership should fail. Not all thought

212

Dan'l Boone was that god simply because he resembled the pictographs that showed, usually, a pale-faced man with shaggy bear-hair and beard. But even if they did not believe, most did not want to take any chances.

So men, women, and children fled from One Eye's village, most in the middle of the night over a period of two days, until the place looked almost deserted. Most of the fledgling warriors who had flocked to One Eye's side were gone, as were even many of the hard-core group who had been with him for a while. Nalin was gone, and Three Tongues, who had been Molly's teacher and interpreter.

Nobody wanted to be there when Dan'l Boone arrived to claim what was his.

One Eye's elite bodyguard, of course—the men he had taken with him to Missouri, and whom he trusted most—not only stayed on but kept reassuring One Eye that they would be ready for Dan'l when he came.

One Eye was furious about the mass desertion, but there was little he could do about it.

"They will come crawling back here when he is killed!" he ranted to his warriors. "And I will cut their hearts out and offer them to true Apache gods!"

One Eye had not touched Molly since the news of Dan'l's arrival in their territory, and that worried her. She still slept beside him in his lodge, but he hardly spoke to her, and when he did, it was only to give her an order. He looked at her differently now, too. She was the enemy again. One evening he said to her, "Are you certain you are not his daughter?"

She understood, but did not know how to answer. She finally replied, "He would come after any of his kin."

He did not seem to like that answer.

Then, on the day following the small battle of the neighboring Apaches with Dan'l's party, a visitor from that other clan came past to report what had happened in the battle, and to relay Dan'l's message to One Eye.

One Eye was meeting with Lone Wolf and his elite bodyguard group when the outsider was shown in and received by One Eye. They were seated around a low fire in the Great Lodge. The visitor, sent by the thin Apache who had attacked Dan'l's wagon, gave the sign of friendly greeting and then was asked his business. He identified himself and reported the confrontation with Dan'l.

"It was Ancient Bear!" the visitor concluded. "I was there and saw him myself! I was wounded, and was allowed to leave with the pardoned ones."

"Pardoned?" One Eye said hostilely.

"Yes, Ancient Bear absolved us of our sins against him and let us live. He is a great god!"

"You damn fool!" One Eye screamed at him. *"He is not Ancient Bear! Can't you idiots get that through your heads!"*

The visitor lowered his gaze. "Please, my

chief. Do not blaspheme with him so near! He may strike us all down with a thunderbolt!"

"You stupid woman!" One Eye growled at him. "Where was his party when you attacked them?"

The warrior described the place to him, and One Eye realized it was just a day's ride or less away.

"That is close," Crooked Leg offered. He sat on one side of the lodge with Gray Hawk, and Little Crow sat near Lone Wolf on the opposite side. One Eye, as usual, sat at a small distance, even from his brother.

"We must strike quickly, brother," Lone Wolf advised him. "And the women must be guarded heavily. Especially Boone's woman."

One Eye turned to him. "She is not Boone's woman," he said darkly.

"Excuse me, my brother. I merely meant to identify her. She will be special to him."

One Eye cast a hard look on the messenger. "You are dismissed," he said acidly.

The man nodded. "There is, however, a message from . . . Sheltowee," he said quietly.

"A message?"

"Yes. He says that the girl may not be harmed. If she is, all here will be stricken down."

Gray Hawk, who had fear of Boone and the legend, cast a quick, dark glance at Crooked Leg. One Eye leaned forward ominously where he sat.

"Stricken down!"

"That was the message, my chief. It was intended for you, I believe."

One Eye was livid. *"You are lucky, old woman, that I do not remove your head for bringing such a message!"*

"Yes, my chief."

"Return to your village of cowards, and tell your chief that I will do as I wish with this Boone woman. And that I plan to ride out with my warriors and rid the world of this impostor god for all time, once and for all! And when I have done that, and have been acclaimed a hero of all Apaches, I will have your village burned to the ground as a place of cowards and morons!"

The fellow eyed him gravely. "I will take the message, my chief."

"Good! Then be gone!"

When the visitor had left, One Eye sat silent for a long moment. Gray Hawk finally spoke to him.

"This is a bad omen," he said quietly. "That he sends this message to you, my chief. Not that there is any truth in it. But that the people may believe there is."

One Eye regarded him darkly.

"If we kill the Boone woman," Crooked Leg offered, "he will have no cause for battle. He comes to rescue her."

"Don't be an idiot," One Eye said. "He has already announced that he will punish any who harm her. He will have to keep his promise to come here, anyway."

"Then give her to him," Little Crow suggested. Like Crooked Leg, he had never liked the idea of having Molly there. "Take her out into the plain, and leave her there for him to find. We don't need her. We don't need any of the white-face women."

Gray Hawk and Lone Wolf gave him fierce looks. They had no wish to give up Isabel or Rachel. They were not the ones causing them any trouble.

One Eye glared harshly at Little Crow. "It is not a matter of needing her. It is a matter of having her. She represents our triumph over the whiteface, don't you see? Do you think I would just give her over to this fake god, just because he demands her release? No, my friends. We will use Pale Dove for our own purposes. If that means her death, then she dies. But not until I say it."

Little Crow nodded. "Yes, my chief."

"We must meet this threat head-on," One Eye told them, looking from face to face with his good eye. "We will go to Boone. Now I will be alone to think on it."

The meeting broke up and One Eye stayed by himself in the Great Lodge, while word of Dan'l's message to them spread around the village like a cold wind. Within the hour, people were once again leaving the village, mounted and on foot, some dragging litters after them with sparse belongings. More warriors disappeared, and at midafternoon, when One Eye emerged from his meditation, the village looked as it had before they went to Missouri.

One Eye could not believe how quickly it had all dissolved around him. All because of one whiteface with a few hired guns. It was becoming very clear that this man must be killed, and not for the reasons that One Eye went to Missouri. Sheltowee had to die so that the Apaches as a people could regain some self-respect and dignity. To grovel before a mere whiteface was bitterly humiliating, and as Running Dog had known so well before his death at Sheltowee's hands, the Kentuckian had to be put to death, and preferably in a dramatic way, to reveal his mortality.

In late morning, One Eye gathered the remaining warriors around him outside the Great Lodge. There were fewer than thirty now, and not all of them were ready for what One Eye was about to announce to them.

"Dog Soldiers of my loyal clan," he began, surrounded by his brother and his personal guard, "you stayed when others left, putting their tails between their legs and running like cowards."

There was some muttering of agreement in the assemblage. No women were present, because they were not wanted. Molly and Isabel watched from inside the entrance of One Eye's lodge, where Isabel was helping Molly sew some rawhide. Rachel was inside Gray Hawk's tipi, keeping out of the way.

Molly was full of excitement about Dan'l's coming, but she greatly feared for his life. She realized that not even he could work miracles, contrary to what some Apache women thought.

"They ran because there is a filthy, defiling impostor out there!" One Eye continued loudly, his scarred face livid in the warm sun, his closed and withered eye looking rather grotesque in its hard light. He pointed toward the north. "This is the same blasphemer who murdered Yellow Horse and his brilliant son, Running Dog! There are even rumors that he has defiled sacred Sioux religious grounds since then! He has been allowed to run amok among us, killing and destroying! Just as he did in the east to the Shawnee and the Cherokee!"

A deep silence had fallen over the bronzed warriors as they stood listening intently.

"This paleface is not a god!"

Some low muttering.

"He is just another black-hearted invader of Apache lands, like so many of his kind before him. He has superior weapons, and it is true that he fights well. But he bleeds when he is wounded, just like us. His heart will stop beating when we stop it, just as an Apache's would. And he will die just as we die when we have the courage to kill him!"

From the lodge entrance, Molly felt terror in her heart. "Oh, God," she whispered.

"I have just received word that he is close by us now," One Eye went on, "coming with a few of his dirty Mexican friends."

They all knew that, but there was still some quiet rumbling among them.

"He is coming after that woman!" He pointed to his own lodge, and Molly ducked back farther inside.

"I know some of you think she should be given over to him. That that would end the trouble. But it would not. And of more importance, it is to our advantage that he comes for her. He is undermanned and outgunned, and we will kill him this time. Look at this as an opportunity and a challenge. Within the hour, we will ride out to rid the world of this scourge of the Apache people!"

There were a few cheering yelps, but many received the news with trepidation.

"I want you to arm yourselves immediately, and prepare your mounts! We will attack Boone's wagon this afternoon, and we will annihilate the party—men and animals. We will leave nothing living. Then we will burn every piece of equipment, all supplies, even the ground they sit on. We will burn Sheltowee's corpse, and will bring his charred head back on a pole for all Apaches to see and spit upon!"

There were a few more cheers. In the lodge, Isabel crossed herself and Molly began shaking. Isabel had understood a lot of it, and had translated for Molly.

"Now we ride out to glory!" One Eye yelled.

Gray Hawk and Lone Wolf cried out their encouragement, and there were more yells from the assemblage. Then the men went for their guns and weaponry, and to the corral for their ponies.

When they assembled again later, mounted, with One Eye at their fore, surrounded by Lone Wolf, Crooked Leg, Little Crow, and Gray Hawk, One Eye noted that the warrior force had shrunk again. There were just over twenty of them now. He acted as if he did not notice. He led his tiny army out of the village with the few Apache women watching, and Molly sitting with eyes closed in One Eye's lodge, her heart pounding in her chest.

About twenty-five miles to the northeast, Dan'l's party had just stopped in the shade of a cottonwood tree for a midday break. Dan'l had already decided that this was as far as the wagon would go, that from this point onward they had to try to use some strategy against One Eye.

Sam Cahill made a fire that would be their last one for a while, and boiled some coffee over it. They ate very lightly, all sitting around or standing in the shade of the tree and the wagon. McGill had been very quiet since his confrontation with the others, and seemed to enjoy keeping to himself. Mountain men were a breed apart, Dan'l decided. Actually, McGill was more like Dan'l than anybody else on the expedition, but the difference was that Dan'l, even though basically a loner, liked people. McGill did not.

Cahill was driving the wagon now, and liked that better than riding. He sat by himself through that morning, bumping along over the uneven ground, recalling good times with Dan'l back in Carolina. Before Missouri, before Kentucky. When they had both been raw kids who liked the outdoors and the woods. But Dan'l had always been the best woodsman, the best hunter, and the finest marksman in the county, even in his teens. That had bothered some young men, and Dan'l had had to defend himself from some bullies. That was when they found out he could fight like a grizzly.

Pedro Rivera had taken on the responsibility of keeping Zarate in line, because they were both Mexican and Rivera figured he had more influence over the quixotic Zarate than most other men would, even Dan'l.

"Maybe it is time now to abandon the wagon, Dan'l," Rivera said to him while they were all gathered under the shade of the cottonwood. "And the extra horses."

The wagon was drawn up close, and McGill leaned against it at the edge of the shade, away from the others. He had just returned from a scouting jaunt, and thought he had seen an Indian on a steep red butte. That did not surprise Dan'l. Dan'l was leaning against the trunk of the dark tree, while Rivera, Cahill, and Zarate squatted and sat around the fire.

Dan'l nodded in response to Rivera's suggestion. "That's what I been thinking. We're sitting ducks with the wagon, and One Eye will come in force." He looked out over the plain. "But maybe we ought to give him one shot at us first."

Rivera gave him a quizzical look.

"Well, that makes sense, when I think of it," McGill said sourly. "You want to give them a sporting chance, I reckon, like you done them other Indians. Who knows, maybe them ones you spared might be with old One Eye when he attacks."

Cahill glared at McGill. "Let it go, McGill."

"McGill is right," Zarate said. "You don't give the Apache any breaks. The only good one is a dead one."

Dan'l shook his head slowly. "I wasn't thinking of giving One Eye no breaks," he said. "I got this feeling at the back of my neck. I think he's coming. Today."

"So?" Zarate said. "That is even more reason to abandon the wagon now. Look where we have placed it. There is no cover here."

"Please," Rivera said sternly. "Let Dan'l speak."

"I stopped here purposely," Dan'l went on. "Just *because* the wagon's exposed."

McGill made a sound deep in his throat, and everybody ignored him.

"Maybe we should give One Eye a sitting duck to attack," Dan'l continued.

Rivera squinted over at him.

"But it'll be a decoy," Dan'l concluded.

Zarate looked over at Rivera, and McGill narrowed his hard eyes. "What's that mean?" McGill said.

"Look around you," Dan'l told him. McGill did, slowly. "We're surrounded by high rocks. Within a hundred yards of the wagon."

Rivera's face changed, and he grinned. "Ah!"

McGill walked out from under the shade and turned a complete circle. "Maybe you got something after all."

Zarate and Cahill were on their feet and looking too. "Maybe," Zarate said. "Maybe. But they will know. They will know the wagon is deserted."

"Maybe not," Cahill said, excitement in his face. "Not if we do it right."

"Exactly," Dan'l said.

"I like it!" Rivera said. "One last, efficient use of the wagon!" He turned to Dan'l. "But if they don't come, how long do we wait for them?"

"They're coming," Dan'l insisted. He rubbed the nape of his neck. "They're coming, all right."

"Do you want a fight at all?" McGill said. "Since what you want is the girl?"

That was the smartest thing McGill had said since leaving Missouri, Dan'l thought. And it was a legitimate question. What Dan'l had essentially was a small guerrilla force, and they were there to accomplish a very narrow task. But even if they melted into the hills and hid from One Eye until the moment they went in for Molly, they would have One Eye's small army to contend with when they got there. This way, they might reduce the odds against success by ridding themselves of some of their opposition.

"Frankly, McGill, I don't know. This might be a big mistake. But we don't know we can hide from them now anyway. I guess we'll find out soon enough, though."

Five miles off to the southwest, beyond some high buttes, a rider came galloping up to One Eye and his cadre of warriors and dusted to a stop.

"I found them, my chief! They are camped under a cottonwood. Just a short distance to the north."

One Eye felt something hard settle inside him. Lone Wolf, beside him on his pony, let out a long breath. "Well," he said. "The time comes once again."

"Let me kill him," Little Crow said from behind them. "I want his scalp."

"I don't care who kills him," One Eye said deliberately. "I just want to see him dead. With my own eyes. I want the corpse burned."

"It will be done," Crooked Leg promised him.

The warriors behind them looked somber. They were tough, experienced soldiers, but they knew this would not be like robbing a stagecoach.

"Let us move on up there," One Eye said clearly.

This time Crooked Leg rode out ahead with the rider who had found the camp. Within a half hour they were hunched behind boulders within two hundred yards of the wagon. A few minutes later, One Eye and Lone Wolf stood beside them, looking slightly downhill into the camp. On either side of them were high rocks, but there was no evidence of any sentry on duty. At the wagon there were five figures. Four were standing around the fire, and one leaned against the wagon. Not far away, horses were picketed to low-growing shrubs.

"That is them," One Eye said. "I think the one against the wagon might be Sheltowee."

"Let's do it!" Lone Wolf whispered harshly.

One Eye nodded and raised his arm, and the warriors came filing out of the rocks and rode up beside him. He made sure they were ready. Then he raised his arm again with a rifle in his hand.

"Now!" he shouted.

Suddenly the hot air was filled with the yelping cries of the Apache warriors, the bloodcurdling yells that had frozen men's insides and made some run in panic. Then they thundered into the small encampment.

As they came, they fired off the rifles at the figures at the wagon, over and over again. One toppled over, and then another. But the scene they rode into all suddenly seemed lifeless to them, and when they stormed into the camp, they saw the error they had made.

The figures were merely coats and tunics thrown over crates and boxes, with hats propped up by loaves of baked bread and other stray items from the wagon.

There were no men in the camp.

The shooting and yelling gradually stopped, and riders dusted about in tight circles, looking bewildered.

Then sounds of gunfire came from the high rocks on all sides of them.

The five defenders were distributed around the camp so that the tree did not obstruct their line of fire. In the next seconds, gunfire blasted out raucously from their vantage points, and the Apaches started falling off their horses, struck in the torso, the belly, the head. Dan'l had taken extra rifles into the rocks, and the defenders were able to fire at least twice before reloading.

Down in the camp, it was a slaughterhouse. Indians were falling all around One Eye as they wheeled their mounts in confusion, not knowing where to shoot to respond to the deadly attack on them.

"There are up there!" One Eye was yelling. *"Return their fire! Kill them all!"*

But it was Apaches that were being killed as One Eye fired wildly up into the rocks, trying to hit something. Dan'l's people were now reloading rifles, and some were firing pistols with surprising accuracy. It was all so easy. The Apaches could not find cover, and most did not yet think of running.

One Eye saw Crooked Leg knocked off his mount, hit in the right ear. The crown of his skull was blown away, and he fell to the ground, jerking spastically. Others lay all over the campsite, dead and dying, turning the sand crimson. Horses were running off in all directions, riderless. A hundred yards away, the Boone party animals were rearing and plunging on their picket ropes, reacting to the noise and melee.

But still the firing came from the rocky heights above them. One Eye had reprimed and fired again, trying to keep his mount from throwing him off. Lone Wolf saw one of the defenders leaning out from a boulder. He fired quickly, and the man went down, hit.

The Apaches, though, were being cut to pieces. A few had dismounted to find cover behind the wagon, but were picked off from the opposite side. One Eye finally had had enough. *"It is over!"* he yelled. *"Get out! Ride out of here!"*

When the others saw One Eye gallop off to the south where they had come in, they all followed him. Gray Hawk was beside Lone Wolf, and Little Crow fired off one last shot, then rode off surrounded by the remaining warriors.

There were just eight left, besides One Eye, Lone Wolf, and the personal guard.

In just moments they were out of sight of the

camp, humbled and defeated. One Eye, leading the retreat, was a different man.

He had learned the hard way what Yellow Horse had known several years earlier.

Dan'l Boone was some soldier.

Up in the rocks, Dan'l was waving toward Rivera and Zarate across the way, on the far side of the low camp area. Rivera waved back, indicating that he and Zarate were all right. Cahill came out from a boulder near Dan'l, holding his left arm.

"You're hit, Sam?" Dan'l said, climbing over the uneven ground to get to him.

"It's just a scratch, Dan'l. God, did you see what we done to them?"

Dan'l looked at Cahill's arm and nodded. "You're okay. Yeah, I saw. I kind of thought it might be a turkey shoot if it worked."

"Looks like we come out fine." Cahill turned toward another boulder fifty yards away. "Hey, McGill!"

There was no reply. Cahill and Dan'l exchanged a look, then climbed over rocks to get to McGill's position, while Rivera and Zarate descended to the camp area from across the way.

It took only a moment to find McGill. He had been the one who leaned out from cover to get a better shot and was taken down by Lone Wolf. He lay now on his back in an awkward position, blood pumping from his jugular onto the rocky surface beside him. He turned his head slightly and looked at Dan'l as Dan'l knelt beside him.

"Damn it," Dan'l muttered.

McGill tried a grin, and his long mustache moved slightly. "It ain't like shooting buffalo, is it? Them damn Apaches shoot back."

Dan'l put his finger on the neck wound to abate the bleeding. "Don't talk, McGill."

"I didn't see none of them other Apaches down there, Boone," McGill said in a choking, gurgly voice. "I reckon you ain't as dumb . . . as I thought."

His eyes closed, his head rolled to one side, and blood wormed out of the corner of his mouth. Dan'l released his pressure on McGill's neck. The bleeding had stopped. McGill's heart had quit pumping.

"He wasn't a bad sort," Dan'l said quietly to Cahill.

Cahill nodded. "I reckon I've rode with worse," he said.

Dan'l figured that was as good an epitaph as most.

Chapter Twelve

It was a shocked, numb knot of Apache riders who straggled back into One Eye's village that afternoon.

A few women and old men had gathered to greet them on their great victory over the white invaders and the killing of the one called Sheltowee. But when they saw the pitiful group of survivors ride in, they knew.

A pall hung over the village unlike any since the death of Yellow Horse.

Molly was out on the compound when they arrived, and was surprised by how few had returned. She knew they had gone to kill Dan'l, and tried to determine whether her cousin had survived their attack. But when she saw their faces, she knew she could not raise the issue.

One Eye went directly to his lodge, alone, as the others dispersed. Molly thought of going to him but decided it was not wise. Lone Wolf disappeared into his lodge, and then Molly heard him beating Isabel. Molly thought she ought to go to Isabel's aid, but realized that might only make matters worse. After a few minutes Isabel came stumbling out of the lodge, her face bruised and her lower lip cut. She collapsed onto the ground, and Molly went to her.

"Oh, God, Isabel!" She held the Spanish girl to her, comforting her.

"I cannot . . . take this anymore!" Isabel sobbed. "I want it to end, Molly!"

"I know."

"They are animals! Just animals!" Isabel exclaimed.

As they sat there on the ground, Molly saw Gray Hawk stride purposefully into his tipi, where the blond Rachel hid from them. There was an awful scream, and Molly jumped in terror. Then Gray Hawk came back out of the tipi, carrying Rachel in his arms.

His knife protruded from her chest.

She was dead.

"Oh, Jesus!" Molly murmured under her breath.

Isabel screamed beside her.

Gray Hawk dumped Rachel's body on the ground not far from them and turned a wild look on them. "Death to all whitefaces!" he cried to the heavens.

Isabel made grunting sounds in her throat, as if she were trying to throw up. Molly began to shake. Gray Hawk strode over to them, and Isabel shrank back, her eyes full of terror.

"This is what will happen to all of you!" he growled. "Prepare to meet your gods!"

But Molly stuck her chin out. "You damn murderer!"

Gray Hawk strode back into his tipi, ignoring her.

Isabel's face was pale. "They will kill us all!" she said, trembling uncontrollably. "Before this day is over!"

"Please, Isabel," Molly said quietly. "Don't give up hope. My cousin defeated them, can't you see? He may still be alive. He'll come for us."

"I cannot . . . just wait to die," Isabel said numbly.

"Stay here," Molly said. "I'll go speak with One Eye."

Isabel did not reply.

Molly got to her feet and walked across the quiet compound. A few women were watching silently from tipi entrances. Over by the corral, a defeated warrior sat on the ground with his head between his legs. An Indian pony limped around the village, shot in the flank, bleeding onto the dirt.

Molly went into the lodge and found One Eye seated there, staring into a low fire. He did not look up at her. He looked very tired. She had never seen his face show such black emotion. She sat down across from him.

"I regret," she said in Athabaskan, "the deaths."

He gave her a deadly look, and she fell silent.

"They fought like cowards," he finally said. "They used trickery and ambush. Like cowards."

She did not understand. She kept quiet.

"Your cousin. Sheltowee. He will come for you now."

She understood that, and felt something release its hold on her, deep down. She tried not to show any emotion in her face.

He let out a deep breath. There was pain in his face that showed clearly in his good eye. He turned partially away from her so she would not see it, and for the first time she felt empathy for this red man who could not deal with the encroaching white man's world.

"Gray Hawk," she said quietly. Her lip trembled and a tear ran down her cheek. "Killed Rachel."

He looked back at her, and she saw what she thought was real regret in his face. "He is a fool."

"Gray Hawk speaks. That all white women must die now."

One Eye looked into her green eyes. He remembered the pleasant nights with her, and how she was so good with Apache children and the old women.

"You will not die," he said.

In that moment, Molly actually felt a bond with One Eye that she had not known existed. She made a sign across her chest. "Thank you."

"You are my woman," he told her.

Molly turned to Spanish. "Maybe it is better if you give me to Sheltowee."

One Eye understood, and surprisingly he was not angry. "Sheltowee cannot have you. You are my woman. You will always be my woman."

She met his gaze, and she thought she saw real affection for her in it. Looking back on all of it, he had never brutalized her. He had taken her physically because she was his, but he had not hurt her.

She went back to Athabaskan, using signs and gestures to help her. "What will you do?"

He grunted. "We will fight him for you."

A sadness welled up in her then that was almost uncontrollable. It was so tragic, all of it. Before she could say anything, Lone Wolf entered the lodge, fearsome in his war paint.

He looked down at Molly with contempt. Then he met One Eye's vacant stare.

"Sheltowee will come now. Today. Tomorrow."

"I know," One Eye said.

"There are few who will fight again," his brother said. "They are convinced he is unkillable."

One Eye looked up at him. "We will go up into the buttes. Make him come for us. Maybe we can do the same to him. I will take only you, Little Crow, and Gray Hawk. It will be an even fight."

"What about her?" Lone Wolf asked him, gesturing toward Molly.

Molly understood most of it, and now looked to One Eye for his response.

"She and your woman go with us," he said. "I am told the fool Gray Hawk killed his."

Lone Wolf sighed slightly. "Isabel is dead too. She just took her own life. Outside. With the knife that Gray Hawk left in Rachel."

Molly rose to her feet and looked into Lone Wolf's brown eyes. "What? What did you say?"

One Eye shook his head and replied for his brother. "Isabel is dead."

Molly felt her heart pummeling inside her chest like a wild thing trapped in there. She turned, ran outside, and looked around the compound. There, not far from Rachel's body, lay Isabel. She had cut her own throat.

Molly felt the dizziness overcome her, and then a great blackness welled in on her and she spiraled down into some dark place where there was no death and no trauma, and crickets sang to her in the night.

Back at Dan'l's camp, there was little cause for celebration. They had lost another member of their party, and they were now down to four. Also, Dan'l knew Cahill's arm wound was going to bother him more than he thought. Lastly, with the devastation they had caused One Eye, he just might be so angry that he would go back to his village and kill Molly out of spite.

"We'll have to ride hard now," Dan'l told them after he had bandaged Cahill's arm. "We'll abandon the wagon and run the extra horses off. We'll carry as many supplies as we can on our mounts."

"Each of us can carry enough food for several days, if we eat lightly," Rivera said.

Zarate was a happy fellow. He had killed several Apaches, and that was why he had come on the expedition. He was sorry, though, that they had not gotten One Eye himself.

Dan'l had gotten only a brief glimpse of One Eye and the others in his house in Missouri before they opened fire on its occupants, but he recognized One Eye among the riders, and later he identified the head-shot Crooked Leg as another of those who had ridden to Missouri with the upstart Apache chief. The dead Indians still lay about the camp area and beyond.

"They will be waiting for us now," Zarate said to Rivera. "It will be different. We will pay a price for the girl." He cast a sideways glance at Dan'l.

"Nevertheless," Rivera said patiently, "that is why we came."

"I say we ride right to the village," Dan'l suggested. "We'll keep off the trail, of course. Maybe they'll still be licking their wounds. We might catch them off guard."

"I am ready to ride," Rivera said.

"Me too," Cahill said.

Zarate drove off the team horses and the extra mounts, and the horses galloped off into the plain. Then Dan'l set fire to the wagon, with its equipment inside, so the Apaches could not somehow make use of it. Fire licked at the vehicle wildly, and black smoke curled into the cobalt sky. They all stood looking at it, their mounts now saddled up.

"They will make this a holy site," Rivera said, watching the smoke rise skyward and casting a look at the dead bodies lying all about. They had piled stones on McGill's corpse, up in the rocks, as a perfunctory burial.

"Let's ride out," Dan'l said.

None of them looked back as they moved out of the camp and away from the burning wagon. That was a part of the campaign against One Eye that was finished. Their goal remained the same.

They still had to find Molly—alive, they hoped.

As they rode south that afternoon, through jumping cholla and saguaro cactus, Dan'l found himself wondering what Molly had gone through since they had taken her off with them back in Missouri. He might not even recognize her when they found her, if she was alive. Some white women stolen by Indians had gone insane, and others had killed themselves. A few had adopted Indian ways and had turned primitive themselves. Dan'l did not really know Molly Morgan, and had no way of knowing how she would react to her ordeal. He could only hope they had not mistreated her badly, and that he could one day return her to her people back in Carolina. Or maybe persuade her to stay on in Missouri and become part of Dan'l's family.

They were not very far from One Eye's village. By late afternoon they were within just a few miles of it, when an Indian appeared on a nearby hillock of sand. Zarate pulled his big pistol from his belt, cocked it, and aimed it at the lone rider.

"Hold it, damn it!" Dan'l said urgently.

Zarate gave him a look, but lowered the gun.

"That's not one of One Eye's people," Dan'l said. "It's one of them we let go in that first skirmish. Look, he's making a peace sign."

"I'll respond," Rivera said. He returned the sign, and the Apache came forward. He wore no war paint and bore no weapons.

"Be careful, Dan'l," Cahill said.

The Apache stopped just a few feet from them.

"Sheltowee," he said, bowing his head. "I recognize you as Ancient Bear."

Rivera translated for them.

"You go to One Eye's Place of White Women?"

Rivera nodded. "Yes."

"We heard of your great victory," the Apache said. "But go with caution. You are very close."

"We know," Rivera said. "Is One Eye prepared to fight again?"

The Indian shook his head. "I know nothing of that. But word comes to us that there are two white women dead there."

Rivera hesitated, then translated for Dan'l. "He says two white women are dead at the village."

"Oh, my God," Dan'l breathed.

"Son of a bitch!" Cahill swore angrily.

"I knew he would kill them," Zarate said.

"One Eye is not one of us," the Apache said. "Our shaman says Ancient Bear will prevail over him."

After some words of parting, the Apache was gone. Rivera then turned to Dan'l, who was slumped in his saddle. "Maybe it was not her. There was at least one other captive woman, maybe more."

"She is undoubtedly dead," Zarate said.

Rivera whirled in his saddle. "Shut up!"

Dan'l sighed heavily. "Let's ride on in."

"All right," Rivera said.

"Give them an open fight?" Zarate asked. "He may have twenty or thirty warriors left here."

"I don't care," Dan'l said. "She could be dying and need our help."

"If Dan'l says we go in, we go in," Cahill stated flatly to Zarate.

They arrived at the village a few minutes later, four abreast, rifles out, side arms primed and ready. Dan'l half expected one or two dozen warriors to rush them, but nobody came. As they rode in, the village looked deserted.

They rode warily, Dan'l at their fore, looking dangerous, holding the Kentucky rifle across his chest. His blue eyes were searching, watching for an ambush.

There was none.

One Eye was gone.

In fact, there was nobody in view. Except for the two corpses on the ground at the center of the compound.

It was two women, Dan'l saw, one with blond hair and the other with dark. He thought the dark-haired one was Molly for one black moment as he stared at them.

"There!" Rivera announced to the others.

They carefully dismounted, still watching the tipis and lodges for any sign of ambush. Dan'l walked over to the dead women and turned the dark-haired one over. Flies buzzed around their heads.

He let out a shaky sound. "It ain't her," he said.

Rivera was averting his gaze grimly. "The goddamn animals!" he hissed.

"She might still be here somewhere," Dan'l said. He rose and moved about the village.

Cahill accompanied him as they looked in tipis and lodges, hoping not to find what they were looking for. But they did not find her.

"He took her," Dan'l said.

"Maybe to bargain with," Cahill said.

Across the compound, Zarate emerged from a tipi with an old man in tow.

"Look what I found!" he yelled.

He dragged an old Apache over to them. He was gray-haired and wrinkled, and when he saw Dan'l he dropped to his knees.

"Spare my life, Ancient Bear!" he said in a weak, cracking voice.

Dan'l recognized the name and shook his head. "Get up," he said, gesturing with his hand.

Zarate pulled the old fellow to his feet, and the Apache turned his eyes from Dan'l. He looked very frightened.

"They left me," he said. "I am not a warrior. Do not take my life, god of the people!"

"He thinks you will kill him," Rivera said.

"Ask him where One Eye went," Dan'l said.

Rivera tried his Athabaskan, haltingly.

The old man pointed to the south. "They rode out that way. Four of them."

"What about the others?" Rivera wondered.

"Gone," the Apache said sadly. "Gone in all directions."

Rivera translated while Dan'l listened.

"It appears One Eye has lost his following," Rivera guessed. "Except for a few close to him."

Dan'l nodded. "Probably the ones he took to Missouri. Ask him about Molly."

The old man did not understand Rivera at first, and Rivera had to repeat the question.

"Ah, the last white woman. This was known

242

as the village of white women. Did you know that?"

Rivera squinted his eyes. "What?"

"The last white woman went with them. She is One Eye's woman. No one dares touch her but him."

"She went with them," Rivera told Dan'l.

Dan'l looked off to the south, thinking. Maybe One Eye had just taken her away to kill her more slowly somewhere else. He remembered his Polish friend, dying on a spit while his screams echoed in Dan'l's ears. That seemed like a lifetime ago.

"There is a place where One Eye camped before he became chief here," the Apache went on, seeming to talk to himself. "We call it Two Buttes. A narrow place sits between them, and it is easily defended. He probably went there."

"I didn't understand much of it," Rivera said, "but I think he mentioned the place we call Black Canyon, because the sun shines there only at midday. One Eye may have gone there. We will see if we can pick up his trail in that direction."

"Good. Let's ride out," Dan'l said.

Rivera stared into his square, rugged face. "It is in high, rocky terrain, Dan'l. It will be very difficult to approach safely."

Zarate came forward. "It is different now," he said to Dan'l. He had lost his taste for the enterprise. "If she is not dead now, she will be, long before we can defeat One Eye in his safe place. It is a dangerous and unnecessary task we set for ourselves."

Cahill scowled at Zarate. "What the hell is the matter with you, Zarate? Is the fun gone, now that you shot yourself a bunch of Indians? Or are you just afraid of old One Eye?"

Zarate's face clouded over. "I have no fear of any man, greenhorn! Would you like perhaps to test my courage?"

"Stop it!" Rivera ordered.

Dan'l looked at Zarate. "I ain't quitting on this till I find Molly," he said deliberately. "If you don't like that, Zarate, haul your carcass out of here. You'll still get part of your pay when we get back to Santa Fe."

"*If* you get back!" Zarate growled.

Dan'l ignored the remark. "Make up your mind, Zarate. We're riding out of here right now."

Zarate hesitated, then sighed quietly. "Hell. I have come this far. Maybe I will get to see One Eye's face when he sucks his last breath. Or maybe when he kills you."

"What a son of a bitch!" Cahill growled.

Zarate tried the crazy grin. "*Gracias, amigo!*" But inside, he was not grinning. He did not like the odds in this rescue attempt. But he also did not want to travel back to Santa Fe alone. They were both dangerous options.

It was midmorning of the following day when One Eye reached one of his favorite hideaways, the deep canyon surrounded by high buttes that the old Apache had described to Rivera and Dan'l.

It was in high, rugged terrain, and the trail in had been precarious. At times the trail was just a few feet across, with a high wall on one side and a sheer drop-off on the other. Molly rode at midline in a single-file procession, and was scared for her life most of the time. They had brought a pack animal for provisions, but the animal had lost its footing on a steep trail and gone over the edge, plummeting five hundred feet before hitting the rocks below. The provisions the horse carried were lost to them.

Now they were past all that, and had entered the canyon and made camp well inside it, setting up two tipis, one for One Eye and Molly and the other for the three other men.

Little Crow was nursing a deep frustration about Molly, and the extra trouble she had caused them in coming here. Both he and Gray Hawk thought she should have been executed back at the village to make things less complicated. Lone Wolf, though, felt that she might be used somehow to give them an advantage when the fight came, so he did not criticize his brother for bringing her.

By noon they were finished making camp and settling their horses in, and their site had finally come into full sunlight. An hour later the light would be gone, as the shade from the high buttes cast its half-gloom over the place.

They were sitting in a very narrow horseshoe-shaped gorge, facing its mouth, about halfway in. Their horses were picketed at the base of the narrows close to a back wall. The side walls rose several hundred feet above them and dropped off steeply to the flat plain on their far sides. The site was almost impregnable from attack. That was why One Eye had chosen it.

The men expected Molly to do all the work once camp was established. She had to gather firewood, make their fire, and cook their midday meal. Even though they had lost some supplies with the packhorse, they had carried dried meat and corn mash on their ponies in cloth bags. A small stream trickled down a cliff face at the rear of the gorge, so there was plenty of water for drinking and cooking.

Lone Wolf was smart enough to let One Eye give Molly most of her instructions and orders, but Little Crow was not so delicate. He yelled at Molly a couple of times as she was building their fire, and when One Eye was otherwise occupied, shoved her to get her out of his way.

Molly decided to make no protests. She was still shocked by the deaths of Rachel and Isabel. She had hoped they would all survive this together and be able to laugh about it all back in Santa Fe, before she returned home with Dan'l. But this was the reality. They were gone, and she did not know how long she would survive if she gave them any trouble. Or even if she did not.

When she had fixed them some food, she took a small amount for herself, retreated to the tipi One Eye had set up for himself and her, and ate by herself there.

The men sat around the fire on big rocks, eating quietly, looking somber. Nobody wanted to speak until One Eye spoke. They kept watching his face to assess his mood.

"All is not lost," he finally commented.

Little Crow made a sour face but said nothing. He was one of them who thought One Eye should have put a bullet into Dan'l's head back in Missouri.

"We are back where we were before we rode to Missouri," One Eye went on. "In fact, we are better off. At that time, we were forced to ride hundreds of miles to kill Sheltowee and claim a glorious victory over him. Now, because we took the girl, he comes to us. We have the same opportunity we had in Missouri, and we are on our own home ground. If we kill him here and show his corpse to our brethren, we will still be worshiped as heroes."

"That is all true, Brother," Lone Wolf offered.

"If we can kill him," Little Crow said.

One Eye turned his sober eye on Little Crow.

But Gray Hawk, looking very athletic sitting there, decided to support his fellow warrior. "He does seem very difficult to kill, my chief."

One Eye did not get angry. "I have seen for myself how tough this Sheltowee is, my friends. He has a large reputation among the Shawnee, who are a noble people. But he still lives because of his skills in warfare, which are very real. And because I did not finish the job in Missouri."

They watched his face to see the emotions in it. It was unlike One Eye to admit any error or failure.

One Eye looked at each of his warriors around the fire. "He does *not* live because he has supernatural powers or has any medicine from an old Apache god."

There was silence among them.

"We know his firepower now. It is equal to our own. And we will not be ambushed by these cowards this time. We will merely wait for his attack. There will be no surprise; he will have to show himself. And he must press the battle, not us. We will have the terrain advantage, and the will to survive. We *will* survive. We will really kill him this time. Him and his Mexican friends. Then this will finally be over, and we will take our place as the leaders of our people."

Lone Wolf's handsome face was etched with sudden fire. "I feel it inside me! This time we will kill him!"

Gray Hawk nodded doubtfully. "Yes," he said.

Little Crow caught One Eye's gaze. "What of the girl?" he said.

One Eye looked at the ground. "The girl is mine. He will not get her back, no matter what happens." He turned to his brother. "Is that clear?"

"Yes, my brother."

"If something happens to me, she must not fall into his hands."

"Have no concern about it," Gray Hawk told him. He remembered plunging the knife into Rachel's chest in his anger and frustration. "She will not."

Chapter Thirteen

Dan'l's party had encamped in high ground the previous night, well behind One Eye. Dan'l had been surprised at how chilly the air had gotten in the middle of the night, but they had not built a fire in case One Eye doubled back on them.

The next morning they were up early and out on One Eye's trail, which led into even higher terrain. It was now all rock and sand and a few scrub bushes underfoot.

Cahill rode up with Dan'l until midday, about the time One Eye was settled into camp in his small canyon. But then, after a quick break, Rivera replaced him beside Dan'l, as Dan'l read sign and kept them on One Eye's trail.

By midafternoon they were getting into sand and red dirt, and Dan'l could relax some. The cliff trail was still ahead of them, and riding was fairly easy for a while. It was during that time that Rivera asked Dan'l about his life since Rivera had last seen him.

"Oh, I added some acres to my place near St. Louis," Dan'l told him as they rode along, Dan'l's eye to the ground. The tracking was easy here, because of the soft earth. "I ain't done much farming on it, though. I ain't never home." He grinned at Rivera through his beard.

"I am sure the *señora* is not so pleased about that," Rivera answered with a smile.

"Rebecca always was pretty understanding," Dan'l said. "She's a fine woman."

"I am sorry that I may never meet her."

"You ought to come back east sometime, *compadre*," Dan'l said. "We'd show you a good old time. Kentucky style."

"I really would like to, and thank you for the offer," Rivera said. "But I most probably will never leave this country now, even to go back to Mexico. I am rooted here, like these red buttes and twisted trees."

"I understand, *amigo*."

"You have the wander fever," Rivera went on. "You cannot stay in one place for very long. Is it not so?"

Dan'l hesitated, then nodded. "I reckon I can't argue with that. I thought I'd finally settle down once I got my family to Missouri. But then somebody asked me to take them west, and then somebody else. It started eating at me inside again."

"We heard that you were in Sioux country not long ago. Up north."

"We done some exploring and mapmaking. Then our party got the gold fever and the whole thing went sour." He rode along, remembering. "There was some old Spanish treasure stashed away up in Platte country. We found it, too, but the Sioux found us. I'm just damn lucky my scalp ain't hanging on a Sioux belt right now."

Rivera laughed softly. He liked being with Dan'l. They had been through a lot together. "The girl, Molly. She lived with you in Missouri?"

Dan'l shook his shaggy head. "She just come there from Carolina. To get married and do some farming. One Eye killed her man."

Rivera cast a sober look at him.

"She's got a lot of grit," Dan'l said. "If anybody can get through this, it's Molly."

They rode along quietly for a few moments. Finally, Dan'l spoke again. "She was so damn happy," he said, staring off into the rocks. "So damn happy."

Rivera sighed. "We will get her, Dan'l. If he gives us half a chance."

"That's how I figure it," Dan'l said.

By late afternoon they were up in high rocks, on the steep trail where One Eye had lost the horse. Cahill was afraid of heights, and closed his eyes in places where there were only three feet of trail underfoot and a straight drop-off on their left. Zarate loved it, grinning and humming odd little tunes.

When they came out onto fairly level ground again, Rivera scanned the area ahead of them and turned to Dan'l.

"We are very close now. The canyon is just beyond that single butte. One Eye is probably waiting there for us."

Dan'l peered at the high butte, wondering what lay ahead. Now One Eye was ensconced in his favorite defensive site, and Dan'l could get them all killed if he led them into the teeth of One Eye's guns. Including Molly.

"Let's camp around here somewhere," he said. "Some place that's well hid. I don't think he'd come at us again now, but it don't hurt to keep out of sight."

Rivera nodded. "There is a small gorge just ahead, with a few trees for cover. We will stop there."

About a half hour later the four of them encamped in the narrow gorge not far from the high butte. There was no water, and Dan'l realized they would have to get along on what they were carrying with them from now on. They did not build a fire. After they were settled in, under the long shadows of gnarled junipers, Dan'l announced that he was riding out to find something to shoot for them. If he found a rabbit or bird to bring back, they could risk making a small fire.

As Dan'l mounted up, Zarate came over to him. "Maybe I will go, too, *compadre*. I am not a bad shot. With two there is more chance to find something, yes?"

Dan'l was surprised at Zarate's change of mood. He had seemed to get more sullen as they came closer to One Eye's canyon. It was obvious he did not like an even fight quite as much as an ambush. In fact, he was now insisting that it was suicidal to go after One Eye in his impregnable canyon. He preferred to presume Molly was now dead, and give it all up.

Dan'l looked down at him from the Appaloosa. "Hell, come on along, Zarate. There ain't nothing much to do here anyway."

Zarate nodded, and mounted his horse. Cahill and Rivera were sitting on a log in the shade, looking very tired. Rivera was sipping some cold coffee, and not liking it.

"You're heading out to the east?" Cahill asked Dan'l.

"There was some buzzards in the air over that way. That might mean small game. I don't know."

"Don't go far," Cahill said. "We don't need no meat."

Dan'l grinned at him. Cahill overworried about Dan'l's well-being. "We won't," Dan'l replied.

"The north-south trail is over in that direction," Rivera reminded him. "Be wary, my friend."

"Would you two try to relax?" Dan'l said. "Anyway, Zarate will protect me from any trouble."

Zarate gave them that crazed grin. "Easterners require some looking after," he said.

Dan'l just stared at him. "Come on. Let's go find a rabbit," he said.

The two of them rode away from the setting sun and were soon out of sight of the camp. Actually, Dan'l was glad that Zarate had come along. It was always better to ride with a partner in places like this. Apaches were everywhere. And there were other kinds of trouble that could jump out at you.

The buzzards Dan'l had seen were down on a coyote carcass, flapping heavily about, tearing at decaying meat. But there was no sign of game. The sun was getting low in the sky, and Dan'l realized they could not stay out there for very long. They rode around to the far side of a small, low butte to see if there was any good ground for jackrabbits.

Rounding a curve in the rock, they almost rode right into a small camp where three men sat around a low fire under a cottonwood tree.

They reined in abruptly, but they had already been seen. The men had picketed their horses nearby, and there was a small, uncovered wagon close to the horses. The wagon suggested they might be traders, but Dan'l thought they looked like a rather grubby lot. They were Mexican *mestizos*, wearing wide-brimmed hats and carrying side arms. One of them rose from the fire and walked toward Dan'l's party holding a rifle in his hands.

"Quién pase?" he called out. He was just fifty yards away.

Zarate gave Dan'l a quick glance. "I do not like the looks of these," he said.

Dan'l nodded, but responded to the Mexican.

"We are hunters. We have a camp nearby." He pointed north, purposely giving them the wrong direction.

A second one had risen to his feet and was staring toward them with keen interest.

"Ah, you speak English!" the first fellow said. He was rather tall, taller than Dan'l and Zarate, and bore a scar at the corner of his mouth. "We do also. We all worked at an American ranch in Texas. Come! We will meet you!"

"I don't like him," Zarate said.

"I don't either. But I don't want to turn my back on him," Dan'l said easily. "Let's ride on over there."

They spurred their mounts and rode into the camp. The tall fellow met them partway, grinning widely. "It is good to meet others on the trail, *sí?*" He looked at Zarate. *"Es mexicano, eh, amigo?"*

Zarate nodded. *"Sí."*

The two at the fire had been speaking confidentially in Spanish, and now they stopped. Dan'l and Zarate rode to the fire and dismounted. Since circumstance had drawn him in, Dan'l wanted to be on foot, not on an unpredictable mount. Zarate got off his stallion too. Dan'l noted that the tall man did not put the rifle down. He also noticed that it was primed and cocked. It was a Charlesville, the kind the Mexican Army was using.

All the strangers were standing now. Besides the tall one with the scar, there was a heavyset man with a gold tooth in front, and a rather small man who had the meanest face Dan'l had ever seen.

The tall stranger turned to Dan'l. "You must share our coffee, *señor!*" Then, before Dan'l could reply, he turned to his companions and muttered something to them in quick Spanish, quietly, so Zarate could not hear.

"No, thanks," Dan'l said, looking them over. "We're out looking for rabbit or quail. You seen any game hereabouts?"

His mind was working quickly, wondering how safe it would be to try to leave. He remembered that his side arm was loaded and primed, and hoped that Zarate's was. The small Mexican had dropped his hand to the pistol at his belt, and the burly one had been using a big, thick knife to cut beef jerky, and still held it loosely in his grasp.

"Where did you say you are camped?" the burly one asked.

Zarate looked over at him. "It is far from here. A day's ride. We intended to camp out overnight."

"That is *extraño*," the small one said. "To go so far *desde su sitio*."

Dan'l wanted to get away from them but did not know how. These men in their tattered clothes were obviously not traders. It was more likely they were bandits. He looked at the beat-up wagon and at the thin horses, which had not even been unsaddled.

"I see you brought a wagon. I reckon you're traders, heading for Santa Fe."

"Traders?" the tall man said. "Oh, yes. Traders. That is exactly what we are, *señores*."

Zarate glanced darkly at Dan'l. Dan'l let his hand drop to the butt of the pistol on his belt, and Zarate put his hands on his hips near his own side arm. Dan'l walked casually over to the wagon, into the shade, and looked in. He was separating himself from Zarate so they would not be bunched together.

"Oh, you got some corn flour here," Dan'l said, feigning interest. "How many bags you got with you?"

The tall man hesitated, then looked at the brawny one. "Oh, there are a dozen there. They will bring good prices in Santa Fe."

Dan'l counted again and verified that there were just nine bags of corn flour in the wagon. And the price of it in Santa Fe was way down, because the Taos Indians brought it in all the time. These men were not traders, and this was not their wagon. They had stolen it.

Dan'l glanced at the buckboard and saw two

dark stains there that looked like bloodstains. He turned back to the threesome and Zarate, and gave Zarate a quick frown.

"If you're traders, how come you don't know how many bags of meal you got for sale?" Dan'l said evenly.

Zarate looked at the bandits, and they looked at each other. Then the tall one got an angry expression on his swarthy face. "I don't have to tell you how many bags of meal we have, *americano*." He edged the muzzle of the long gun up toward Dan'l's groin. "We don't have to explain anything to you!"

The last thing Dan'l wanted before he caught up with One Eye and Molly was other trouble. But it seemed he had found it anyway. So he had to deal with it.

The rifle was now aimed at Dan'l's belly.

"That don't seem very friendly," Dan'l said. "I thought you was going to give us coffee."

The tall man snorted out a laugh. "It is you who will give to us, *señor*," he said. "Your horses. Your guns. All of your possessions. After you tell us exactly where your camp is located."

The small man had drawn his side arm, which he held on Zarate, and the brawny one turned the knife over so he was holding its blade.

"You dirty *cabrones!*" Zarate hissed.

"Take their guns," the tall fellow said in Spanish to the heavyset one.

Dan'l moved his hands away from his body.

"Hell, take them if you want them. But you'll never find that camp without our help."

"We will see," the tall man said.

The brawny one came over to Dan'l and reached for the gun on Dan'l's hip.

"Here, take it," Dan'l said, pulling it out and proffering it to the other man.

But when the brawny man grabbed for it, Dan'l swung it against the side of his head in a deft, liquid movement. The hard metal connected dully with flesh and bone, and cracked audibly there. The Mexican cried out loudly, but before he could fall, Dan'l grabbed him and swung him around between himself and the tall man.

The tall Mexican had already squeezed the trigger of the long gun, though. There was an earsplitting explosion, and the brawny man was hit full in the chest with the hot lead, and both he and Dan'l went crashing back against the side of the wagon.

Zarate had drawn his side arm and cocked it quickly. The small Mexican saw the movement and swung the barrel of his old one-shot pistol toward Zarate and squeezed off the round. Zarate felt a tugging at the cloth of his left sleeve. But he did not even blink. He returned fire in a split instant, and the small man was jerked off his feet as if pulled by a rope. He hit the ground on his back, his heart exploding in his chest.

In the next moment, while the tall man was going for a gun on his waist, abandoning the rifle, Dan'l cocked and fired his Annely without aiming. The tall man was struck low in the chest and staggered backward a step, holding his hands over the bloody hole. He looked at Dan'l as if a dirty trick had been played on him, then collapsed onto his face.

The brawny man had slid to the ground now, out of Dan'l's grasp. He lay there moaning quietly, not dead. Zarate came over to them, aimed his reprimed pistol at the man's head, and fired again. The shot blew part of the fellow's face off, and he jerked there for a moment and was dead.

Zarate kicked the corpse twice in the side while Dan'l watched silently.

"Goddamn *cabron!*" Zarate said harshly.

Dan'l went over to their rearing mounts and quieted them. Zarate was repriming.

"Nice shooting, Zarate," Dan'l told him quietly. "I'm mighty glad you come with me."

Zarate looked at him and nodded.

Dan'l looked inside the wagon again. He felt wetness on his left arm, and looked down to see blood coming from it. The brawny fellow had cut him with the big knife as Dan'l pulled him around to use him as cover.

"There's some jerky in here," he said to Zarate. "Reckon that's better than fresh game in our situation. We'll take it back."

Zarate came over, his side arm still hanging loose in his hand. He looked in too. "Good idea. Are you wounded?"

"Just a scratch," Dan'l said. "The knife."

"You had good instincts," Zarate said. "You knew they were bandits, didn't you?"

"They didn't look like merchants," Dan'l said.

He reached into the wagon, picked up some small wrapped bundles of jerky, and headed back to his mount with them. He slid them into one of his saddlebags.

"This stuff ought to last us till we get Molly back," he said as he worked. "I'm hoping this will be over in a few days, and we'll all be celebrating in Santa Fe."

He turned back toward Zarate, who was holding his pistol trained on Dan'l's chest.

Dan'l's eyes narrowed. "What the hell!"

"You will not be celebrating in Santa Fe, *amigo.*"

Dan'l looked into those crazy eyes and saw that Zarate meant it. "No?" he said carefully. He had reholstered his own gun without even bothering to reprime it.

"You were thinking clearly back in Santa Fe," Zarate explained to him. "You seemed a reasonable man to ride with. But you have lost control, *amigo.* You have beaten One Eye, destroyed his power. Yet you will continue this fight until you kill him. Because he almost killed you in Missouri. Because he abducted the girl, who is now dead. You cannot kill One Eye in The Place of Two Buttes. He will kill you. And everybody with you. I will not let that happen."

"What's the matter with you, Zarate? Rivera wants to go after One Eye. So does Cahill."

"The colonel will lose interest when he knows what happened to you. That we ran into bandits and killed them. But not until the little one put a bullet into you. It was a very unfortunate thing, this chance meeting. But there was nothing I could do to save you. I almost was killed myself, see?" He pointed to the bullet hole in his sleeve. "I was fortunate to get away with my life. You were not so lucky."

"Cahill won't believe you."

"Cahill will have no proof to the contrary," Zarate said, showing part of the crazy grin. "Anyway, nobody cares what Cahill thinks. I know you have money with you. I will take that now, after I kill you, as the rest of my payment. And the Appaloosa, of course."

Dan'l shook his head slowly. "You really are crazy, Zarate."

"It is well-known, *amigo!* I like being *loco,* you see! In a world such as this, it helps to be just a little crazy."

"Put the gun down, Zarate, and let's talk about this."

Zarate shook his head. "I have thought about this, Señor Boone. It is why I came riding with you for this hunt. It is finished between us." He aimed the gun deliberately. *"Adiós, compadre!"*

Dan'l could tell when a man was about to fire a gun, and Zarate was ready. His eyes changed, and his mouth drew into a straight line. Just at the moment of firing, Dan'l dived to the ground off to his left and rolled once. The gun exploded loudly in his ears and dug up dirt between his right arm and his side. Then he was lying there with his own gun in hand, trying to prime it. Zarate, swearing, was doing the same thing. But Dan'l beat him. Just as Zarate cocked his gun and aimed to fire, Dan'l rose up on his elbows and fired with both hands on the Annely.

The ball of lead struck Zarate just beside the heart. He jumped backward, his pistol cracking out a last shot that hit nothing.

Zarate hit the ground hard on his back, his eyes wide for a moment in surprise as he tried to understand what had gone wrong.

Dan'l was still on the ground, on his belly. He rose slowly to his feet. "Son of a bitch!" he muttered.

Zarate lay within a few feet of the brawny bandit's corpse. Dan'l walked over to him, and Zarate was staring up at him, bleeding from the hole in his chest.

"It seemed like . . . a good idea at the moment." He grinned up at Dan'l.

Dan'l knelt beside him, his pistol still dangling from his right hand. He shook his shaggy head again.

"What got into you, Zarate?" he said heavily.

Zarate arched his dark brows, and his black mustache moved when he tried the crazy smile, and he showed the space between his front teeth.

"It was . . . fear," Zarate said. A worm of blood crept from the corner of his mouth. "I like shooting Apaches. Not being . . . shot by them."

"You could just have left us."

Zarate shook his head. "I would have lost face, *amigo*. I figured Rivera . . . would give it up. Without you."

Dan'l sighed. "I reckon you never was the smartest *hombre* I ever met."

"My mistake was . . . trying to kill you," Zarate admitted. He coughed up some blood. "The Indians are right. You are . . . unkillable."

Dan'l grunted. "You just can't shoot straight enough, Zarate."

A small nod. "That was part of it. Well. I give you . . . my guns, *amigo*. And my horse. *Cuidado*, he bites."

"I'll remember that."

"Tell Rivera that—"

He coughed again, and his eyes were becoming dull.

"What?" Dan'l said.

"Tell him—"

A spasm wracked Zarate's body, and a raking breath came from deep inside him. Then he was gone.

Dan'l closed his eyelids.

"You didn't know no better," Dan'l said to the lifeless figure at his knee. "I reckon a man can't hardly hold that against you."

Dan'l rose again and slowly holstered his side arm. He looked around him at the carnage. If Zarate had not been with him, he would undoubtedly be one of the corpses decorating the landscape.

That counted for something. That, and the way he had fought when they were attacked twice by Apaches.

Add to that the great embarrassment Rivera would feel if he learned that one of them from Santa Fe had turned on Dan'l and tried to kill him.

Yes, he would lie. He would tell Rivera and Cahill that Zarate had been killed by the bandits.

Zarate would have gotten a big laugh out of that.

Chapter Fourteen

At One Eye's camp, darkness was falling all around them.

In the narrow gorgelike canyon, it was never sunny, but when dusk came, it was almost pitch black. Looking out from the canyon was like looking out from night and seeing daylight beyond the buttes.

Molly had brought the Apaches their food again and had done all the camp chores herself. One Eye was very quiet now and very tense waiting for Dan'l's arrival, and Molly kept away from him. In the tipi by herself, she began to think about all that had transpired, and how Dan'l had survived a great battle with One Eye. But she knew this would be different. Dan'l would have to ride into the teeth of One Eye's guns to rescue her, and even if he succeeded, she sensed that one of the Apaches would probably kill her rather than allow Dan'l to take her alive. But the worst scenario was that Dan'l would be killed in the attempt, and for nothing.

Molly thought that maybe it would be better if she made the first move. If she could somehow escape from the canyon—there were just these few men to watch over her, and Dan'l was out there close somewhere—she might reach Dan'l and abort this final bloody confrontation. Escape from the village earlier would have been futile, even if immediately successful. But now all that had changed. If she could make it past the one sentry One Eye had set out, she might be able to find her way to Dan'l before being discovered missing and brought back.

That idea formed inside Molly all evening, while the men sat outside around a fire and talked in low tones. By the time One Eye returned to the tipi for sleep, the notion had taken complete control of her. She would try again to escape.

One Eye came in carrying his long rifle, looking very dangerous. He set the rifle down at the entrance of the enclosure and sat down beside her in the near-blackness. He looked into her face for a long moment.

"I did not know, when I took you, that you would be this much trouble," he said in his native tongue.

Molly watched his face for meaning, not understanding some of the words.

"If I had, I would have killed you there."

Molly looked away from him.

"But now that I have you," he went on, "I do not regret the taking."

Molly understood most of that, and met his gaze. She saw a tiredness in his marred face, and a humanness that touched her. She almost responded, but decided not to.

"You possess fine qualities," he continued. "Under the Apache moon, you are Apache."

She understood all of that, and felt something for him in that moment that was akin to affection. But she could not forget his murder of her fiancé on that terrible afternoon in Missouri.

"You are a great chief, One Eye," she managed to say in Athabaskan.

He smiled at her. "I think that we may both descend into the Nether World before the sun rises twice more. Do you understand?"

She hesitated. "Yes."

"It is an honorable thing, to die defending what is yours. But you must share my honor. You must stay at my side when I cross over."

Molly understood all too well. "Yes."

"On the other hand, I have pledged to kill Sheltowee. I regret this for your sake. But if I do, I will ascend to power among my people, and you will also share in that glory."

She did not get all of it, but she did not like

what she heard. She knew that One Eye lusted for Dan'l's death, and that the chief was a very dangerous man.

"Now we will sleep," he told her, lying down. "And hope your cousin does not come in the night, like the Thunder Spirit."

"Yes, my chief."

Not much later, One Eye fell into a restless sleep.

Molly lay there beside him, wondering how she had gotten caught up in this drama. One moment she had been in Dan'l's cabin, laughing and joking with the man she loved and making plans for a gala wedding. The next, it seemed, she was here in some wild wilderness, lying beside a dread horse warrior of the dry country, with all their lives in the balance—hers, Dan'l's, and One Eye's.

She had seen them ride off to murder white settlers. She had witnessed Rachel's violent death at the hands of the volatile Gray Hawk, and Isabel's by her own hand. It all seemed like some terrible nightmare that she ought to wake up from soon, and be in her own bed at Dan'l's house, with visions of wedding gowns in her head.

But that was not going to happen. This was reality. This was the harsh and primitive world she had been dragged into, and she would be there until some cataclysmic event ended it one way or the other. Or until she found a way to end it herself.

The idea of escape took her by its iron grip again as she lay there beside her lord and master. She listened to One Eye's even breathing for a long while, until she was certain he was in deep sleep.

Then she rose quietly.

He moved slightly but kept on sleeping.

Molly tried holding her breath through it all, but could not. She inched her way to the open flap of the tipi and looked out into the black night. The fire nearby was very low, and Little Crow sat on a rock beside it, his head slumped on his chest.

He was the early-night sentry.

Molly was glad it was not Gray Hawk, who would have been much more alert than the brawny, older Little Crow.

She crouched in the entrance for a long moment, watching and listening. Up in the rocks somewhere, a coyote yelled at the moon. Crickets rasped out their nocturnal songs all around her. The moon was not visible in the high canyon.

Little Crow's head pressed heavily to his chest, and she could hear his regular breathing. He had fallen asleep. Now was the time, if ever.

She looked back at One Eye, who was still in the same position and breathing deeply. She moved very quietly through the entrance on her knees.

Little Crow continued to sleep in the same position. Gray Hawk was obviously asleep in the other tipi with Lone Wolf. She heard a sound from there, and froze. After everything was quiet again, she rose to her feet.

Slowly she moved across the camp area, past Little Crow, in the direction of the rocky plain a hundred yards away. Little Crow mumbled something. His head jerked up and he seemed to look right at her. She stood immobile, waiting. He nodded again, then his head fell back on his chest.

Molly breathed again, feeling her heart beat in her chest. She started walking slowly, trying to be as quiet as she could. She was twenty yards from camp. Thirty. She kept walking.

A coyote howled at the top of the butte to her right, and one of the horses at the back of the canyon heard it and whinnied loudly.

In half a moment Little Crow was awake and on his feet, rifle in hand, looking about, not knowing what had happened.

Molly turned to look at him, and in that moment he looked right at her again.

"Hey!" he yelled.

Molly let out a little cry of dismay and started running toward the mouth of the canyon.

"Stop, woman!"

Lone Wolf appeared outside his tipi and saw Molly running. Little Crow lifted the rifle to his shoulder and aimed it at Molly's back.

Lone Wolf came over and knocked the muzzle of the gun down. "Are you crazy!" he yelled. Then he started after Molly in a fast run.

Molly saw him coming, stumbled over a low-growing shrub, and fell to the ground, bruising and cutting herself. When she looked back again, Lone Wolf was halfway there, coming fast. She got up awkwardly and kept going. But she never got to the mouth of the canyon. Lone Wolf was on her in just moments, grabbing at her from behind. She yelled and fought him, but he held her easily. When it was clear to her that she had been stopped, she broke down and cried.

Now Gray Hawk and One Eye showed themselves back in camp, looking toward Molly and Lone Wolf. Lone Wolf began dragging Molly by the arm back toward the campsite.

"You are a stupid whiteface woman!" he said angrily to her as they moved back to the camp. "Little Crow was going to shoot you! You would have deserved it!"

"I don't care!" Molly said tearfully.

They arrived back at camp with One Eye staring somberly at Molly. Gray Hawk was shaking his head slowly, and Little Crow just glared at her.

One Eye came over to her as Lone Wolf released her.

"She tried to run," Lone Wolf said curtly to his brother. "I had to keep Little Crow from killing her."

One Eye did not look at him.

"I knew she would be trouble," Lone Wolf added.

One Eye came up to Molly deliberately, and

in a surprise action, suddenly hit her with his fist. She yelled and went down, dazed. She landed on her backside, then just lay there breathing raggedly.

"Is this the way you repay me?" One Eye shouted at her, standing over her menacingly.

Molly lay there, tears staining her pretty face.

"I feed you and clothe you! I make you a queen! You have the protection of myself and all of my *akacita!* I speak my innermost feelings to you! And now you embarrass me by fleeing from my tipi!"

She got most of it, and was not impressed. "I want it all to end," she said thickly in English. "All the killing and the hatred!"

One Eye looked toward his brother for a translation, then grabbed Molly and pulled her to her feet.

"We live by rules, just as you do!" One Eye gritted out. "You do not break our rules!"

"Kill her," Little Crow said in a guttural voice.

Gray Hawk grunted his approval of the suggestion. Lone Wolf wisely kept his silence.

One Eye turned a brittle look on Little Crow but did not reply to the remark. When he turned back to Molly, she saw a new sadness in his face.

"You are my woman," he said, and she heard the doubt in his voice. "You must accept that fact. You will always be my woman. You will go to my ancestors with me."

"Kill her now, and I will deliver her body to

Sheltowee," Little Crow said, growing bolder, forgetting what had happened to Eagle Spirit.

One Eye did not even look at him this time. He just stood there, staring into Molly's face, wondering why she would act in this manner. It was an honor to share his tipi. Even for a white woman.

"Give me your gun," he said finally to Little Crow.

Little Crow's face exhibited smug surprise, and Lone Wolf's showed shock. Gray Hawk nodded. "Good," he said to himself.

Little Crow gave Lone Wolf a slight grin and handed over to him the rifle that he had almost killed Molly with. It was reloaded but not primed.

One Eye threw it back to him. "Prime it, you fool!"

Little Crow nodded, found a flint, and fumbled with it. "She can wait a moment," he said with a crooked grin. He handed the rifle back.

"Brother—" Lone Wolf said.

"It is all right," One Eye said tightly. He cocked the rifle and turned its muzzle toward Little Crow's head.

Little Crow was suddenly wide-eyed and dry-mouthed. He stared down the barrel of the long gun and felt his stomach turn inside him. "My chief!"

Lone Wolf saw One Eye's finger whiten over the trigger.

"*No!*" he called out, almost in One Eye's ear.

One Eye turned to his brother. "Yes?"

"If you kill him, we have but three guns against Sheltowee!"

There was a deadly look in the chief's good eye. "I can defend this canyon by myself!" He turned again toward Little Crow, intent on blowing his head to pieces.

Lone Wolf grabbed his brother's arm, and One Eye whirled on him fiercely. If anyone else had done that, he would have killed him immediately.

"You dare interfere, my brother!"

Lone Wolf spoke softly. "Apache warriors do not kill each other over women," he said.

One Eye knew he was right. He lowered the muzzle of the rifle. Little Crow breathed a sigh of relief. Then One Eye whirled and swung the rifle barrel up against the side of Little Crow's head.

It smacked loudly, and Little Crow fell heavily to the ground, half-conscious. He lay there, groaning. One Eye kicked him savagely in the side, and Little Crow yelped in further pain.

"My brother has saved your life, you worthless piece of buffalo dung!" he growled at the fallen man. Little Crow barely heard him. "If you had killed her, I would have roasted you over a spit!"

Molly had huddled, scared, through the whole exchange. She was trembling all over and understood why Isabel had taken her own life. That way it would be finished. All of it.

"Go to the tipi," One Eye said to her.

She turned and hurried to the skin tent just to get away from them. One Eye watched her go. Then he went over and threw a piece of wood onto their fire. The moon was just now cresting the top of the nearby butte, throwing an eerie light into the canyon.

"I know she is trouble," he said, facing away from them. Little Crow was sitting up, groggy, holding the side of his head.

Gray Hawk caught Lone Wolf's eye, and they both were somber.

"Women are trouble. That is their nature," One Eye went on. "Even Apache ones. I will not give this woman up. I have grown . . . accustomed to her."

"It is natural," Lone Wolf said.

"They get into your blood," Gray Hawk said. "They are the moon, and the stars their children. They can cast spells."

Lone Wolf gave him a hard look. "Shut up," he commanded.

Gray Hawk shrugged and walked to the far side of the fire. One Eye turned to Lone Wolf.

"I am not blind in my good eye, too. I see your loyalty, brother, and your patience. My hope is that they will be rewarded."

Lone Wolf smiled. "I do not seek reward. You are my brother."

One Eye went into the tipi to join Molly, and Lone Wolf pulled Little Crow to his feet. Little Crow was wobbly.

"You are a fool, and lucky that I was here," Lone Wolf said. "You are relieved. Go to the tipi. Gray Hawk, take the guard for the rest of this trouble-filled night. Maybe we may yet get some sleep. I suspect we will need it."

Gray Hawk nodded, a cryptic grin on his face. "Just as you say, Cousin."

When Dan'l had reported the confrontation with bandits to Rivera and Cahill, he omitted the part where Zarate had tried to kill him. Rivera expressed regret at losing such a brave fighter, with no stigma attached to Zarate's memory. That was the way Dan'l wanted it. He had brought Zarate's body back with him, and they all helped bury it before they went to their bedrolls.

Dan'l had not discussed plans that evening. He had said he wanted to sleep on it. He now figured that if Molly had survived to reach One Eye's hidden camp, she would undoubtedly do so for another twenty-four hours.

The next morning, the one after Molly's attempted escape, he finally did bring up the subject of going after One Eye. They were sitting around on boulders, waiting for the air to warm up. They still had not built a fire, and Cahill was missing his morning coffee. He looked five years older than when he had set out with Dan'l from Missouri. They chewed on some hardtack and the beef jerky that Dan'l had brought from the bandits' wagon. It was what hunters called a hardship camp.

"Zarate had one thing right," Dan'l said while they were eating. "If we don't go about this right, there ain't none of us coming back from there."

Rivera nodded. "If we are to be successful in rooting this devil from his hiding place, perhaps we should wait until tonight. I know the canyon terrain. We could manage a little surprise."

"Ain't a bad idea," Cahill agreed. "I don't see none too good in the dark, though. I might end up shooting one of you instead of the Apaches." His face broke into a dry grin.

Dan'l returned the grin, but appreciated the truth in the comment. There could be a lot of confusion in a night raid, and anything could happen. They could end up shooting Molly.

"They will have us outgunned now," Rivera went on. "And we are dealing with One Eye's best men. We must work out some advantage for ourselves."

Dan'l stared into the distance for a long moment. "I gave it a lot of thought last night," he said at last.

The other two looked at him.

"I don't think we ought to ride in there and fight it out with One Eye now. It's putting too many odds in his favor."

Cahill frowned. "What?"

"The best chance of bringing Molly out of there alive is to send one man in. Try to get in past their sentry. And be out with her before they know it."

"Hell," Cahill said. "That ain't possible."

"It is even more dangerous than if we all ride in with guns blazing," Rivera agreed.

"But there might be a better chance of getting Molly out alive," Dan'l said.

Rivera looked into Dan'l's blue eyes above the shaggy beard. Those eyes, he decided, had more strength in them than any others he had ever seen.

"You want to be the one to go in, don't you?" he said.

"Who else?" Dan'l said. "She's my cousin. I couldn't ask you or Cahill to do it. No, it's my job."

"You have never been there," Rivera reminded him. "I know what it looks like. How to hide myself in the approach. I am the logical candidate."

"Let me go, Dan'l," Cahill said. "At least I know what Molly looks like."

Dan'l smiled. "She's probably the only woman with them, Sam." He turned to Rivera. "Maybe you do know the terrain. I'll have to learn it as I go. But I done this kind of thing before, Colonel. It's my kind of action. If I don't make it, I only got myself to blame."

Rivera sighed. "Hell. We may never see you alive again."

"He'll skin you, Dan'l, if he catches you," Cahill said solemnly. "He'll skin you alive."

"I know who he is," Dan'l assured them. "But I escaped one time from a Shawnee village with three guards on me. They chased me through the wilderness for two days and nights, but they never caught me."

"That's a whole different situation," Cahill argued.

"I know that. This will be ticklish. Especially if I'm to get Molly out unharmed. But it's got to be done this way, I think, and I'm the one to try it."

"Damn," Rivera grunted. He fingered his dark mustache nervously.

"Hell, don't count me out till it's over," Dan'l said in mock annoyance. "Anyway, I got a good feeling about it. I got some plans that just might work."

"One Eye will have her close to him," Rivera said. "Sleeping with his good eye open, probably." He tried a grin.

"I know," Dan'l said. "You can help me by describing the canyon to me. And the ground between here and there."

"I will do that today," Rivera said.

"How far is it now?" Cahill asked Rivera.

Rivera pursed his lips pensively. "It is a two-hour ride at a cautious pace. You could start out in late afternoon to be able to find your way with some light. When you get there, you would have time to assess the terrain before making your move."

"Dan'l, let me go with you," Cahill pleaded.

"No, it's a one-man job, Sam," Dan'l said. "Two wouldn't never get in there without being seen." He looked away, then caught Cahill's gaze again. "If I ain't back here by dawn, I didn't make it. You two go on back to Santa Fe. You'd never get her with just two guns."

"I won't never leave this country without her," Cahill said.

Dan'l smiled at his old friend. "Don't make promises you can't keep, Sam."

"We would bring others out here," Rivera agreed. "We would make another try, and another, Dan'l. But you will succeed. I feel it in my belly." He was lying.

"Good. Now, let's talk about that canyon," Dan'l said.

Molly and One Eye sat cross-legged in his tipi, facing each other. It was midafternoon now, and One Eye had forgiven Molly for her ill-fated escape attempt. Women were not predictable, not even Apache women. It was obvious that this cousin of Sheltowee still had not accepted her position with One Eye's people. She still thought of herself as his prisoner and not his woman. That troubled One Eye, but he assumed her feelings would change with time. He must be patient with her.

Molly's face still hurt from the blow she had received at One Eye's hands, and she was now even more afraid of him. He could see that fear in her face, and had come into the tipi to try to explain things to her.

"Apache women must obey rules," he said carefully and slowly. "Do you expect me to treat you differently because you are related to Sheltowee? Because you are white? We do not consider such things in our tribe."

Molly would not meet his gaze. She was miserable, wondering how all of this would end.

"You are no longer related to the Kentucky man. Not under Apache law. You are Apache. My ancestors are yours. When you die, you will go to our sacred place in the Nether World. You will be buried with me."

Molly stared at the floor, understanding some of it, but not trying very hard. She was withdrawing into herself.

"If we survive these next days, you will once again take your place at my side. You will learn how to make tobacco pouches, and powder flasks of buffalo horn. You will become an expert preparer of our food. You will learn the dances and the songs, and will play Hide the Bone. You will pray to Child of the Water and White-Painted Woman. You will drink the blood of our slain enemies."

Molly looked up at him. He was so good with her when it pleased him to be. And yet he was a savage. He was the murderer of her Jock Parrish.

"Your cousin will come soon," One Eye continued. "I must prepare for him. You will remain in this tipi until I tell you that you may leave it. Is this understood by you?"

Molly did understand. She nodded weakly.

He got to his feet. "Good. I will speak on this later."

He went out into the late-afternoon light, which was rather limited in the narrow canyon. Lone Wolf was out there, pacing, looking worried. Gray Hawk was out at the mouth of the box canyon, watching for trouble. Little Crow was inside the other tipi, recovering from his beating.

"It is not her fault," One Eye said as he came up to his brother. "She does not know our ways. She does not understand what is in our heads."

Lone Wolf turned to face him. "May I speak frankly, my brother?"

One Eye's good eye narrowed slightly. "Please proceed."

"The gods have frowned on this whole enterprise."

"What gods?" One Eye demanded.

"I know you are not religious. But there are forces out there that control our lives. Call them what you want."

"Continue."

"If we did not have her, we would be in control here. Sheltowee would not have come after us. We would not even know he was alive, I suspect. Now it gets worse and worse. Because of him. Because of her."

"I regret the trouble I have caused you personally with this," One Eye said to him. "You know the affection I hold for you. I will never have a person closer to me. We are bound by blood."

"It is a bond I cherish," Lone Wolf said.

"But you see, Brother, the bones are cast. I cannot turn the sun back and make things some other way. She is here, and I have made her mine. There is honor involved here. I will fight him for her to my dying breath."

Lone Wolf searched his brother's face.

"If you wish to leave me, Brother, I will not keep you here. But I must make this stand."

Lone Wolf understood. "I would not leave you, One Eye. We are one. We always will be. I will protect your life with mine for as long as there is breath in me."

One Eye smiled and put his hand on Lone Wolf's shoulder. "Your words are like the eagle's cry to my ears."

Lone Wolf looked toward the canyon mouth and saw Gray Hawk moving about. "I am not certain in my mind how much help we will get from Little Crow now when Boone comes."

One Eye glanced toward the tipi. "I know."

"Or, for that matter, Gray Hawk," Lone Wolf added.

"What do you propose? That we release them to go their own way?"

"No, of course not. We need them. Whatever they contribute in a fight is better than being alone. But there is, of course, an alternative."

"Yes?"

"We can leave here and travel into Mexico. There are places there where he would never find us. He would eventually give up and return to Missouri. And with a little luck, we would never see him again."

"You would have me run from him?" One Eye asked in surprise.

"Not run. Beat him at his own game. Make him always be the pursuer, always the vulnerable one."

"He would follow us," One Eye said. "And if he did find us, the situation might not be as defendable as this one." He looked out toward the plain, as if he might get a glimpse of Dan'l out there. "But there is something else, my brother. You forget why we went to Missouri in the first place. If we kill him here, we will have it all back. We will be revered in Apache history."

"And if we do not?"

One Eye lowered his voice to make sure Molly could not hear him. "I had this dream last night, my brother. I saw us engaged in a fierce battle with Sheltowee. When it was over, I held his scalp in my hand."

"But it was only a dream."

"I have this feeling that we will defeat him. That he will lie at my feet and I will take his life slowly. I will slice his skin from his body, pluck out his eyeballs, and stuff them into his lying mouth. Then I will cut out his liver and cook it for our evening meal."

Lone Wolf smiled at his brother. "Let the gods make it so," he said in a half-whisper.

Chapter Fifteen

It was a warm, airless night. One Eye had expected all day to see Dan'l appear at the canyon, but it had not happened. It was possible that Dan'l and Rivera had not been able to find his hiding place, but he largely discounted that scenario. One Eye was uneasy about the quiet time. Maybe Rivera was recruiting One Eye's enemies to join in the attack. Perhaps Sheltowee was finding a way to get onto the high cliffs overlooking One Eye's camp, and would shoot down on them from above. Restless and tense, he decided to send Little Crow up on the western butte, over a difficult path at the rear of the canyon, to stand guard above them. He could also gain a wide view of the dark plain from there.

But Dan'l had not approached the canyon directly.

Two hours after dark, Dan'l had circled around in back of the canyon to approach it from the dead end.

Dan'l figured they would not be looking for one man to be coming at them from that direction, and he was right. When he crested the precipice after a long walk on foot, all was quiet in the canyon below. His eyes were like those of a hawk, and he could see the small fire at One Eye's camp, and a figure sitting near it. It was Gray Hawk, a second sentry on duty below. One Eye and his brother had promised to relieve the two guards halfway through the night.

Inside his tipi, One Eye tried to sleep, but was finding it was difficult. A thong of rawhide bound his ankle to Molly's, so he would wake if she tried anything foolish. It was just until the emergency was over, he assured her.

Molly, lying awake beside him, had a feeling deep inside that something big was about to happen, and the excitement of that kept her from falling asleep.

Up on the crest, Dan'l hunkered beside a boulder and looked around. He did not see Little Crow at first, but then spotted just a part of his silhouette. He was propped against a rock near the head of the canyon, watching out toward the plain.

"You're looking the wrong way, Indian," Dan'l said under his breath.

Then he started down the precipitous face of the cliff, along a rocky trail that Little Crow himself had used earlier to get to the top.

It was a slow and arduous descent, and took most of an hour. Little Crow would be no problem. He was staring out toward the plain before the canyon. It was the camp sentry that Dan'l had to get past.

When Dan'l reached the level canyon floor, he blended perfectly with the dark of the canyon wall and the ground. He stood there for a long moment, peering into the camp just fifty yards away. Gray Hawk was sitting beside the fire, looking toward the entrance of the canyon. Dan'l glanced up to the rim, and could not see Little Crow up there from this angle. He figured that if he kept to the western wall, the one that Little Crow sat atop, the Apache could not see him as he entered the camp.

Dan'l's Appaloosa was picketed well back from the crest, out of sight of Little Crow.

Dan'l picked his way along the base of the cliff, in deep shadow, hugging the cliff wall. When he was within thirty yards of the camp, he paused, crouching. Gray Hawk sat immobile at the fire.

Dan'l moved forward again, watching Gray Hawk as he went. He came to within ten yards of the nearest tipi, the one in which Lone Wolf was sleeping alone. The fire, and Gray Hawk, were less than fifteen yards away.

Gray Hawk suddenly rose and stretched.

Dan'l pressed himself into deeper shadow against the wall. Gray Hawk turned and scanned the entire canyon floor, looking right past Dan'l but not seeing him. He looked up toward where he knew Little Crow was keeping watch, but could not see him. He glanced toward One Eye's tipi and thought of One Eye in there, tethered to Molly like a goat. He shook his head. If it were up to him, he would slit her throat, and that part of it would be over. He sat back down and rubbed his hands over the fire while Dan'l held his breath at the canyon wall.

Dan'l waited. Gray Hawk let out a long breath and hunkered into himself. He was very pleased that he had killed the woman Rachel. He had set an example that not even One Eye was man enough to follow. Someday he might succeed One Eye in power.

Dan'l moved forward to the nearest tipi and looked inside silently, like a cougar. He saw Lone Wolf inside, sleeping soundly, and knew Molly would be in the other tipi with One Eye.

Dan'l drew a big skinning knife from his belt and crept toward Gray Hawk, who was heavy-lidded again. Ten feet away, then five.

Dan'l lunged soundlessly, grabbed Gray Hawk's head, and drew the big blade across his throat, all in one motion.

Crimson spurted from Gray Hawk's throat, his eyes saucered, and he grabbed at Dan'l's knife hand, which was slippery with blood. But Gray Hawk was too late to save himself. His jaw worked a couple of times, and he collapsed to the ground at Dan'l's feet, dead.

Dan'l wiped the blade on his rawhide trousers and crept toward One Eye's tipi. All was quiet.

He stuck his head into the entrance and squinted. There were two figures on a ground cover, and one was obviously female. He took a deep breath and crawled inside.

He heard a gasp from Molly and saw her sit up beside One Eye. Her eyes widened, and Dan'l put a finger to his lips.

"My God!" she whispered. The feeling she had had was right. Her cousin was here!

One Eye had finally fallen into a troubled sleep. He was breathing deeply beside Molly on her far side. Dan'l realized it would be risky to try to kill him. If One Eye managed to cry out, both Lone Wolf and Little Crow would be alerted, and he might not get out of camp with Molly.

Molly sat straight up, slowly, watching One Eye. He mumbled something in his sleep and moved slightly, but kept on sleeping. Molly pointed to the bond that held her to One Eye.

Dan'l looked at it. The knot was on One Eye's ankle, so that undoing it would wake him. Dan'l moved forward, took hold of the thong, and severed it with one easy slice of the knife's blade.

Molly was free.

She did not move. She looked over at her captor, and had a small pang of guilt as she watched him sleep. Then she slowly, very slowly, began inching her way toward Dan'l and the entrance of the tipi.

Dan'l backed away as she came toward him, and in just moments they were outside.

Even then they did not get to their feet. They crawled slowly and silently toward the fire. Finally Dan'l rose and Molly followed suit. She glanced at Gray Hawk and gasped again.

She looked at her cousin and was reminded how deadly he could be. He touched her shoulder, put his finger to his lips again, and pointed toward the western wall. They sneaked past Lone Wolf's tipi, where he was still asleep. Then they were at the wall, in deep shadow.

Now Dan'l hurried her. They walked swiftly to the rear of the canyon and found the narrow trail Dan'l had used to descend. Dan'l helped Molly get started on it, but the going was difficult for her. At one point, halfway up, she slipped and sent some pebbles cascading downward. They both stopped, holding their breath, but nobody woke. A few minutes later, they were at the top.

Dan'l pointed toward Little Crow, a small silhouette up at the head of the canyon. Molly nodded her understanding, and they turned and walked quickly away from the canyon rim, toward the Appaloosa.

Only when they arrived at Dan'l's mount did he finally speak to her. He looked her over carefully.

"Are you all right, Molly?" he said softly.

She nodded. "God, I'm so glad to see you, Dan'l!" Tears were streaming into her eyes suddenly, and she wiped them away. It all seemed so unreal, this midnight rescue. It was less real than lying beside One Eye and listening to his deep breathing.

"Let's get out of here," Dan'l told her.

They mounted the Appaloosa with Molly on the horse's rump behind Dan'l. Then Dan'l spurred the mount gently and they headed away from the entrance of the canyon in a wide circle that would put them out of sight of Little Crow.

Nobody came after them. There were no shouts of alarm from the camp.

Dan'l had stolen Molly right out from under One Eye's nose while he slept. His life among the Shawnee and Cherokee had given him the incredible skills he needed to save Molly's life.

They made their escape without speaking further, but Molly held on to Dan'l's waist as if she would never let go. Soon they were headed back toward Dan'l's camp a short distance to the north, and Molly's heart was filling quickly with a happiness she had not known since that fateful day in Missouri.

An hour later One Eye awoke, turned toward Molly, and saw that she was missing.

He swore loudly in his language when he saw the cut thong. "That damned woman!" He sprang to his feet and rushed outside.

The first thing he saw was Gray Hawk's corpse beside the fire. He stared in disbelief at it, noting the cut throat, then looked around fiercely.

"By the ancient gods!" he murmured.

Lone Wolf appeared at the entrance of his tipi, looking sleepy. "What is it?"

"Look at this!" One Eye sputtered. "He has been here!"

Lone Wolf came and peered down at Gray Hawk. It was all bewildering to him in his drowsy state. "Sheltowee?"

"Of course Sheltowee!" One Eye exclaimed. "He came and took her! Right out of my tipi!"

He went to the tipi and grabbed the rifle that was propped on a rock outside. His Mortimer pistol was still on his ground sheet inside. He cocked the long gun and stared up toward the western crest of the canyon.

"Little Crow!" he yelled at the top of his lungs.

There was a brief silence, then the reply.

"Yes, my chief!"

"Get down here, you fool!"

Lone Wolf ran for the mounts, which were picketed in gnarled trees on the eastern side, and which Dan'l had spotted only when leaving with Molly. When he came back with his and One Eye's horses, they could see Little Crow starting his descent at the rear of the canyon.

"Stay here until we return!" One Eye called up to him.

"What happened?" Little Crow called back.

Neither brother replied. They swung aboard the ponies and galloped at full tilt out of the canyon. In the darkness it was difficult to see tracks on the ground, but after they had ridden for a mile or so, it was obvious to One Eye that the only tracks out there were their own, from when they had ridden in.

After another couple of miles, they stopped and looked at each other.

"How did he do it?" Lone Wolf said. "He cannot walk on air. Can he?"

One Eye glared at him. "It is obvious, brother. He came in from behind us. If we ride far enough, we will pick up his trail. But there is no point. He is already back in his camp. With the woman."

"How could he do it?" Lone Wolf exclaimed. "She was tied to you! Beside you, in your tipi!"

One Eye was not pleased with his brother's sudden awe of Dan'l. "I was fast asleep. He cut the rawhide. Yes, he was very clever. Let us return to our camp."

They went back very slowly, and in complete silence. One Eye's head was hanging, his blood boiling inside him. When they rode into camp, Little Crow stood there watching them come, looking stunned beside the body of Gray Hawk.

"Is she gone?" Little Crow asked as they dismounted in heavy silence.

One Eye turned and backhanded him across the face, and Little Crow flew back, landing at the edge of the fire. He yelled when he felt the flames on his bare back, and scrabbled away from it, holding his face.

"You are a disgrace!" One Eye yelled down at him. "You let him come in here and steal her away from us! You got Gray Hawk killed!"

Little Crow rose awkwardly to his feet, glaring at One Eye. He was becoming tired of One Eye's abuse. He had become a different man since he had abducted the white woman.

"He did not come past me! I was watching for him!"

"I put you up there to watch both the approach to the canyon and our camp!" One Eye said angrily. "He came right in here and did what he wanted in plain sight of you!"

Little Crow shrugged his broad shoulders. "Gray Hawk was on watch down here. Why did he not see him?"

One Eye looked as if he might hit Little Crow again, but Lone Wolf put a hand on his arm. "Forget it, Brother. It is done."

"If Sheltowee now has the girl, let it be over," Little Crow said quietly, averting his gaze.

One Eye gave him a scathing look. "He was in my *tipi!* He could have killed me in my sleep!"

"He was afraid to rouse us," Lone Wolf said. "He might not have gotten the woman out alive."

One Eye stared out over the plain to where he imagined Dan'l's camp to be. "He is very clever. We expected an attack by several men, and he came in alone in the night."

"The Shawnee believe he can make himself invisible," Little Crow said. He had never known when to keep quiet.

Lone Wolf turned toward him and stared at him for a long moment, assessing the comment. One Eye saw the look, and came over to his brother. "I will hear no more of his magical powers! He is a man, like all of us here! He can be killed, and I will kill him!"

They both looked over at him.

"Let her go now, Brother," Lone Wolf said in a low, soft voice. "She is not worth it. We have nothing to prove. We had her all this time. Made him worry over her, forced him to ride a thousand miles to retrieve her. It is he who is humiliated, not us."

But it was as if One Eye were not hearing him. "It is not finished," he said deliberately.

"Not finished?" Little Crow said.

"Do you think he will just ride away now? Return to Santa Fe and forget what has happened?"

"He has the woman to consider," Lone Wolf said.

"He will take her out of harm's way. But then he will come for me. When the Shawnee killed his son, he returned to the place of battle and killed twenty Shawnee to avenge the death of his offspring. He thinks like an Indian."

"We can go to Mexico," Little Crow said. "He will give up and return to Missouri."

Apache Revenge

One Eye gave him a brittle look. "I have little left now but my Apache pride," he said slowly. "My honor, and the honor of my ancestors. Of Yellow Horse. I will not run from him; I told you that. So I must fight him."

"You will attack him?" Lone Wolf asked.

"Should I sit here and wait for him to come again?" One Eye demanded. "No, it is not the way of the Apache. We will find their camp when the new sun has risen, and we will attack them while they are drunk with their small victory. We will go for Sheltowee first, and the woman."

Lone Wolf took a deep breath. "We may be outgunned, One Eye."

"Then our ancestral spirits will give us the courage to overcome any odds," One Eye pronounced solemnly.

Little Crow was shaking his head. "This has gone too far. I will not do this. I have given you my loyalty; you cannot deny it. I went to Missouri with you. I put up with the woman. But now you ask too much."

One Eye cast an ominous look at him. "You ride with us, or you join Gray Hawk," he said simply.

Little Crow looked to Lone Wolf for support, but Lone Wolf would not desert his brother in this important matter.

"Your chief has spoken," Lone Wolf said. "He asks only that you conduct yourself like an Apache."

Little Crow looked away for a long moment, then turned back to them, resignation in his square face. "Very well. I will fight beside you to honor our long friendship. But why must we turn to a different strategy? We are secure here if they come to fight. You brought us here because of that."

"The situation is different now. They might come now, or a month from now. We know that if we ride out now, we will find them at a time when they may not expect us. And the woman will still be with them. It is important to me that she die with him."

"You do not want her back? Even if it is possible?" Lone Wolf asked.

One Eye shook his head. "She is dead already in my heart."

Lone Wolf nodded his approval. "Then there is much to fight for. We will ride to finish what we began in Missouri."

One Eye smiled a grim smile. "Prepare to break camp!"

When Dan'l arrived back at camp with Molly, Cahill and Rivera welcomed them with shouts of excitement. Cahill had already counted Dan'l with the dead, so it was like a miracle to see Dan'l ride in with Molly on the rump of the Appaloosa. Dan'l dismounted and took Molly off the horse, and they embraced for the first time.

"Molly!" Cahill exclaimed. "I'll be damned! I'll be *damned!*"

Molly turned to him and smiled with tears in her pretty eyes. She was wearing Apache rawhides, skirt and leggings, and a cloth blouse they had given her. Her hair was pulled back in the Apache way, and she looked leaner than when they had taken her. But she looked healthy.

Cahill embraced her too. He had met her just days before her abduction, but had felt as if she had been a part of the family forever.

"It's good to see you again, Sam," she said with a smile.

Rivera came up to them. "You don't know me, Molly. I am an old friend of your cousin Dan'l. But I am extremely pleased to see you back here."

Molly took his hand in hers, hesitated a moment, then planted a kiss on his cheek. "I know you came with Dan'l to help get me back. *Muchas gracias, amigo.*"

"*Mucho gusto de ayudar,*" Rivera said with a little bow, in the Spanish way.

Molly turned to Dan'l. "I knew you would come, Dan'l," she said, the tears returning. "I knew it."

Dan'l nodded. "We rode out soon as I could. My worry was that you wouldn't be alive when we got here."

Molly let out a little sigh, thinking back over all of it. "After we got here, he treated me pretty well," she admitted. "He . . . married me, Dan'l."

"I figured."

"I'm kind of spoiled . . . for a church wedding," she said, trying a small laugh. But her lip was trembling.

"There is no dishonor in it, *hijita*," Rivera told her soberly. "You were a victim, a prisoner. Like the other white women at his village."

Molly shook her head. "I miss them already. Isabel. And Rachel. Did you find them?"

"We did," Cahill said. "They got a Christian burial, Molly."

"I'm glad of that."

In the next hour they gave her hot coffee— they had finally built a fire—and made some porridge for her. Then they sat around the fire talking about her time of captivity and all she had been through.

Before they knew it, it was almost dawn.

"I wish I could offer you some sleep now," Dan'l told her after they had talked it all out. "But old One Eye might come out after you. You're pretty important to him. For a lot of reasons."

"Won't he just stay in his hole?" Cahill said.

"Maybe, maybe not. His pride's been wounded. He's lost a lot of face," Dan'l said.

"He is a very proud man," Rivera agreed. "We cannot stay here. We will just be taunting him."

"When the sun is up," Dan'l said to Rivera, "I want you to take Molly and ride back to Santa Fe. Cahill, you can go with them."

Cahill frowned heavily at his old friend. "What?"

302

"I'm staying," Dan'l said. "I'm going after One Eye."

Molly furrowed her pretty brow. "Why?" she asked.

Dan'l met her quizzical look. "I know he didn't hurt you, Molly. You might feel some gratitude toward him for that. But he can't get away with what he done. He took you by force. He killed your man, and Uriah Gabriel. I was just lucky he didn't kill me. He has to answer for his deeds."

"Hell, you can't ride after him alone!" Cahill said. "You ain't getting rid of me that easy, Dan'l!"

Rivera intervened at that point. "Look, Dan'l. One Eye must be brought to justice, *verdad*. But not this way. We have Molly now. Let us all return to Santa Fe with her, and then recruit some more guns to go after One Eye. I will ride out with you again, I promise you. One Eye is the scourge of this territory."

Molly found herself surprised at the way they spoke of One Eye. Having slept with him in his tipi all this time, and having had him give her the long talks, explaining her responsibilities as an Apache woman, she found that she did not see him in quite the same way they did, as a dark, evil figure. For Molly there were shades of gray when she thought of One Eye.

Dan'l shook his shaggy head. "I can't wait for all of that, Colonel. There's only three of them now. If I do it right, I ought to make out fine. I

303

just wish I could've cut his damned throat when I got Molly. But there might've been noise. And Molly could've been killed. If I'd been there alone, the bastard would be dead."

"Three to one ain't good odds, Dan'l," Cahill argued. "If you're a-going, then I'm a-going."

Dan'l looked at his friend. "Hell, Sam. You always was a stubborn farmer. But look at it this way. Molly will be safer heading back to Santa Fe with two of you watching over her. And her skin is a whole lot more important than mine. She's why we come out here."

Cahill did not know how to reply. He looked toward the eastern horizon. The sky was brightening, and the sun would be up in a few minutes.

"For God's sake, Dan'l, listen to the colonel. This ain't the way to go about it, damn it!"

Dan'l did not like arguments. He got up from the fire and walked over to the horses picketed nearby. He looked toward the south and One Eye's hidden camp. The night sounds of insects had quit, and there were still no morning sounds. It was that dead time of morning when you wondered if anything was really alive out there, or if the earth had stopped turning entirely and would require a great act of faith to get it moving again, as some Indians believed.

Rivera's white stallion nickered nervously.

Dan'l had been about to go over to Cahill and explain his position on One Eye more carefully, but now he studied the horse. His Appaloosa, just recovering from the long ride, also was looking restless again. Off in the distance, an eagle screamed, the first sound of the new day. Dan'l frowned at the sound.

"Something's going on," he said to the others.

They all rose, one by one, Molly last. "What is it, Dan'l?" she asked.

"I don't know."

Rivera came and stood beside him, and they both looked toward the south. "Is it him?" Rivera wondered.

With that question, Molly felt a little chill skitter through her, and she was suddenly short of breath. "Oh, God!" she whispered.

"It's probably coyotes out there," Cahill said, but he sounded nervous now.

Dan'l surprised them all by turning suddenly. "Get the rifles, and get them primed!" he said in a hard voice. "Molly, get over there between them boulders and stay there."

"Is it One Eye?" she said tightly.

"That's my guess," Dan'l said.

"Oh, no!"

She did not want a confrontation now. She wanted it to be over. To go back to Missouri and try to put it all behind her.

In the burgeoning light, Rivera saw a lone vulture to the south, making tight circles over an unseen something.

"I believe you are right, *amigo*," he said. "Let us arm."

"Damn!" Cahill swore. He looked toward

Molly. "Do what Dan'l says, Molly!"

They went for their guns. Molly reluctantly hid herself between the rocks, kneeling on the hard ground, watching the horizon.

"It looks as if our discussion is irrelevant now," Rivera mused, priming a Charleville rifle. "One Eye has taken our options away, it seems."

Dan'l was primed and ready. He focused on the horizon again and narrowed his eyes. "Look!" he said.

Rivera did not see them at first, but then they became more visible. Three Apaches rode hard toward them, One Eye in the lead.

"Here they come!" Rivera said loudly.

Dan'l had thought One Eye might try to sneak up on them, to make the most of the element of surprise. But it was too late for trickery, he guessed. Now it would be a battle of emotion, and the winner would be he who wanted victory most.

The three men took defensive positions away from the horses and Molly, behind rocks and a small tree, checking their side arms and ammunition. Dan'l glanced toward Molly.

"Stay put, Molly! No matter what happens!"

She swallowed hard. "All right, Dan'l." Her relief of a short while ago was gone now, replaced by a tension that was almost unbearable. It could still end up badly for all of them. Dan'l, his friends, herself. She had thought she was finally safe.

The riders came in swiftly and in silence. No

firing of guns, no war cries. Somehow it seemed deadlier this way.

"Don't fire until they're right on us!" Dan'l told them. "I'll take One Eye. Colonel, you try for the tall one riding close to him. I think that's his brother."

Rivera nodded, and then the three Apaches were riding right into their camp like a whirlwind. Just before the shooting started, Dan'l could see One Eye's face, grim and resolute, his rifle aimed right at Dan'l.

Then the guns exploded on both sides.

One Eye's first shot hit Dan'l in the left arm and spun him around. But Dan'l had already fired the Kentucky rifle and knocked One Eye off his charging mount. Lone Wolf fired at Cahill, who had just moved slightly after firing at Little Crow. Lone Wolf's shot creased Cahill's rib cage; Cahill missed Little Crow completely but hit his pony in the head and sent it sprawling with Little Crow still astride. Rivera opted to use his Mortimer pistol, aimed carefully, and hit Lone Wolf in the right cheek, destroying his handsome face and killing him immediately.

The mustangs were stampeding through the camp, with Little Crow's mount sliding along the ground as it died, kicking up a lot of dust. Lone Wolf hit the dirt hard at Dan'l's feet. Dan'l regained his balance and drew his Annely revolver just as Little Crow got to his feet, drew a tomahawk from his belt, and rushed Dan'l, yelling crazily. Dan'l fired and hit him in the center chest, and Little Crow went hurtling past him, hitting the dirt on his face. He jerked once and died.

Cahill was sitting on the ground, holding his side. Dan'l was repriming as Rivera walked over to One Eye, who had been hit in the belly but was very much alive.

"No, he's mine," Dan'l said from behind him.

Rivera moved aside, and Dan'l walked over and looked down at One Eye. Dirt was smeared on One Eye's hard face, and he looked very defiant lying there. He looked around for Molly but could not see her.

"Now, you son of a bitch!" Dan'l growled at the Indian. "This is for Jock Parrish, and Uriah Gabriel, and all the rest of it!" He aimed the gun at One Eye's head.

"Where . . . is she?" One Eye gasped.

Dan'l did not understand the Athabaskan, but Molly did. Just as Dan'l was about to squeeze the trigger, she came out from behind the rocks.

"No, Dan'l! Wait!" she cried.

Dan'l turned to her curiously.

Molly walked over to them and looked down on One Eye. He met her gaze and smiled. "You are my woman," he said, choking a little. "Tell him so!"

Molly took hold of Dan'l's arm. "Hasn't there been enough killing, Dan'l? Let him ride away. Look, what harm can he be to anybody now?"

Dan'l could not believe his ears. Rivera was shaking his head slowly.

"I can't do that, Molly. There's too much water under the bridge. Stand away."

Molly's eyes teared up. "Please, Dan'l!"

One Eye understood the exchange, and a hard grin came on his scarred face. He was vindicated, no matter what happened now. In a moment of desperation, he drew a Mortimer pistol that had lain hidden at his waist and quickly aimed it at Dan'l.

Dan'l heard the sound of the hammer cocking, and in the next split second turned and fired in one motion. The Annely roared loudly, and One Eye was hit in the chest, his heart burst by the hot lead. He widened his eyes in shock, took one last look at Molly, and, with a shudder, died.

"Oh, God," Molly whispered. She knelt over One Eye and touched his arm gently.

"I'm right sorry, Molly," Dan'l said.

"You had no choice." Molly sighed. "He was not a good man, Cousin. But he had his moments."

"Yes, ma'am," Dan'l said, holstering the gun.

Rivera sighed heavily. "Well. It is really over now. Let's get started back to Santa Fe. We all have a lot to think about."

Cahill was on his feet. His wound was shallow, as was Dan'l's, and they would both be fine. Rivera looked Cahill's wound over and went to get some gauze.

"Are you all right?" Molly finally asked Dan'l.

"We just got scratches, Molly," Dan'l said. "We come out of it lucky. Compared to One Eye."

"He didn't really have much luck," Molly commented.

They rode out a half hour later. Nobody spoke of One Eye again on the way back.

They figured it had all been said.

One way or the other.

A mighty hunter, intrepid guide, and loyal soldier, Dan'l Boone faced savage beasts, vicious foes, and deadly elements—and conquered them all. These are his stories—adventures that made Boone a man and a foundering young country a great nation.

DAN'L BOONE: THE LOST WILDERNESS TALES #1:

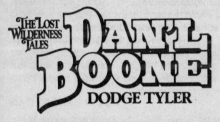

DODGE TYLER

The colonists call the stalwart settler Boone. The Shawnees call him Sheltowee. Then the French lead a raid that ends in the death of Boone's young cousin, and they learn to call Dan'l their enemy. Stalking his kinsman's killers through the untouched wilderness, Boone lives only for revenge. And even though the frontiersman is only one man against an entire army, he will not rest until he defeats his murderous foes—or he himself goes to meet his Maker.

_3947-8 $4.99 US/$6.99 CAN

Dorchester Publishing Co., Inc.
65 Commerce Road
Stamford, CT 06902

Please add $1.75 for shipping and handling for the first book and $.50 for each book thereafter. NY, NYC, PA and CT residents, please add appropriate sales tax. No cash, stamps, or C.O.D.s. All orders shipped within 6 weeks via postal service book rate. Canadian orders require $2.00 extra postage and must be paid in U.S. dollars through a U.S. banking facility.

Name_____

Address _____

City _____ State _____ Zip_____

I have enclosed $_____in payment for the checked book(s).

Payment <u>must</u> accompany all orders.□ Please send a free catalog.

CHEYENNE GIANT EDITION:

BLOOD ON THE ARROWS

JUDD COLE

Follow the adventures of Touch the Sky, as he searches for a world he can call his own—in a Giant Special Edition!

Born the son of a Cheyenne warrior, raised by frontier settlers, Touch the Sky returns to his tribe and learns the ways of a mighty shaman. Then the young brave's most hated foe is brutally slain, and he stands accused of the crime. If he can't prove his innocence, he'll face the wrath of his entire people—and the hatred of the woman he loves.

_3839-0 $5.99 US/$7.99 CAN

CHEYENNE

JUDD COLE

Follow the adventures of Touch the Sky as he searches for a world he can call his own!

#3: Renegade Justice. When his adopted white parents fall victim to a gang of ruthless outlaws, Touch the Sky swears to save them—even if it means losing the trust he has risked his life to win from the Cheyenne.

_3385-2 $3.50 US/$4.50 CAN

#4: Vision Quest. While seeking a mystical sign from the Great Spirit, Touch the Sky is relentlessly pursued by his enemies. But the young brave will battle any peril that stands between him and the vision of his destiny.

_3411-5 $3.50 US/$4.50 CAN

WHITE APACHE

Jake McMasters

Follow the action-packed adventures of Clay Taggart, as he fights for revenge against settlers, soldiers, and savages.

#7: Blood Bounty. The settlers believe Clay Taggart is a ruthless desperado with neither conscience nor soul. But Taggart is just an innocent man who has a price on his head. With a motley band of Apaches, he roams the vast Southwest, waiting for the day he can clear his name—or his luck runs out and his scalp is traded for gold.

_3790-4 $3.99 US/$4.99 CAN

#8: The Trackers. In the blazing Arizona desert, a wanted man can end up as food for the buzzards. But since Clay Taggart doesn't live like a coward, he and his band of renegade Indians spend many a day feeding ruthless bushwhackers to the wolves. Then a bloodthirsty trio comes after the White Apache and his gang. But try as they might to run Taggart to the ground, he will never let anyone kill him like a dog.

_3830-7 $3.99 US/$4.99 CAN

Dorchester Publishing Co., Inc.
65 Commerce Road
Stamford, CT 06902

Please add $1.75 for shipping and handling for the first book and $.50 for each book thereafter. NY, NYC, PA and CT residents, please add appropriate sales tax. No cash, stamps, or C.O.D.s. All orders shipped within 6 weeks via postal service book rate. Canadian orders require $2.00 extra postage and must be paid in U.S. dollars through a U.S. banking facility.

Name _____

Address _____

City _____ State _____ Zip _____

I have enclosed $_____in payment for the checked book(s).

Payment <u>must</u> accompany all orders.☐ Please send a free catalog.

THERE WAS A SEASON

T.V. OLSEN

Winner Of The Golden Spur Award

A sprawling and magnificent novel, full of the sweeping grandeur and unforgettable beauty of the unconquered American continent—a remarkable story of glorious victories and tragic defeats, of perilous adventures and bloody battles to win the land.

Lt. Jefferson Davis has visions of greatness, but between him and a brilliant future lies the brutal Black Hawk War. In an incredible journey across the frontier, the young officer faces off against enemies known and unknown...tracking a cunning war chief who is making a merciless grab for power...fighting vicious diseases that decimate his troops before Indian arrows can cut them down...and struggling against incredible odds to return to the valiant woman he left behind. Guts, sweat, and grit are all Davis and his soldiers have in their favor. If that isn't enough, they'll wind up little more than dead legends.

_3652-5 $4.99 US/$5.99 CAN